BLACK HEART(S)

Calliope Daniels

Books to Hook Publishing, LLC.

This book contains an excerpt from *Dare Me to Love* by Calliope Daniels. The excerpt is for this publication only and may differ in the original edition.

Cover art designed by *Covers by Jules* www. coversbyjules.crd.co

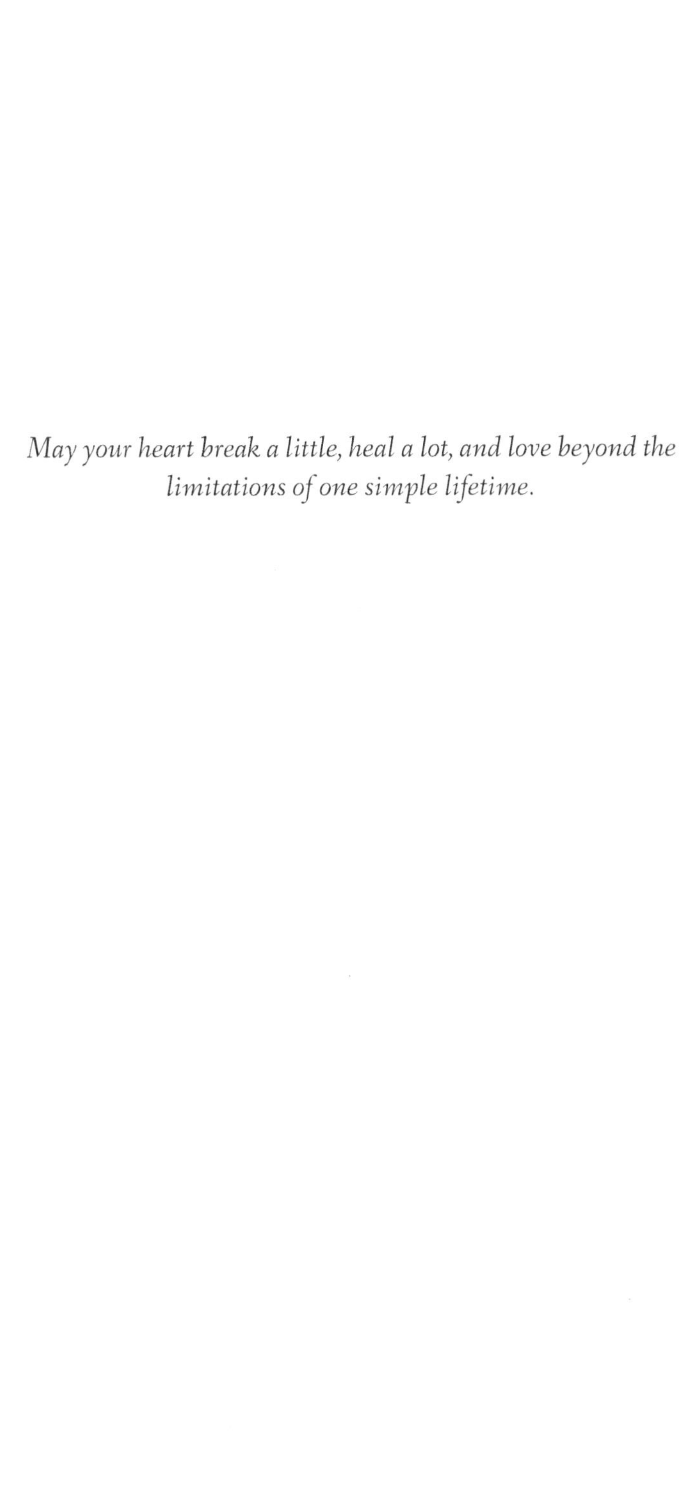

May your heart break a little, heal a lot, and love beyond the limitations of one simple lifetime.

BLACK HEART(S)

Prologue

I'm going to die.

Simple as that.

Chapter One

Another exam table in yet another medical office. This is becoming a habit. It's the millionth time in a month I've been stuck in this antiseptic purgatory. Might be a different room, but they're all the same. Why are they all so uncomfortable? Rolled out bleached white tissue paper crunches underneath as I try to relax the ache building between my shoulder blades with every worried breath I take.

Hospitals and doctors' offices have always made me nervous. There's sterility and a heavy undercurrent of despair and agony from every soul to grace a medical campus. No one ever goes inside without a purpose, an ailment, something they cannot cope with to some degree. I'm not sure it's anyone's thing, but it's definitely not mine.

At all.

The waiting adds to this wholly unbearable experience, and I squirm as each minute ticks by on the clock over the doorway, paper rustling with every breath I take.

My eyes scan the whole room, around the clinically clean environment, while I'm wringing my hands then rubbing the length of my arms with clammy palms. The room stirs with recycled air, the astringent scent of rubbing alcohol, scrubbed metal instruments and disinfectant stinging my nostrils. Even with the cabinet doors closed across from me, it's clear there are tools inside of it, tools to which I'd rather not be introduced.

My jacket was shucked off the moment I was escorted in the room and now regret fills the chilled air. I'm wearing only a tank top and jeans after the medical assistant had me remove it for the blood pressure cuff. She urged me to keep it off so I didn't have to change into a threadbare, open-backed gown—a small victory.

The table is winning, my legs going numb, dangling six inches off the ground. I refuse to move the little step stool out, choosing instead to shift slightly, the nasty paper wrinkling even more until it's a clump of waxy paper hell. Why the hell is it so cold in here? It can't be good for anyone to be freezing like this. My hands rub at my arms again but it's practically arctic and warming them seems futile.

Tap-tap. A soft knock raps at the door adorned with the poster of various structures, showing the anatomy of the heart. Another plastered underneath is an instruction guide.

'Know the Signs of a Stroke'

All the little characters on the stroke information poster display each step in a cheerfully cartoonish and tongue-and-cheek way. It's so distasteful. Why are all hospital-issued leaflets and posters so childish? As if we're idiots.

The door pushes open even though no words of permission escape my mouth in response to the knock.

A blur of a man in a white coat rushes in, parking himself on a rolling stool before swiveling my way. "Miss Rachel Heltin? I'm Dr. Trenton."

A well-practiced smile flashes, and he waits for me to

nod. He doesn't really see me, doesn't really register my face or the anxiety clawing me. I'm only another patient sitting on the exam table to him, but at least he's got the correct name.

I give a half-hearted lift of my chin, and he spins away again, sticking his nose in a computer and hitting a few keys as my chart pulls up. It's like some weird dance that we've all been conditioned to endure. I give him a little, he backs away. Then he moves forward, and we meet in the middle again. Two strangers sharing intimate details under the premise of a doctor/patient relationship.

"I'll be right with you. Just pulling up your chart. Then we can discuss what's been going on with you. Shouldn't be too long."

He's attractive, and although that should be the last thing on my mind, I'm happy for the momentary distraction. There's something about men in scrubs. The sky-blue material is partially hidden under a white lab coat adorned with a stethoscope draped around the nape of his neck.

Dr. Trenton's perhaps a little older than me, but young by most doctor standards. Mid-thirties, or so. He's trim, which is expected when you're a cardiologist. At least I would hope that's the standard.

An overweight doctor with crumbs that rest atop a bulging belly wouldn't command so much respect. Except the thing that really catches my attention isn't his appearance at all but his all-too-quick dismissive glance.

Doctors are well practiced in this art form. They must receive specialized training in medical school, the same with how they always ask, 'how are you?' but never wait for *any* kind of a response before they ignore you again.

His dark blue eyes meet mine for only a millisecond

while I gawk, but their intensity commands enough to make me gulp and avert my gaze anywhere else.

His nose goes back to the computer, and I haven't said a word, only working my hands in my lap, trying not to crinkle the paper anymore and not think about his eyes. He frowns and nods several times to the screen then plants his palms on his thighs, twisting the stool top to face me.

"So, my colleagues asked me to look into your case and I wanted to make sure I read through all their notes. Why don't you tell me what's been going on?" A dark brow edges up enough to know he is waiting for a quick reply.

I wipe my hands down my thighs, a little frustrated he's read my entire chart and still expects me to recite my whole life story in a nicely packaged condensed thirty-second version.

It's evident he only wants to dismiss me so he can duck out of the room and onto another patient.

I swallow once more, in an attempt not to let my gaze drift to those blue eyes a shade or two darker than his scrubs. "I'm sure it's all in there." I point to the computer. "What more do you need to know? Everything from the past several appointments are in there, aren't they?" I nod at the screen. "In front of you."

His eye twitches, but he likely doesn't realize it's noticeable. "I'd like to hear it from you. Starting from the beginning, to make sure we don't miss anything. Even the slightest bit of additional information can make a difference for diagnosing a patient. Every detail is critical. It happens sometimes that patients have told their primary care physicians or other specialist something the doctor never wrote down." His shoulders pull back and he scoots a little closer. With a dip of his chin, he looks up at me on the exam table. "Miss Heltin, I understand this is a lot for one person to deal with. From the looks of it, you've seen quite a few doctors. The process of elimination in the medical world can make anyone jaded, but I promise I want nothing more than to find you a solution."

Now, he has my focus. What he's said makes sense and because of that, he deserves the benefit of doubt despite how exasperating this whole ordeal's been so far.

I puff my lips out and exhale.

"A few months ago, a kind of lightheadedness came over me during a run. Dizzy, you know? And sweaty and nauseous, normal sort of stuff until the flutters started." I touch my chest, remembering the first time the odd sensation took over. "Felt as if I might pass out, all coming over me in waves. Anyways, I stopped and took a breather, and when things got a bit better, went on my way. My runs aren't difficult, only a light jog at most so it's weird but it kept happening."

I coast on autopilot, reciting all the boring details left. It's the fourth time telling the same thing to a different specialist. I'm interested to hear what he thinks, to hear if there was 'something missing' from my notes.

"Pretty sure it's anxiety, but my primary doctor gave me anti-anxiety meds and they haven't helped. In fact, the anxiety or the stress or whatever it is... it's getting worse."

"Sounds like it," he mutters.

"I've stopped running and started walking, but it's even happening while doing that. There're days I think I'm going to pass out and I'm just sitting at my desk minding my own business. It comes on even when I'm not pushing myself. Sometimes my vision goes in and out and other times it's a tightness in my chest or both."

He leans forward, propping his elbows on his knees, studying me, but it's still an obligatory habit as if he's actively rolling through my symptoms in his head, trying to go down a mental checklist. "Do you consume alcohol, recreational drugs, or caffeine?"

I shake my head. "None."

His face does this thing where it pinches together toward his lips, like he's suppressing a knowing smile. "Not even a glass of wine after a long week or a cup of coffee in the morning? I'm not talking excessive amounts here."

"No," I reiterate, frustrated he's calling my integrity into question. "Nothing since this started happening. None at all."

With a bob of his head, he rolls back over to the computer, clicking into several files.

I stare at his profile. How do doctors always seem to get the best of everything, even genetics? An aesthetically straight nose that curves at the tip, and full soft lips in stark contrast to the rigid line of a square jaw. It all comes together, working in spectacular fashion. The man needs to be in a calendar dedicated to shirtless men in scrub pants. June, perhaps.

His tongue runs over his perfect white teeth as he taps a pen to the desk, examining the reports. *Definitely June.* He pushes up suddenly and slinks his stethoscope from around his neck, positioning it to hang along his collar bone. "May I?" he asks as he approaches, gesturing toward my sternum region.

I nod.

Dr. Trenton stands so close I think he might tuck his hips between my knees, but he stops just shy, adjusting the stethoscope on his ears as the smell of mint and clean laundry overtake my senses.

There's something else there I can't quiet pinpoint, a sweet, comforting fragrance swirling between us.

The base of the instrument finds my heartbeat easily as one of his tan knuckles brushes the bare skin near the start of my tank top. It isn't inappropriate in the least, just the nature of trying to find the right spot.

Goosebumps return peppering my limbs, and I have to actively resist the urge to rub my arms that are still chilled to the core.

His eyes meet mine as he listens through the stethoscope, and I wonder if he can hear my heart rate speed up at the way I am hypnotized by him. If anyone's inappropriate in this moment, it's me.

I can't break free of this lock as my lips tuck behind my teeth, realizing too late that my stomach is hollowing out on each exhale.

How am I seriously thinking about anything other than trying to get answers?

The stethoscope moves to my back, and he breaks our standoff to shift around to the side of the exam table, telling me to take several deep breaths. His hands are warm through the fabric of my shirt, feeling comforting.

Again, it's the merest of appropriate touches, a fleeting fingertip resting on cotton as he positions the scope. He listens, repositions the instrument, listening again. "All right," he proclaims. "All done." Without flair, he loops the scope around his neck once more and plops down in the stool, rolling away while at the same time, expertly swiveling to park at the desk.

He begins typing a windstorm of notes, glancing between the keyboard and screen periodically.

My palms won't stop sweating, but I'm freezing. "Anxiety, isn't it? Stress?" I murmur, reaching behind to grab my jacket, putting it on to try to get the new layer of goosebumps under control.

He stays silent, trying to focus on the task to notate my file, but I can't help starting to ramble as my damp hands try to yank up the zipper.

"I'm healthy otherwise. Didn't think there even was much stress in my life. I mean, it's great minus this ordeal. Maybe I sleep more than normal, but that can't be bad, can it? I've always liked my bed, my mom used to say—"

"Mm-hmm." His fingers fly across the keyboard, interrupting my train of thought.

"Anyway, I'm a travel blogger, and there are a lot of self-imposed deadlines so that must be where the stress come in. Though I make my own hours and take on whatever current trend appeals to me and leave the rest. It's not a bad way to earn money. Not at all."

Dr. Trenton swivels a quarter turn toward me, fixating on me intently, waiting to speak patiently, a smile creeping up one corner of his mouth.

But I press on. "There are people who have to commute hours every day and I get to fly around on someone else's dime. How stressful is my job other than dealing with trendy influencers and going through customs coming back into the States? Sometimes, they're both a fucking bitch to deal with but come on, it's not like it happens every day."

My hand comes up and slaps against my mouth, eyes growing wide when I realize the slip of my sailor's mouth.

The other side of his mouth tips upward. "Anything else you'd like me to add? Or delete?"

"Yeah," I hear myself say, trying to ignore the heat in my cheeks. "Just that it'd be great to get back to my life as it used to be before this started. I've got plans and this is really getting in the way. Can't you prescribe me something to get back on track? Something to calm me down?"

He turns all the way toward me, his expression unreadable, as though he's conducting research on my mood. "I'd like nothing more than to get you back to your exciting life. But first, I'd like to run two more tests before clearing you of any cardiac issues. One's a stress test on a treadmill and the other's an MRI."

"But there's already been an MRI. It'll be in your notes."

He nods and glances back at the computer screen. "I'm fully aware of that, Miss Heltin. I want to double-check an area they didn't image the first time. You know, dot all the i's and cross the t's. Or as they say across the pond, belt and suspenders."

"Belt and suspenders?"

"A double precaution to stop your pants from falling down. It's a..." He shakes his head. "We're getting off track. Let's get you this additional test to confirm nothing has been missed and then I will give you the all clear."

My eyes squint at him and I don't realize it, but the paper underneath is scrunching in my fists. "What are you checking for though?"

He waves his hand in the air between us. "Nothing to worry about. Only want to mark something off the list."

My shoulders slump, hands finally unclenching. "Am I crazy? Is this all in my head?"

His stool rolls back under the desk with a gentle kick of a shoe then he walks over and offers me a hand down from the table.

"You aren't crazy," he reassures me as my hand slips into his. "We'll figure it all out and get you back to your life."

Chapter Two

TEN DAYS LATER.

"You *are* coming to the concert tonight, right?" Azzy whines through my earbuds as I track my usual path through Golden Gate Park, coming to a walk and turning up the volume to hear better.

It's nippy but normal for any time of the year in San Francisco. And today, I'm enjoying the mist from the overlayer of fog as it cools me down. This is my happy place. Trails are serpentine shaped, making for a far more enjoyable feeling than running at some infinite pinpoint in the distance down a straight and level line. The redwoods and grass, and all the little hills make each turn more interesting, while each incline and corner hides what's coming ahead. The surprise keeps me engaged and looking forward to my daily runs.

"Are you kidding? I've been looking forward to this all year." My grin is a little too wide. I might be twelve years out of high school, but the music from those days still appeals. Rebellion Death has been a non-stop listening ritual since living under my parents' reign.

Growing up, I studied everything about them and at one point in my teens, it seemed fate had destined me to marry the band's dreamy eyeliner-smudged lead singer. If I weren't in my early thirties and trying to project a more mature image, I'd probably still line my walls with their posters and stalk them mercilessly online.

Azraelia Lilliana Warren has been my best friend since grade school, and she's also *really* into Rebellion Death. Maybe obsessed, even. Who am I kidding? We are infatuated to the extreme. It's all we've been talking about for weeks so when she asks if I'm coming, I find the question a little odd.

Azzy never grew out of her goth phase like her parents had hoped, but in all fairness, they did name their firstborn after the Angel of Death, Azrael. So, what else could they expect?

Apart from our similar musical taste and the unwavering devotion to this one band in particular, we're total opposites in almost all respects. We're also total contradictions to our own identities. It's what I love about us the most.

I, brunette and petite, enjoy my name-brand running tights, fancy yoga classes—when I can afford them between paychecks—and chewing with my mouth wide open with absolute, zero regard to manners unless my mom is in the room. I'm carefree with a lot of things, but my mom's look of disapproval is the one thing that has the ability to scare me into submission...at least temporarily.

Azzy, on the other hand, bleeds all things darkness.

But then she's also the very definition of cultivated refinement and prim and proper. To complicate her identity, Azzy thoroughly enjoys her weekly thrift store dumpster-diving therapy—her words, not mine. And her hair is always dyed with two bright purple streaks down the sides to complement raven black strands that match the color of wing-tipped makeup around her golden doe eyes, whereas I hardly wear makeup at all.

Our ongoing joke is that we share a black heart in two opposing bodies, minds, and souls.

Now thanks to her teasing, I'm mulling over what I'll wear at the concert even though I'll end up settling for my normal go-to outfit full well knowing she'll have something to say about it.

"I wonder what you're wearing, but fear the answer," I say with a smile.

She coughs out a laugh, the sound warming me. "You already know what I'll wear. Have I changed in the past twenty or so years?" No, Azzy has not. "Want to borrow anything? I can make something out of nothing. Why not change it up and let me decide?"

"Hmm, that feels almost insulting. No, I think I'll stick to my boring stick-out-like-a-sore-thumb outfit if you don't mind. Maybe this time, I'll even bring a fanny pack with all the essentials like hand sanitizer and ChapStick. I might throw in a snack too. How's a juice box sound?"

She makes a gagging sound. "Rache, you're embarrassing not only to me, but to yourself. I hope you know that. You'll get us kicked out because they'll think you're a mom chaperoning her teenage kids. I'm doing your makeup at least, to try and salvage your image. No use in even protesting. It's happening."

My mouth forms a response that never makes it to out before she's talking again.

"I'll be at your place an hour before. Mind if LC comes with us too? She was able to get a ticket last night."

LC is a recent but welcomed addition to our twosome.

Azzy and her have been getting more and more serious as the months go by and I can't help but love LC and all her head-to-toe tattoos and piercings that cover every inch of her skin.

Despite her stealing most of my best friend's time, she's great.

"Is this why you're calling me? Because you thought I wouldn't want her to come along?" The other end is quiet for too long. "Azzy..."

"I don't want to make you feel like a third wheel," she blurts out.

"Not at all, I'd love her to come. Listen," I say, looking at the reminder alarm vibrating my watch. "Shit. I have an appointment I have to run to, but I'll see you later tonight. And I promise I want LC there."

"Appointment for what?"

"Just a physical." The lie comes out way too easy, but it's enough to get her off the phone without more questions as the guilt settles in my gut.

As I jog back home, spots start to fill my vision and my chest flutters enough that I stop several times to try and calm them. By the time I'm unlocking the door to my apartment, my vision is almost completely speckled by dark gray blurs.

Ignoring the spots in an attempt to will them away, I strip down and head into the shower for a quick rinse.

The moldy wall tiles form a resting spot for my back and shoulders as yet again the faintness comes over me, the room dissolving into a spin.

Breathe, breathe nice and deep, I tell myself. If this is a panic attack like one of the faceless doctors suggested, then it's my breathing I have to perfect.

Inhale...one...two...three... exhale. Soon, the room is the right way again, my heartrate settling back to normal and I'm able to finish my shower.

After that near incident, energy eludes me, so I dab on minimal makeup, then toss jeans and a sweater on that still carries perfume from another day—it's only been worn a few times and there isn't enough time to search through my semi-clean pile of clothes for something different.

Presentable enough, an Uber whisks me to the University of California, San Francisco Medical Center. Despite plenty of traffic I'm actually two minutes early when I check in at the front desk.

The waiting room and those two extra minutes really wreaks havoc on my nerves. I hate these tests. I hate medical facilities. And I *really* hate that Dr. Trenton still holds a spot in my head rent free a week and a half later.

He barely acknowledged me. We didn't even speak about anything outside of my condition.

So why do I even care about a cute doctor when all I need are answers?

A medical assistant in a faded SpongeBob scrub top calls me back and I follow her through the maze of exam rooms and offices. Passing one of those random doors, I instantly recognize the dark-haired doctor hunched over a desk, scribbling notes at a furious pace.

As if he senses I'm passing by, he glances up from the stacks of papers and frowns. The medical assistant is quick to usher me away, but that brief interaction perplexes me.

The assistant takes me farther into the maze of rooms and we end up in one with a treadmill and a bunch of weird machines. Here, she passes me off to an older nurse who is disconnecting leads and scurrying about, the wires looping over the arm of the main machine.

I already did my MRI earlier in the week and today's

test will hopefully be the last before I get firm answers. It may sound odd, but I hope they'll find something—not too serious—just something that they can treat with something simple like a pill.

I'm instructed to change into the workout clothes I brought. Why did I bother taking a shower at all?

Before she shuts the door to give me privacy, a hand stops it from closing and Dr. Trenton squeezes through the opening. This time, his mop of black hair looks a little more disheveled than five minutes ago. He casts the nurse one glance—only one—and she dematerializes out of the room.

"Do you have cold feet?" he asks with no hello, no other greeting.

I don't get it. "What? You mean was I scared to come here again? I'll be honest I'm not a fan of—"

He waves a dismissive hand. "No, no. Medically, do you suffer from cold hands or feet, anything like that? Cold extremities. And has your weight fluctuated at all lately?"

With my nod, he leans against the door frame, half facing me, a hand pushing into that messy hair.

Dr. Trenton is eyeing me, the color slowly draining from his face. "We don't need you to do this test anymore."

He stands there, staring at me. Not that I'm any better. I stare back, not sure how to interpret him and why I no longer need the test, and why the decision wasn't made beforehand, saving me a whole annoying trip here.

He clears his throat as if to embark on answering the questions inside my head. "It's not been a wasted trip for you," he says. "There *is* one more test, but not this one. Someone will come get you to administer it. I'm going to arrange it right now. Shouldn't take too long. Then we'll be in touch."

The doctor turns to leave.

"Is something wrong?" My voice sounds frail and not my own and I can't ignore the goosebumps scattering across my arms. "Did you find something?"

"No, no. Not yet. We need to conduct one more test."

He exits before I can say anything else. My heart sets off in palpitations again—the man's set me even more on edge.

Not yet? What the hell does 'not yet' mean?

The nurse sneaks back in. "All right, if I could have you pop over to the room across the hall."

It's a mandate, not a question and I trudge after her with heavy legs.

A few minutes later, the same nurse returns to have me change into a gown and escorts me to an adjoining procedure room.

In the other room, a technician is waiting. And I'm cold yet again in a hellishly thin gown.

"Hello there," the tech says as he urges me into the room and onto an awaiting gurney. "We would like to run an echocardiogram. Nothing to worry about."

"Um. Ok."

He's nice and walks me through a breeze of a procedure, and other than my boobs almost lolling completely out of a threadbare gown and him rubbing warmed gel over the center of my chest, it isn't too bad.

And seeing as I haven't dated in over a year, I consider this second base, logging it as a win.

As he finishes, I try to read the tech's face, to see what he sees in all that scattered gray matter on the screen, but he gives away nothing.

"Alright, ma'am. All done. If you'd like to change back into your clothes, we are all set here."

Back in my clothes a couple minutes later, I drop my

butt onto the small chair by his desk as he sits tapping at the keyboard. As if we're on a seesaw, the moment I hit the plastic seat, he leaps up.

"No, we're all done," he says, obviously eager to get me out of there. With one wave of his hand, he ushers me out the door.

Planting my feet, I corner him. "We don't talk about the echo...echo..." *Hell, what was that machine called?*

"Echocardiogram. ECG," he offers, pushing up his glasses. "No, no. Dr. Trenton will have a good look and a discussion with me if needed, and someone will be in touch. Urgently if necessary."

With that, he politely forces me out the door and shuts it, leaving me in an empty hallway. I feel the faintness coming over me again like a huge and heavy cloak. But despite it all, somehow, my feet find their way down the cold corridor where the chill seems to whistle through every bone in my body.

As I pass another consulting room, a doctor's distinctive voice drifts to my ears, sounding an awful lot like *my* doctor, discussing a case with another member of the medical team.

They have hushed voices. But somehow, not hushed enough. Nowhere near enough to miss one word and one word only.

"Fuck," he says.

I have to admit to sporadic inappropriate words flying from my mouth on the regular. But coming from who I believe is a doctor—and one who has said *not yet* when I asked if anything was wrong—I find it deeply concerning. They are talking about me. I know they are.

Call it a sixth sense if you like or call it plain crazy. Call it stress or fear or anxiety... but I am sure they are discussing me. There is something terribly wrong, something deeply frightening.

My ears strain to listen while my confused heart—now no doubt in arrhythmia—and my feet take every ounce of my remaining energy to flee and get the hell out as far and as fast as I can. Cute doctor be damned.

Chapter Three

Azzy arrives at my apartment exactly one hour before the concert, delivering on her promise to do my makeup, although I only let her transform my eyes into dark wings of kohl. I have no intention of looking like a porcelain doll with the white foundation and the deep purple lipstick like she and LC and both wear.

My attitude is sour and I'm exhausted, but I try as hard as I can to not let her see. I don't want her to worry, and I don't want the endless line of questioning. I only want to enjoy a night out with my best friend and her girlfriend.

As I walk out of my bedroom, both women frown at my clothes. After today's earlier events, I'm not in the mood for their judgment. "What? I couldn't find my fanny pack."

"You look like you're going grocery shopping at Trader Joe's at three in the afternoon with the PTA moms," LC giggles into her girlfriend's arms.

I look down at my outfit. Over-washed gray Rise Against band T-shirt, jeans, and well-worn combat boots. I'm two-thirds edgy. The other third went missing and my suspicion is that Azzy soaked it up. I shrug off the so-called insult and gather a jacket, putting my ID, money, and ticket into my pocket and head for the door.

The girls walk in front of me, both in short, pleated leather skirts leaving little to the imagination. Their matching chunky platform boots, torn fishnet stockings and exposed tattoos on every inch of skin exposed to light have them looking like they are almost twins as they sway hips in sync.

Azzy doesn't have as many tattoos but even their dual-sided French braids match and look as if they've been dunked in a quart of years-old motor oil.

"At least your heart is black," Azzy calls back to me and I wince at how right she might be, but she doesn't notice. Luckily, she's distracted by LC which has kept her out of my comings and goings this past month. If she had been made aware of all my appointments, there is no way we'd be doing anything other than excessive Googling my symptoms and lounging on the couch with aging leftovers.

I was not about to miss this show or put my life on hold for whatever was happening. This is what we do and I'm not changing that now.

The first time I went to a concert with Azzy, we were fifteen and I had to beg my conservative parents to allow me to go, lying to them by saying it was a Christian rock concert. There was a cross at that concert, but I do believe it was set on fire sometime during the show.

Not sure that's exactly what they had in mind, but my parents wouldn't have approved and when they eventually found out the truth, they attempted to ground me—I say 'attempted' because I snuck out and didn't come home for the entire weekend that I was supposed to be in lock up.

I think they were so relieved to see me after that time

that they forgot all about my transgressions. Or they chose to ignore it.

Either way, my parents' ability to control me continued to spiral through my teen years, even into my twenties. Although things have grown so much better over the years, a streak of rebelliousness still runs through my veins, as well as a lot of things I should be apologizing for. But going to a concert where there's more screaming and yelling than singing, that wasn't one of them.

We make it to the warehouse district in Berkley. Our Uber unceremoniously throws us out practically at the entrance of the venue with its aged bricks and dented steel doors. As soon as we scan our tickets and head inside, Azzy and LC disappear into the crowd. Some people would be upset about their friends leaving them so soon but for us, it's nothing new.

She enjoys the up-close view but for me, it's more fun to let loose in the back, avoiding getting smashed by crowd surfers or involuntarily forced into the mosh pit. Running into each other, kicking, pushing. Not for me.

The minutes before the show allows barely enough time to grab a beer and find a suitable spot to see the opening band start. I edge into the crowd, listening to a repetitive bass drum—likely due to the sound engineer carrying out final tweaks—when someone taps me on the shoulder.

My body spins toward them, taking in the venue at the same time. It smells somehow gritty, like spilled beer, puke, and sweat. It makes me grin, bringing me back to the nostalgia of my high-school days.

My mouth drops open when I realize I'm facing the one and only Dr. Trenton, only he no longer wears scrubs or a stethoscope. Dressed in a plain black t-shirt, jeans, and relaxed shoulders, he gives off the vibes of someone I would normally be drooling over at a place like this.

He forces an awkward half-smile—which I return—before a guy with a fire-engine-red mohawk steps between us, causing me to get absorbed into the crowd, looking back for the doctor.

But he's gone.

My heart dips, disillusions, downbeat, but only for the briefest moment as it makes no sense. My eyes probably deceived me anyway. It couldn't have been him. Not here.

How could he possibly have the same taste in music? The guy seems way too square for that. Never once did he crack a genuine single smile in all the time we were in the exam room. But then I remember that even right now, I'm sporting an afternoon grocery shopping outfit, so maybe he thinks exactly the same about me, hardly Miss Trendsetter or posterchild for heavy metal.

Thankfully, the opening band starts the first set, allowing me to push Dr. Trenton out of my thoughts and focus on the task at hand. I rock out to the first band, the music thumping deep into my chest. I have no idea who they are, but it doesn't matter. This opening band, whatever they're called, has definitely set the tone for this evening in the lead up to the headline act. The sea of people floods the place with energy and about the time my band takes the stage, the crowd is at a fever pitch.

I don't spot the doctor again, but I convince myself he's watching me from somewhere in the shadows, wanting to question the beer I've been sipping on for an hour. Doctors are so judgy, and I got the impression at my appointments that Dr. Trenton might be worse than most.

An opening riff and ear-piercing scream belt out from the stage, along with coordinated lighting effects adding to the electric atmosphere. I shout with my fellow strangers, finishing off my beer sometime between their first two songs, jumping around and throwing my hands in the air, bumping into others and singing at the top of my lungs. We all rock out together as one, barely a gap between hundreds of people.

The lyrics to each song are embedded in me from years of listening to each track religiously and I let all my walls down to exist in this perfect moment.

This atmosphere takes me back to the many times I've witnessed this band play live. The sound is so loud but free of any distortion. It's immaculate. Every chord, every cymbal and range of vocal is crystal clear.

I'm spinning in circles when I feel the familiar fluttering and at first, I think it might be the bass from the music reverberating off my chest wall, but a wave of anxiety takes control.

My senses... they are leaving me. The noise fades out to nothing. My vision is near blackness, only the tiniest bright light in its center. Nausea overtakes me, and my breathing comes in gasps as I stumble.

Help me, help me, help me runs through my confused brain.

Has someone spiked my beer? I don't know but it's going to be too late for any assistance. Something that feels like death tugs a heavy curtain over my body, shading the rest of my vision.

Panic sets in, knowing I need a place to quickly sit to catch my breath and I'm in a standing-room only warehouse. I rush toward where I recall the nearest wall, plowing through the crowd, smashing toes and shouldering my way through the mass of bodies, bulldozing straight into someone at one point, then pushing my way past them to get to the wall so I can lean against it before collapsing.

My arms are outstretched and inches from falling into the concrete wall, and I only hope I can make it with enough time to slide down to the ground gracefully. People die underfoot in these places all the time, trampled by the shoving, oblivious crowds.

I hope for a miracle.

But before making contact with the grimy floor, someone grabs at my wrist, tugging me in the opposite direction.

What the hell's happening? Please. Please help me.

I don't have time for this, not when I feel as though I'm going to pass out. I try in vain to scan through the crowd for Azzy or LC, but that's a longshot at best. My vision is pretty much gone and even if it wasn't, the place is packed, and Azzy always tries to be right in the front.

The stranger's hand on my wrist is firm, dragging me, tugging me. Now, I'm moving through the crowd, unable to stop this person from taking me wherever they are going.

I can't even see who holds onto my arm, the blackness growing ever darker if that's even possible. All of this should be alarming, especially the part of being towed by a stranger.

My body's fight-or-flight response should be revved into full force, but I'm just allowing it to happen, hoping to be led to safety. A tiny glimmer of vision at one side of the left eye is all I have, and even this comes and goes, making me even more nauseous.

The more exertion with rubbery legs, the worse my sight and sickness become. I just want to lie down.

The crowd is so thick, and all I can see is that long arm attached to me, somebody's right forearm—a man's—dragging me through the mass of people, being rough and uncaring, relentless. On a mission.

Their body keeps absorbing into the crowd ahead, melding and merging.

My vision blurs over the last spot I could see, and my chest squeezes tighter. I trip and stumble to my knees, breaking off the stranger's grip. He retreats back to me, lifting me into strong arms and cradling my body as he's yelling over the riffs for people to move out of his way, using my feet and his elbow to make his way through.

"Get out of the way!" he hollers, authoritative, urgent. "Move!"

I still don't know who he is because my face is contorted by the pain and pressure but what he shouts is a little reassurance.

I'm pressing my palm against my chest, hoping it will alleviate the burning and squeezing, but it does little more than remind me of what lies beneath thudding wildly.

Whoever is carrying me—hopefully to some place safe —pushes through the bag check and security guards. Cool air hits my flushed cheeks as he sits me down on a half brick wall that probably used to hold plants but now only forms a welcome place for discarded cigarette butts and trash.

I attempt to bend myself in half, wanting to collapse on my thighs, but he adjusts me to sit up straight, moving my palm off my chest, not allowing it to move back again. He's replacing it with his.

A firm, warm hand lays over my shirt, spread wide across my breastbone.

My silent voice cries out to get away, but it's a voice no one can hear because the words never leave my lips. I am rendered disabled, at the edge of unconsciousness.

I should be appalled by the unwelcome touch, but I

can't breathe. My eyes slam shut tighter to block off a new wave of dizziness.

His hand moves again, and two fingers go to my neck.

"Shit," he breathes out.

All my senses are locked down except one. I smell him leaning into me. Clean laundry and mint and something else I can't figure out. But it's nice all the same, and I'm grateful my brain is registering something other than pain and anxiety. My eyes pop open, my vision returning and relief envelopes me as I notice his hair is not so disheveled anymore. Dr. Trenton's plain black T-shirt is a tad too tight in all the right places and a tad too close to my nose.

His biceps flex as he moves his fingers around the thumping on my neck.

Now at rest, I slowly improve, the sight returning almost fully, the nausea slightly waning.

"Dr. Trenton?" I force out, but he doesn't respond while staring at his watch, taking my pulse. "Why are you here? I'm not dying, am I?" I joke, chuckling as I say it on a weak breath, trying to lighten the mood of the stern man who moments ago carried me through a concert and has one hand on my throat and the other supporting me.

His brows come together and then flatten again, not meeting my eyes. I straighten at this as he releases my wrist and I move to create a little space between us.

"You said *fuck*," I say. When he frowns, I add, "As I was leaving your office earlier today. I heard you say it." I'm trying to stand up, clutching my chest when I can't quite get to my feet.

"Easy there, don't move too fast. Thought you said you don't drink?"

The snarl is involuntary. "It was one beer and the first in a really long time."

"Everyone says that," he replies with an eyeroll. I smirk at him. But his face doesn't crack a smile even now.

His comment was a serious one.

"Were you spying on me?" I ask. "If you're so concerned with a patient's personal health and safety, I'm sure there are better ways then following us around to see if we've fibbed."

Something else is bothering me more. This time, I won't wait for him to respond to my ridiculousness, and this time, I won't let him get away without answering me.

"Dr. Trenton, why did you say that in your office?" I leave it as a simple question. He knows what I'm asking. The concern flickering through his features is too easy to read and the look on my face is all worry, no play.

"It was about me, wasn't it?" I guess. Scowling at him, my lips slightly tremble though I don't know why.

"Miss Heltin," he murmurs, eyes darting to the cracked concrete ground. "Might want to call it a night. Can I order you a ride home? Or do you want me to find your friends?"

I come to my feet, steadier than before. He's so much taller than me when he stands at the same time, and I have to look up at a sharp angle, but that also might have to do with him standing so close that I can still feel the warmth radiating from his broad chest.

He still won't meet my gaze, looking somewhere over my shoulder as if trying hard to be disengaged and appear disinterested.

"What's your first name?" I try to steer his attention toward me.

His chest inflates and I'm not sure he's going to answer. He exhales through his nose.

"Dave," he says after some time. "My name is Dave."

"Well Dave, I'm Rachel." I plant my hands on my hips,

waiting for him to look at me. "Now that we got that out of the way, will you answer a question for me?" He's still looking away, frozen in place. "Hellooo? All I'm asking is for you to answer one question." Still nothing from Doctor Dave. "I'm not asking for too much, am I?"

A grunt comes from him, and he shakes his head like he already knows. Because *he knows*. "Not here. There's a protocol. You have a follow-up appointment. I suggest you come to it." He takes a step backward, but I grab the hem of his shirt with my thumb and two fingers.

He easily could have stepped out of it, but he halts, his head tilting in my direction, navy eyes clouding when they skim over mine.

"Please," I whisper.

With a swallow his Adam's apple bobs twice. "This isn't appropriate. Unprofessional. I have an ethos to follow, Miss Heltin."

"Rachel," I correct.

"*Rachel*," he mutters slowly, lowering his gaze to his feet, hands tucking into the pockets of jeans that fit a little too well.

The air is charged with electricity between us.

I feel the thumping of the bass of my favorite band but have zero desire to be anywhere else than standing in front of Dave, waiting for my sentence to be handed down to me.

"Please don't make me wait until next week. It's bad, isn't it? Your body language is giving it away." Releasing his shirt, I brace my palms on the brick ledge to hold myself upright. "Oh god, it is."

I look up to him, seeing his brows squish together. He seems on the same verge of the same emotions I also feel. "Please," I plead once more. "You can't expect me to wait until the appointment to find out. Think about it, Dave.

Think about the added stress and anxiety—two things I don't need at the moment—for having to wait until that appointment."

He nods as his head rises. "Look Rachel, I understand your frustration and in hindsight, maybe I should have been more aware of all this at the hospital. Mea culpa. It means—"

"I know what it means. My mistake. But please..."

"Rachel, can you not leave it alone? I just...I can't," he says, almost inaudible.

"I can't handle not knowing. I can't deal with this. Tell me. Please—"

"Okay!" His fingers interlace on top of his head, and he twists away. The muscles above his shoulder blades flex several times until he finally spins back to me. "Fine. I'll tell you, but you must know that I am adamantly against telling you this way. You have to promise me right now that you'll still come into the office for a proper run-down. All right? You can't just hear what I'm about to say and ignore it."

The air between us is still, cold, but the wind is gathering when I nod.

His head shakes back and forth. "I won't tell you anything until you promise me. I need to hear the words."

I take a step closer, saying, "I agree—I promise. You're only being kind to me by not making me wait."

A deep inhale inflates his chest. He releases it into the breezy night then looks me direct in the eye. "I'll give it to you straight, no bull. It's bad, Rachel. You have a tumor in your heart, it's called a primary cardiac sarcoma."

The floor drops out from under me, making me feel as though I'm sinking in gelatin, and I can't surface, but haven't moved an inch. Thoughts race through my head at lightspeed.

With a stumble, I slide down the brick wall until I'm planted on the ground, dizzy and in utter shock. I don't say anything for what feels like forever. My mouth opens on the verge of words and then I snap it shut again.

After a couple of staggered breaths, I shake my head. "I was expecting—*hoping*—to have a diagnosis, something tangible instead me thinking it was all in my head...but I wasn't expecting *that*." I try to process the jumble of emotions. "But I'm glad you told me. Really, I am. The wait would have killed me."

I stare at my shoes, searching for more words, but they're absorbed into the chaos.

Next to me, Dave nods. "I'm very sorry," he says in a soft voice, the gentlest tone I've heard from him.

Thoughts zap me into action. "Okay, but it's treatable, right? A surgery? Medication? I mean, in today's world, everything is treatable. I mean, they've come so far in treating tumors and some of them are even benign. So, we don't know anything until you biopsy it, right? It might be something...nothing major. Right?"

He eyes me, an emotion I can't quite interpret overtaking him. His lips form an awkward purse as he presses them hard together then he squats down until at eye level with me. "I'm so sorry," is all he offers.

"Definitely not benign?"

"No, Rachel. A sarcoma is always bad news anywhere on the body. But in the heart, it's..."

I put up my palm. "I get it. Thanks."

His hand drags over down his face, and he shakes his head.

I nod mine in acknowledgment of the gift he just gave me, the gift of not waiting and worrying.

Panic rises in my chest, and these flutters aren't from my

heart for the first time. "Transplant then?" I sound as though I'm begging, pleading with a stranger for my life as though it's his choice whether to administer mercy or to let me die. "Is there a research study I can join? A trial? I don't mind if it's not fully developed yet. There has to be something...something to fix this."

He swallows again, moving next to me and sits, hands flattened on the concrete, looking straight ahead at nothing. "Rachel, I understand your concerns and if I had an answer or solution, then rest-assured I would suggest it because making people better is what I strive to do. But a transplant won't work."

"Why not?" I say too loud, a little too angry. "I'm sure I've read somewhere that—"

"It's rare and it's spread already. Even if we swapped your heart out tomorrow, we wouldn't get it all. You'd only be prolonging the inevitable and not by much. Plus, the transplant list is a year long, best case. It's far too long a wait."

"But I'm cool with that. Really, I am. I already said to you I'd do anything, I'll wait." I force a smile at him.

He exhales, a loud submission, a sign of an impossible defeat. One I hope never to hear again. His head tips backward to the brick wall and he closes his eyes.

"Rachel, I think you misunderstand."

"No. You said it perfectly fine. I know there's a *really* long wait. I can be patient," I say.

This time, he simply gazes my way, sympathy and anguish filling his eyes. He rests a gentle hand on my shoulder.

"Rachel..."

Oh my god.

A cold chill tracks down my spine, all the way to my toes. The blood shrinks back from my fingertips.

"You mean I don't have a year? A year is too long *for me.* That's what you mean, isn't it?"

To this, he simply nods.

The finality in that confirmation rips through my gut. I turn to him, and now he has his face in his hands, scrubbing at his jaw as if he were the one getting bad news.

"How...worst-case scenario, how long do I have? Months, weeks?"

The hair is standing up on my neck as he cocks his head sideways through his fingers. A deep sigh comes out through his nose. "It's impossible to say exactly, but I'd say six months, give or take."

Chapter Four

My first rebellious act occurred when I was five years old. There must have been times before that—had to have been—but it's the first one I remember. My family lived in a farming community in Hammett, Idaho, and everyone I knew had a horse. Except for our family, that is.

Every birthday and Christmas, I begged for one, but by the time I turned five, it became clear that it wasn't going to happen unless I did something to change that. So, one afternoon, I snuck out and went over to our neighbors' corral and picked out the prettiest horse with a sleek sorrel coat and long shimmery mane. Carefully climbing on the fence, I encouraged the horse over to my position, bribing it closer with a bouquet of weeds plucked from the around the fence posts.

Then, I plastered myself to the massive beast's back, proudly parading myself around the paddock for a solid hour, declaring the beauty as my own and shrieking with delight.

My parents were flustered when they finally found me, Dad's eyes wide and full of fear as he approached the corral with caution, hands up as though negotiating with a hostile kidnapper.

I still recall the tremble in his voice as he spoke softly.

"Rachel, hun, why don't you come over here slowly, hook your arm onto that fence when you walk past it. Go steady and try not to make any sudden movements. Easy."

I only giggled at him, kicking at the horse more, sending it into a gentle canter and my dad's hands into his hair, pulling at the roots. But he didn't come get me. In fact, he never came close to the corral as my trusty steed would snicker and pin its ears back anytime Dad shifted forward.

Mom, on the other hand, was busy crossing herself and praying at the sight unfolding in front of her, watching her child awkwardly seated high upon that lofty beast.

Unbeknownst to me, I had picked out the one horse the Jones family used strictly for breeding, precisely because his temperament was so unpredictable. Not even the handlers could get a halter on him without him kicking out or rearing up, and they said he was impossible to control.

And here I was, a little five-year-old girl, bouncing my brown wavy hair around the pen atop a lethal weapon. I suppose it could have ended a lot worse than it did.

After a little more coaxing from my dad, I relented and slid down the horse's side and over its stomach, plopping to the ground as if it wasn't a big deal at all.

When I crossed under the fence, my dad raced to me, skidding on his knees to envelope me in his arms as if he had been so close to losing his first born. My mom came behind and joined us, thanking the Lord for keeping me safe while my new friend reared his front legs into the splintering fence, whinnying and snorting when my parents yanked me away.

Chapter Five

Back then, I was too young and too naïve to understand all the trauma I'd put them through. The look in my father's eyes that day is one I never want to see again. That terror and anguish were enough to see only once.

Which is why I haven't told them about my diagnosis.

Instead, I am yet again sitting in the increasingly frustrating UCSF Medical Center waiting room.

Alone.

After missing out on most of the concert, Dr. Trenton eventually helped me—dazed and confused—into an Uber. It was a week ago he released me only against a solemn promise to come to this follow-up appointment.

"Bring someone with you," he said more than once. "Someone you feel you can trust."

Trust. More like someone who'll pity my predicament. *Is a death sentence a predicament?* I scroll through my phone not looking at anything, just passing the minutes that tick by, waiting.

You'd think for someone with an overactive death clock, that they'd hurry up so I can use whatever precious minutes

I have remaining doing something other than *this*. But no. The system operates the same way for everyone, and I don't matter anymore than the other patients in the waiting room. As irritating as it is to hang around and wait, at least it passes some time outside of my apartment.

It's all been so surreal.

I spent last week mostly in bed, the city and I finding ourselves caught up in a perpetual fog. Unmoving, thick with tears, but unable to let a single one form to trickle down my face—just trapped inside, unwilling to vacate.

All part of the grieving process, so they say. Maybe I skidded right past denial, bumped into anger and bargaining, and went headfirst into depression, slamming into an abrupt and unwelcome brick wall.

Looking at it now, I imagine acceptance will arrive in the near future, likely the worst stage of them all. That's when it's over. Finality.

This depression is bad enough, but I need to prepare myself for what's coming. No time is right, but when do I tell everyone? When do I tell my best friend I'm no longer going to be around for random seedy diner dates and midnight memes? When do I tell Mom and Dad or my sister Chloe?

When is the 'right' time to explain to them that I have months to live and break all their hearts?

As any parent would, my dad and mom are bound to want to take care of their child and while I understand it, I really don't know if I can face the constant attention...the pity and obligation wrapped in a nice little bow disguised as help they will no doubt wish to gift me.

At present, my thoughts should be focused on the next half hour, and on what I'm about to hear for the second time. There's no way it will be any easier to stomach, especially hearing it in an official capacity with lab coats and chart notes.

The same medical assistant I saw last time calls me from the waiting room, breaking me free from my spiraling thoughts. My throat tightens as she—attired in a pastel pink Dora the Explorer scrub top—leads me into an exam room where I again take my seat on the scratchy paper.

I already know the results, but somehow, coming in here and seeing Dr. Trenton—Dave—in a lab coat and scrubs makes it official. He enters in his usual brusque manner, sweeping in from the hallway's open door with a gust of wind chasing his movements. He looks terrible as he approaches, eye bags hanging in bruising shades as if he hasn't slept since we last spoke.

Is that how I look too?

Probably worse. I haven't dared to stare in the mirror for days, and if I do look as bad, it will only be for a few more months anyway. The thought feels oddly distant, as if it's someone else I'm thinking of.

The doctor holds a tablet to his chest when he enters the exam room, at first standing in the opening, not coming any closer to either me or the stool he had so effortlessly slid onto last visit.

It's as though he sees me as diseased, not wishing to share the same air.

It's total nonsense, of course. He might seem avoidant, repelled from me the way two magnets of opposing polarities won't come together and spring away, but the only logical conclusion that comes to mind is his fear that I will somehow spill to everyone at UCSF that he gave a brutal diagnosis outside a grungy venue.

Dr. Trenton surveys the small exam room, his brows

matching his frown. "You're alone? Thought I told you to bring someone with you?"

His tone is clipped, mirroring my own sour mood but setting me even more on edge.

I can only look at my hands and dangling feet. "You did but I'm fine. I don't need anyone here. I'm not a child."

He's glowering at me, judging me as though he can't quite comprehend there wouldn't be a single person in the world for me to bring to such an important appointment.

"Most of my patients aren't children, Miss Heltin, but I still ask them to bring someone. You are no exception. You need the support," he says. As if I mustn't have a different view. "You shouldn't go through this alone," he offers, slightly softer now. "Plus, it's not only about you. It will help your loved ones if they can go through the process with you."

Thoroughly chastised, his words burn.

If I glance up at the doctor now, I'll see pity because he'll be seeing my eyes welling up, blurring all reasonings I had to come alone.

And I don't want that either. So, I avoid him and try to take steady breaths to shove the growing emotions down. This is such an alien experience. I avoid him, and he avoids saying anything in return. Yet somehow, we can still communicate to each other, barely managing to survive. This is inhumane in itself, this awkwardness, this absence of true connection at such a horrible time.

"Not in here," he tells me after a minute goes by without words. "Let's go to my office."

I slide off the circulation-restricting table, resigned to follow him into the office that I've noticed already is plain and dull, devoid of any character and boasting only stacks of papers and no personal effects. Nothing to show him as a man with family and friends.

No degrees or certificates framed in gaudy wood. Nothing homely such as a potted plant or an interesting paperweight, or a sweater hung over the back of a chair. Not even a hook to hang a lab coat.

It's as if he's exactly what I see—that this defines all of him. The desk is sad and bare other than charts, two empty coffee cups and a large bottle of water. A placard on his desk reads: David L. Trenton, MD, FACC, FACP, FAHA. I don't know or care what that all means, aware only that each extra letter after his name shows I'm in decent hands.

Someone comes up behind me as I take a seat.

"Come on in and join us," says Dave to the stranger, ushering in a man wearing a similar lab coat over a pressed collared shirt and snappy purple and gold tie.

The man takes a seat next to me and the door shuts.

The two men share the briefest of handshakes as if it's something they repeat a few times a day. Dave moves around our chairs and takes a seat behind the desk.

"Miss Heltin," Dave starts, acting as if we aren't already on a first-name basis. "This is Dr. Juan Santos, the head of the Oncology Department and specializing in cardiac oncology. We have been poring over your case trying to see if there is anything either of us can do to..." He stops speaking and it's all visibly written across his face. Pity.

Inside, something other than my heart breaks. "To not let me die?" I finish for him, his mouth growing tight and forming into more of a wince.

"Miss Heltin," Dr. Santos tries, crossing an ankle over his knee in my direction. I break from Dave and look at the man speaking. He's older, dark eyed and with his hair trimmed close to the scalp, but his smile is kind and sympathetic. In his line of work, I'd think that's a must.

"Dr. Trenton has asked me to review your case notes for anything we can do on our end. There are several options that I urge you to consider."

He keeps talking, but I stop listening when the words and phrases jumble into the same conclusions like 'may only prolong for a month', 'severe side effects', and my personal favorite, 'deteriorating quality of life'.

"If I may," I interrupt him while he's lecturing me on the potential side effects of a treatment involving too many needles and chemicals. He looks a tad put out that a mere mortal would dare to interrupt an oncology god mid-word. "I appreciate you both trying to figure something out, but I refuse to spend the time I have left hooked up to machines and taking medications that will offer only minimal improvements to my life and no real chance at making me better. Living a month longer while going through all those treatments is madness, isn't it? What's the point? I mean do people really *see* a point in it?"

"I assure you they very much do," Dr. Santos promises. Dave nods his head in silent affirmation, swiftly and with an unhappy look as if I've offended his colleague.

"Almost every person I see, except very geriatric patients, tend to opt for longer life. That's the case even if for a brief time. It gives you more time to prepare," he answers.

Prepare for what? What they mean is it gives relatives more time to get used to it. I'd say for someone like me, the less they draw it all out, the better. Why would I want to hang around and make it more difficult for myself?

It makes me think of all those painful and embarrassing family gatherings where someone says, 'well, I must be going now', but they're still standing there in the open doorway in the moonlight for another hour or so, freezing cold and making pointless small talk.

No one knows how to say goodbye these days. No one knows how to exit gracefully.

Amusing. And quite pathetic.

Scratching at my scalp I try to make sense of everything. "Isn't there anything either of you can offer me besides 'might be's' or 'could try's'? Anything that makes more long-term sense? Or are these my only options, to be medicated and violently sick into death?"

That bizarre sense of disconnection rears its ugly head again, as if I'm talking about someone else. Maybe it's not a bad thing. Perhaps it's self-preservation.

"There are clinical trials, aren't there?" I hear myself inquire again even though Dave already told me there wasn't. "That's something I would consider. At least I'd help out future research and maybe give myself more time. I've donated to plenty of them. Someone's got to be studying this, right?"

Dave looks as though he wants to say something, but holds it in, thinking better of it. He gestures toward Dr. Santos with a slight wave of his arm as if to say, *you might want to answer this one.*

Dr. Santos appears indifferent. He shakes his head then gives me an answer to a question I never asked.

"You will feel relatively normal for a while, but one day very soon, it will start taking a real toll on your body."

This is what I came to hospital for? To be told nothing. "But how does this relate to clinical trials?" I ask a second time.

"Well, it doesn't but I want to make clear that you won't be able to reconsider the options we've given you at that time, and that's going to happen soon. This is unfortunately all we can do. It's all we can offer. Clinical trials and research studies are not an option for you. The disease has progressed too far for them to be useful to you or the scientists. Now, if you are certain you don't want to move forward with these treatments offered today, we will respect that decision."

I huff out of exasperation. "So, reading between the lines, it sounds like you're saying I'm too far gone to participate in any trials. You know, I'm stronger than you think, and I feel fine other that the dizziness." Before even having a chance to rethink what I'm saying, I push more. "I can't wrap my head around the fact that I am only left with terrible options and that you're not willing to try a little harder to help me. It sounds like my only options are things that have no chance of working."

"You may be right, Miss Heltin. You are absolutely entitled to a second or even third opinion on this, but I'm afraid they will all come to the same conclusion," says Dr. Santos. "Dr. Trenton and I reached out to multiple colleagues to make sure we are advising you properly," he adds, conceding defeat as if he's tired of the verbal tussle with me. He clearly thinks he's caught up in some kind of an argument that he can't win no matter what he says. I must be coming across so abrasive, but it's unintended.

I'm terrified. Can't they see that?

"I'm sorry you have to even think about this," he says next. "And I apologize for taking up your time. And of course, I'm very sorry there are no clinical trials we consider suitable for you."

It suddenly feels so imbalanced and unjust that I cannot make my own decisions about suitability—as if all decisions are taken, stripped away by the system. Left with nothing but a countdown clock.

Dr. Santos falls quiet and nods politely, giving Dave a quick glance.

He tries to excuse himself without another word.

The door is already closing behind him when I speak, spinning toward it as if given a new rush of adrenaline.

"Doctor Santos!" I cry out, after him. "What would you do if you were me?"

Dr. Santos turns the upper half of his body toward me. "Miss, I get asked this question almost every time someone is given a terminal diagnosis. My answer is almost always the same. I tell them that I'd fight like hell."

His throat rolls back a swallow, his gaze drifting to Dave before settling back on me. "But with all due respect to you and Dr. Trenton's opinions, none of those patients have had a primary cardiac sarcoma that's metastasized into other parts of the body. In your case, I'd live my life the best I could while there was still time left. Spend it with the people you love. I wouldn't waste a precious minute on anything else." He doesn't wait for my response. "All the best."

The door shuts behind him with a soft click.

Deflating into the chair, I face forward and stare at Dave long after Dr. Santos leaves, waiting for him to say something, whatever seems as if it's right on the tip of his tongue. He stares back at me as if waiting for the same. I finally give in, lowering my head to focus on my hands that I can't stop twisting and squeezing.

Finding my voice amongst my crushed thoughts, I say, "Thank you for helping me the other night. Wasn't really in a great headspace to communicate that. My friends also thank you for not kidnapping me and for insisting I text them."

It didn't really happen that way, not exactly. In my haze that evening, I recall him forcing me to give the passcode to my phone and making me find Azzy's text messages as he pounded out a quick message to let her know I went home. Dave also went with me in the rideshare as I stared out the window the entire way, devoid of any emotion other than shock.

He didn't bother getting out of the car when the driver pulled up to my apartment. We didn't even speak at all, other than him making me promise to show up today.

He nods, but his mouth is in that same clenched tight line when he leans an elbow on the desk, fingers resting on his chin. "What are you going to do now? Have you told anyone yet?"

I shake my head. "I haven't thought of a creative way to say, 'hey Dad and Mom, funny story, I'll be dead in six months.' I'm still working on it. I'm still sorting through the finer details."

"Don't do that," he says, and I flinch at his tone as if this doctor has any right to discipline my behavior. He senses my rising anger, probably from the daggers I'm shooting him across the desk. "This is scary, and I get that you are dealing with it in your own way, but this is not a joke."

My anger flares to life, the wood on the arms of the chair digging into my palms as I squeeze until my fingers turn white. "You have no right to tell me how to feel right now."

He sits back and nods. "You're right, but I've been on the other side of someone that went through something similar, and I can tell you firsthand that those jokes are barbed when they land. You can't pull them back out without causing extreme pain. So yes, I respect the way you deal with it, but all I'm trying to do is provide a different angle of *how* to deal with it."

My cheeks flush and I'm not sure if it's the anger or embarrassment, but I don't care. I stand, my head held high in his direction. "Anything else before I go, doctor?"

He straightens a stack of papers. "If you need anything further from the cardiology department, I recommend Dr. Wu. She's brilliant and will be a great replacement. I've already briefed her about—"

"Replacement?" My stomach drops and I don't know why I'm letting him affect me.

Probably the fucking scrubs.

"Yes, replacement. I'm taking a sabbatical. I have some personal things I will be attending to."

I nod slowly, my neck flushing along with my cheeks at how cavalier he sounds.

"Well, enjoy your long and healthy life."

I salute him and turn to leave, my hand finding the door handle.

"Rachel," he calls out.

I don't face him, only remove my hand from the handle as I lock onto the fake wood grain pattern on the door. Tears fill the well along my lash line, and I have no clue why they decided to show now.

There's rustling behind me and I feel his presence near my back and hold my breath.

He slips a card into my palm and leans close to me.

"Anyone who listens to the same screaming bands I love, is a friend of mine. It's not often I meet someone with the same taste. If you ever need anything, give me a call, even if you only need a friend. Someone to talk to."

Gripping the card until it's almost crumpled, I turn to

him. Tears free fall down my cheeks, and I glance down at the wrinkled business card. A sob bubbles out as Dr. Trenton's arms wrap around me before it even escapes my lips, pulling me into him.

I nearly collapse in his hold.

He's the first person to know of my illness and the first to comfort me.

His chin rests on my head, and I cry into his broad chest, my arms wrapped around his middle as I come undone. He pulls me in tighter, gently caressing my shoulder.

I don't know much about the medical field, but my guess would be that this is completely inappropriate, but Dave doesn't seem to care. And I don't either.

Chapter Six

One Month Later.

We're sitting at an outdoor café along the southern coast of Portugal in the sleepiest of villages. It's wonderful, the temperature perfect, the villagers going about their daily chores and off in the distance, a fishing boat faintly chugs across the gentle swells.

Salty air fills the patio along with the recent catches of fish brought to the restaurants along the coastal strip. There are probably sardines in the breezy mix too, and I wonder how all these restaurants got the best views in the village of Praia da Luz. When I dip my head to the right, I watch a couple devouring a plateful of the tiny fish and it's not even ten in the morning.

The briny breeze coats my hair in the best way possible, turning my shoulder-length mousy brown mess into wavy curls kissed by the salt of the ocean.

The tan I earn by extending my bare legs into the sun doesn't hurt either.

I've been sipping on a Galão even though it's hot enough to be dipping in the waves. The frothy coffee leaves foam on my lips, and I lick it off, my hands hugging the porcelain. It's pure heaven—the sweetest nectar of the gods in the simplest form of espresso and milk.

Honestly, why can't America get its act together to produce something with so much more depth than a drive-through coffee pumped out in ten seconds? If coffee is one of our supposed national treasures, is that the very best we can do? It's shameful. A Galão tastes so different. I can't pinpoint it, but I've never tasted anything like it.

Mom laughs, rich and genuine, making me smile into the sun baking my face.

I don't even bother to lower my sunglasses to protect my eyes.

She's sitting across from me under the shadow of an umbrella and has been chatting up a woman named Helen, someone I'd guess is the same age as Mom.

Mom holds onto her wide-brimmed straw hat as a gust of wind picks up while the woman slides over half an egg custard pastry that she can't finish. They both revel in how delicious these incredibly simple things taste when so far from home and I can't disagree.

They've been chatting since before I came out of the hotel, and now they have started to compare their itineraries and restaurants to try that dot the enchanting landscape of the Algarve region.

Helen's dark hair is peppered with time and cut into a perfectly angled bob, tilting toward where she points to the beach in front of us. As it sways in the breeze, she goes on about how lovely the coastline looks in the morning light.

"It's so beautiful, isn't it? I could take up residence right here in this chair and never move again," she declares.

My mother leans into Helen's aura as if the other woman were a magnet full of knowledge.

They move on to the all-important contest of whose family is more successful, a competition most parents partake in, though to tell the truth, neither woman seems that competitive. Mom's face beams with pride as she tells Helen about my younger sister Chloe.

Chloe... with her perfect husband and two spoiled rotten boys and a little girl on the way.

Helen's face lights up almost identical as she tells Mom of her son who invited her on this trip, and of a daughter, but she doesn't say much about her.

I smile politely when mom points in my direction then take another sip of the Galão.

"My daughter's a *travel blogger.* You wouldn't believe all the places she gets to see. She's got more passport stamps in that book than I ever thought she could fit in there. She even had to ask for more pages to be added. There must be three or four dozen. She's a very talented writer. We're so proud of her," she says, beaming my way.

The other woman smiles, a genuine and warmhearted smile that reaches her eyes—rare these days among strangers. "What exactly is a travel...what was the word again?"

"Blogger," Mom says.

Helen nods with the revelation. "What exactly does 'blogger' mean? I hear all the young people using it, but I never understood it."

Mom is silent. She's thinking, mulling over the question, probably not sure of the answer herself. She raises her sunglasses to look my way. "Rachel," she calls across, apparently not worried whether I'm dozing.

I raise my head and give an exaggerated glance over my drink.

"Forgive your old and out-of-touch mom for disturbing

you, but Helen was asking. What's a blogger? I suppose I should know really, shouldn't I? What does it mean?"

"What's a blogger?" I repeat, toying with them. "It's what I am, Mom. Do you even know your daughter at all?" I giggle and adjust my sunglasses out of my hair and position them on my nose. "It just means I write and review my travel experiences and put the online."

They're still trying to interpret what the word really means, but I tune them out. I mean, no one ever wants to talk about work when down on the beach and soaking up the sun.

Then there's Dad, less than thrilled and sitting next to me on a flimsy plastic chair that can barely take his weight, his pasty-white farmer's legs stretched toward the ocean like mine but crossed at his loafers. Has the sun ever seen him in Wrangler khaki green shorts? I'm not sure *I* have. And I'm not sure I want to again, either.

Hell, since when did Wrangler make shorts?

The limbs are a little blinding, but I'm glad he's taking such a risk for a lifelong 501 Levi's man.

He's been ready to go do something for a while. I can tell, seeing his eyes flitting left and right across the beach, and watching his right leg and foot jiggle as if they have a mind of their own. He's waiting to be off and doing something a little more productive than passing the day on the hot sand.

Like any good farmer, he's been up and ready since 4 a.m., and this lazy lifestyle is not his thing. Regardless, he indulges Mom's chattiness despite the awkwardness of attempting to sit still at the table. Secretly, he loves that she takes such pleasure in talking with strangers. It's that twinkle in his eye that gives him away. The same one that whenever Mom glances his way, the whole world stops for him, just so he can shoot her a playful wink.

And he takes even more pleasure in recognizing how every person seems to adore his wife as much as he does.

Plus, there have been plenty of times Mom's chats have proven to be worth so much more than pleasantries and he knows this.

He picks up a newspaper, unfolding it, eyeing each page and scrutinizing each line, sighing and nodding, looking fully immersed in the printed ink. A huge grin spreads across my mouth, hidden under the protection of my coffee cup.

It's a Portuguese newspaper.

Unless I've been living under a rock for the last thirty years, my dad doesn't read or speak Portuguese. In fact, I'm not sure he could say thank you to the waiter if put on the spot. Which means he's doing more than pretending to read. He's biding his time and waiting for my mom to wrap up and he's doing it without pushing her. I find it incredibly endearing as he attempts to reread the paper again, all the way from the beginning.

On my final sip, the breeze picks up enough for me to set the cup of what's left of the froth back to the table, shielding my eyes from the morning sunbeam as it comes sneaking under the yellow umbrella trimmed in white cordage. It flashes alternating light and shadows across my face.

Eventually, the material stops flapping about and I'm cast into the shade. It's the moment I see *him* walking up to the table. Tall, with near-black hair that's not quite messy, but not quite put together either. Shoving my sunglasses up, I squeeze my eyes closed and pop them back open, wondering if his perplexed cobalt eyes connecting with mine are an illusion.

It's also the same moment that the woman, Helen, tells my mother, "Did I mention that my son is a cardiologist? Oh, here he is!"

A bombardment of emotions hits me all at once as Dr. Dave Trenton approaches our little slice of quiet paradise.

Or maybe it's more like a tsunami. Either way, all I can do is watch him approach, feeling my already red and burning face flushing even more scarlet, my heart in palpitations—this time not caused by a terrible disease.

In fairness, my entire system seems to be on red alert, wanting to run, yet yearning to stay.

The pull of his own confused gaze sucks me out toward him before I'm about to get slammed with the big one. His eyes skim over to mine, but as I gawk blankly, he only smiles enough to be polite and pivots to the group.

He shakes my parents' hands the same way I'm certain he would if they'd stepped through the door of his consulting room, addressing them as Randy and Carol. Then he approaches me in a businesslike fashion, tentatively, saying, "Hello. How are you?"

"This is our daughter Rachel," I vaguely hear Mom say.

"Rachel," he repeats slowly. He extends a hand toward me. "A pleasure."

The heat of his hand brands mine, fingers sending searing delights to places I shouldn't be concerned with. He's touched me before, professionally—mostly, but this is the first time it really hits me that Dave, not Dr. Trenton, is touching me.

If I didn't already have an issue with heart palpitations, I'd swear mine were skittering all over the place. While I should be grateful a cardiologist stands in my presence to keep me safe, he's the absolute last person I want to see.

My first instinct is to run away and lock myself in the hotel until he's gone.

Then in the next moment, I am longing to stand and hug him tight in relief, the same way he embraced me in San Francisco. Like a craving, I want more than a handshake. I want his comfort as the only person that knows.

The emotions of it all are muddled to a pulp inside me. My heart leaps and my eyes want to well up. My stomach is nauseous and churns, and my inner voice sings. But like before, I realize something unpalatable: he's robbing me of all of my strength and power, something he's done twice before. Once at the concert and once in his office.

This is the third time he holds me in his control. I can't run. I'm paralyzed by him. This is uneasy, peculiar, and we're in the spotlight too, everyone looking at us both wondering why neither of us are doing anything other than facing each other with odd expressions.

Finally, he seems to take in our silent audience and forces his mouth into a cringe of a smile before turning to the group.

"Dave has taken some time off after a particularly difficult case and came out here to recharge. He asked me to join him," his mother explains.

Am I that case?

Of course not. That's impossible with the caseload I assume all the doctors at UCSF take on.

My case is a drop in the doctor's bucket.

Once introductions are done, he won't meet my wandering eyes anymore, taking the one free chair between Helen and me. "You don't mind if I take this seat?" he asks with that same forced politeness.

"No," I mutter. But I do. I really do. Every nerve in me is firing at once until good and frazzled.

My mom is eating this up, seeing an attractive young doctor and her single daughter ogling at him, and she smells an opportunity. "Your mother said you're from the Bay Area," she says, her voice a touch too high. "So is our Rachel." As she glances at Dave's mother, there is something conspiratorial going on and it's enough to pull me away from him and snap my jaw shut.

Luckily, he picks up on it too and gives Mom a forced smile. "I doubt we'd ever run into each other. It's quite a large area."

Mom looks momentarily crestfallen, as if the bottom's dropped out of her world.

I almost let out a sigh of relief, but then he speaks again and all the blood rushes out of my face. "What's the occasion for coming all the way out here? Something important?"

His head swivels to me, eyes lingering, but I just want to snatch the newspaper my dad is reading and hide behind it. It's as if he sees right through everything.

Fuck you, Dave. Fuck your judgmental glances sent from your perfect face. You might think we have some weird connection, but you aren't getting anything from me other than an attitude and a permanent flight risk.

"Rachel was given a free trip for her blogging business, and she's invited us along. Even though I still don't really know what blogging is." Mom often pokes fun at herself and she and Helen laugh. I give the best fake smile possible, noticing Dave's eyes crinkling at the corners before he gains back his solemnity.

"Hmm," he hums out, not taking his attention off me. "That's great."

My mother angles over to Helen, cooing to her new friend, "Isn't it wonderful to have kids who care about their parents enough to bring them along on these adventures?"

Dave's fingers drum across the table, his knee bouncing next to me. Without warning, he shoves back his chair in a huff that has my dad folding the corner of the paper over, eyeing the doctor as he towers over me.

"Rachel, is it? Would you like to go for a walk down there?" He tips his chin to the beach beyond a parking lot and thrusts his chair under the table with a loud ear-splitting screech.

Maybe I don't want to hide behind the paper at all. Perhaps I want to swat him with it. Thinking Dad might not appreciate me ripping his paper away, I sink deeper in my seat and try to drain whatever foam is left in my coffee, hoping my face isn't flushing again.

"No, I'm good thanks. I feel a bit dehydrated, so I'll stay here in the shade."

He rakes a hand through his hair, unmoving. "I'd really like to go for a walk with you."

"And I'd really like to finish my coffee."

Dad lowers the paper even further.

"You can take it with you."

"Thanks, but I think I'd rather enjoy it here."

Dave snatches my coffee cup from out of my hand and turns it upside down on the saucer, the porcelain clanging. I could swear his mother gasps.

"Oh look. Your coffee's finished." Dave turns toward the sea. "It's a nice day for a walk."

"No *thanks*," I retort back, folding my arms across my chest. "Like I said, I'm fine sitting here."

He lets out a frustrated sigh, yanking the chair back

again, about to sit. "Okay, it's your choice. Guess we can chat here in front of everyone."

All this is going on with my parents and Helen volleying their glances between us. This is the only reason I spring up, my face redder than it should be this early in the morning. "Fine," I snap, marching off through the parking lot and into the sand, my flowy white tank top flapping behind me.

Looking back to make sure he's following me, I'm met with three sets of wide eyes staring back from their yellow café umbrella. I wave them off and trudge far enough toward the water that my parents and Helen can't hear. Once I dig my heels into enough sand, I turn sharply to him, almost slamming my nose into his chest.

My neck cranes straight up to look him in the eye. "What the *fuck* is your problem?"

His eyebrows shoot up and he points at himself. "You ask me about *my* problem? Have you even told them? Because the way it looks to me is that you are on a perfectly normal family vacation. Tell me, how did your job afford to pay for this trip? Is travel blogging covering family expenses nowadays? How long has it been now?"

"That's none of your business!" I screech. "You are my doctor, not my conscience. I have a little under five months to live and I don't need your approval to handle this the way I want to handle it."

His shoulders slump. "How are you being fair to them? To yourself? Come on, Rachel. Before long, your parents"—he looks back to the café and even though we're far enough away he still lowers his voice—"they're going to notice your deterioration. Look, I'm only trying to pass on some advice, that's all. Personally, I think you need to tell them."

Squinting at him, I can't find an argument worthy of his

observation. "Why are you even here? How do you keep turning up where you're not welcome?"

He flinches at this. "Do you think you have some sort of monopoly on Portugal?"

"And the concert?" I remind him.

He snorts. "What, do you think I've devised some scheme to follow you around the world? Why would I even do that? You think I want to keep running into you?" Dave's face contorts and his jaw locks, then releases. "All I've been doing is trying to get you out of my goddamn head!" His eyes go wide, and he spins away, striding down the beach as if he can't get away from me fast enough.

I stay in place, paralyzed and forced to process his words. Am I really that off putting? After I regain my senses, I go after him, jogging in the direction he's gone. When I come up alongside, he glares down at me.

"You shouldn't be running. This is serious, Rachel."

"I'll add it to the ever-growing list of things I *shouldn't* be doing."

His jaw clenches so tight I can't tell whether the rumble is coming from his bone grinding together or of the waves hitting the shore. He collapses into the sand, wrapping his arms around his knees, not seeming to care about the sand still attached to his skin.

I'm not sure what I should do so I remain standing, hands on my hips.

"I don't want to tell them. I tried once and it was... I can't do it," I finally say with a release of breath, then drop my ass into the warm grains, burying my pink toenails, sandals and all, underneath. Folding my arms across my chest, I take in the waves. "Not here, at least. I want two weeks of genuine happiness before I destroy it all. I need them to have positive memories before I rip that all away. I cashed out my pathetic savings and decided to make one last trip out of it." I turn to him in time to see that scowl soften minimally. "Can you please not make me feel guilty about that? I can't spend my money where I'm going next, but I can make memories that might help to get them through the worst of all of this."

He brushes away the sand on his hands onto his shorts.

"Look, I've been in their position, Rachel." One eye finds mine even though he's facing the water. "No matter when you tell them, it's going to hurt, but the longer you wait, the more all your options dwindle."

"What options though?" My hands fly in the air and my lungs burn from the ragged desperate breaths of frustration. "Tell me, doctor, what options are left for me, because at that last appointment, it sure seemed as if there weren't any meaningful ones. I refuse to pump my body full of chemicals that have a 'minimal chance' of changing the outcome—other than making me feel like shit for the next five months."

He sighs. "I know, I only meant that your family could help."

Inhaling another deep breath, the weight of my secret consumes me. "And for the love of god, don't you dare even hint at me being sick around them again. Don't you have the Hippocratic Oath to follow? Isn't there a law about patient confidentiality? As I said, I will tell them, but not here, and it'll be in my time, not yours. Mind your own damn business."

He focuses back on the waves, so much smaller than the ones at Ocean Beach in San Francisco, calmer, not as much seafoam and far less chaos. The breeze is warmer than it probably should be in late April, sweeping up into his hair, twisting those short dark ends skyward.

I think he's finished talking and I go to push myself up to stand, but he grabs my wrist, preventing me from leaving my seat in the sand. His eyes pin me in place. "Promise me you won't wait any longer than necessary, for their sake. Please, Rachel. Imagine only just getting the words out and while they're still trying to process it, you die."

Such cruel words. In the moment, I detest him for that brutal bluntness.

"I won't wait that long," I whisper into the breeze between us. "Once we're back home, I'll break it to them."

The frustration of promising a stranger anything has me getting to my feet again and plowing back through the sandy beach and up to where my parents and Helen have been no doubt eyeballing us. Dave is on my heels and when I chance a glance back, his head is tucked low between his shoulders, both hands shoved into khaki shorts.

It looks as though I've spent the last ten minutes berating and beating him down.

A frown is forming on my mouth.

Mom wastes no time pulling me out of my guilt and slamming me right into panic as we approach their grinning faces. "Helen and I have decided we should tour some of the sights together. What do you think? There's so much to see here. It'll be nice as a little group."

She's giddy at the idea of having someone interested in the churches and castles she wants to see. Dad goes along with it, but his enthusiasm usually only bleeds through at mealtimes.

I don't have the heart to tell her that I'm dreading anything to do with Helen and her son. *Especially* Dave.

Dad's peeking one eye over the newspaper again, no doubt trying to decipher my reaction.

Hell, I can't even figure out what I'm feeling at the

moment, but Dad keeps glancing at Dave, and I register the question in my father's face: why does this man have me so worked up? I suspect his dad-perfected spidey senses are taking in the whole mood of the table. I give him a weak smile and half an eyeroll. Hopefully, my discomfort isn't as plainly written across my face as it feels and it comes across as indifference.

There is no point whatsoever in making Dad worry about me.

Not yet. Not here in Portugal.

I grab my purse, slinging it over my shoulder and intent on finding our rental car in the cobblestone parking lot between the café and beach. The two older women fall in step ahead of me, wandering away from us arm-in-arm. Dave and Dad are the last to vacate the table, some passive aggressive peacocking going on between the two of them.

Dad pushes a chair in, and Dave does the same then pulls the coffee cup and saucer from under Dad's nose, taking them to the nearest bin on top of a trash can.

Dad's voice does this peculiar thing when Dave returns to grab the discarded newspaper on the table. "I've got it," Dad tells him. It's a little deeper than normal. Am I the only one noticing? It's not quite a warning but comes close.

More like, *I'm watching your every move, Doctor Dave.*

Dave stands there, one finger holding the paper to the table, but Dad yanks it out from under his touch and tucks the newspaper into his armpit, leaving Dave more perplexed.

I'm watching over my shoulder. Why has Dad even taken the damn thing as if he's going to continue to read it later? Or maybe he wants to use it to swat at Dave. Either way, it's out of character for my normally calm and collected father. He can obviously sense something's amiss and Dave's the cause.

As annoyed as I am, the interaction between them causes a grin to spread across my face, replacing the frown. When they both head toward the rest of us, I quickly conceal it again.

"Rachel," my mom says, retreating back to snake an arm in mine, her new mid-life crisis auburn and honey-streaked pixie haircut tickling my ear when she leans against me. "Helen and I were thinking that the Castle of Castro Marim is the best place to start. It's the farthest one. After that, maybe we'll drive over to Alte for lunch and tour the other church and castle in that little town of Silves. What do you think? We can all ride together. It will be so much fun, an adventure with new friends!"

She wants me to agree with her and be just as excited, but I'm already so damn tired. Can she not see my exhaustion? Is my makeup concealer that good?

The lightheadedness and blackening vision have been in and out for days now and weren't aspects I factored into this trip. I want to glare at Dave for sucking out my energy reserves before the day even gets started. Arguing is so senseless, and it's left me depleted.

But Dave's moved away from the group and is busy examining Dad's rental car.

"Randy, it seems a little bit tight for five, don't you think?" Dave calls over to Dad, but he's ignoring Dad's pinched face and instead staring at me as if he can see the energy bar draining across the video game of my life.

He's giving me an out.

"Why don't Rachel and I follow you in my car and if anyone gets tired, they can come back with me? As much as I'd love to, I can't stay out all day because I have some work to catch up on later. It's up to you." He looks between us. "But it makes sense. And rather than cut short your trip, I can come back on my own. What do you think?"

The women both jump at this idea and giggle in unison. As for Dad?

He's clearly unsure, not saying a word but in one look, his eyes ask me a hundred questions.

I give him a nod and it's enough for him to get into his car.

The smallest of European cars sits a few spots away from Dad's, and I open the door while Dave walks around to the driver's side. How two adult-sized humans could fit into this tiny and ridiculous thing is beyond me. The fact that there is even a backseat is laughable.

Somehow, this vehicle doesn't meet my idea of what a medical professional might drive—not flashy enough. If I were to venture a guess, I'd think he'd go for something sportier for all the sharp turns and curves of the coastline. He seems like someone that would take every shift into a new gear with precision while making it look easy.

The image of Dave relaxed behind the wheel of a sports car flashes through my mind. I snicker and he eyes me, his demeanor as serious as ever. Does this man ever smile?

There're books as thick as my thighs and a backpack on the passenger seat as Dave climbs through the driver side to toss them in the back. "Give me a moment while I move these."

"You do know they think we're screwing," I say from outside the car.

He jolts up and bumps his head on the roof of the low ceiling. "Jesus, Rachel."

I shrug at him and chuckle while he rubs the top of his head. "What? It's true. My God-fearing mother is plotting with your mom. Do you not see the way they've been giggling like little schoolgirls since we came back from the beach?"

"No, I haven't noticed," he snips at me, but it sounds a little more playful than sour. "I've been too preoccupied with the death glares from your dad." He motions for me to sit, the seat now clear. "Jump in. There's not much room, but it works for these narrow roads."

"You have to know that by the time we get to Castro Marim, they'll have our whole life planned out. They're hoping for a quick engagement and a herd of kids, I'm sure. I think my mom likes the name Ian for a grandson." I drop my hands into my lap as he starts the car, but he doesn't put it in gear.

He turns the upper half of his body toward me, his face hardening. "Well, she can have a grandson called Ian, but he won't be *my* kid. I don't date patients. It kind of goes against my ethos."

I'm sure it applies even more to patients who are dying. I want to say, but I don't.

"That's not where I was going with that," I say instead. "It was just a joke, but I'm still sure we are the topic of conversation in that car. Plus, Ian is more of a middle name, don't you think?"

He looks mortified and glances behind. Then he slowly reverses the car out of the space. The pinking of his cheeks makes me smile, as if I've tangled him up in a web of words.

Dr. Dave Trenton doesn't seem like a man who gets embarrassed easily.

My fingers pick at the hem of my black shorts, keeping me occupied for the first silent thirty minutes of the ride through the narrow village streets. I don't bother looking out the window. What did I need to see anyway?

This trip wasn't and isn't about me. It isn't my bucket list to rush through while my candle is close to the end of the wick. It's for them. For them to know we spent some quality time together.

To Dave's credit, he stays quiet as we merge onto the main highway, staying a few car lengths behind my parents and Helen.

"Would you mind?" he asks, not waiting for an answer before dropping his phone in my lap after we've been cruising down the uncluttered highway for a while.

I almost leap into the low roof. "You scared me."

"Sorry," he says as a throwaway remark, not sounding at all empathic.

"Uh sure. What do you want me to do?"

"Two-five-five-four-seven-eight," he says, nodding toward the screen. I look at him once then enter the numbers, the password flicking away to his home screen.

A beautiful woman with long sleek hair the color of a raven's wing and his same dark cobalt blue eyes stares back at me. She's in the middle of a laugh, her face scrunched and mouth wide open while a much younger Helen and Dave have their arms around her as though this hug was a surprise.

"Your sister?" I tilt the screen toward him.

"Go to my playlists," he says, ignoring me.

467 unread emails catch my eye and the phone icon with a red twenty-two on it, but I don't ask. He doesn't seem in the mood to chat and that's fine by me.

When I open the app, he pushes a cord at me that's plugged into the dash, and I fumble to plug it in.

The first playlist is titled 'Calm Me Down' and the next one 'Pump Me Up'.

"The first one," he directs, as if he knows I want to question the playlist names and he only wants to stop any conversation. I hit it and then the shuffle button, shoving the phone in the slit between our seats. As music begins to play, I turn, almost involuntary, toward him, mouth agape. The music is dark, heavy, and definitely not what a sane person would describe as calming.

It's perfect.

"Beartooth? Seriously?" I shake my head, grinning. "Nobody knows who they are. I love them. Was this the reason you wanted us to travel together? I don't think the three up ahead would approve, do you? Or is Helen a closet fan?"

A smile tugs at his mouth, but he remains focused on the road, tapping a thumb against the steering wheel as I crank up the 'evil incarnate of music'—Mom's description, not mine.

I even sing—well scream—out a few one-liners, a rush of adrenaline racing through my veins as we cruise the coastline of Portugal in the stupidest looking of cars while listening to devil music.

And for the first time in longer than I care to admit, I feel happy. Carefree. Almost enough to forget. As if a few weeks of this would take away all the depression and impending doom weighing me down.

We are loud and raucous, as Dave and I sing a final song from one of the A Day to Remember albums at the top of our lungs. We pull into the parking lot, and it's more shouting and growling, but still hardcore as tiny beads of sweat collect on my forehead despite the A/C being on max. Dave is wildly thrusting his fist into the air, hitting the headlining of the tiny car to really drive home the last seconds of our shared final song.

Our parents are watching us, slack jawed while they

wait outside their car for us to park. Dad's arms are folded across his chest. And I don't even register that familiar scowl. I'm a giggling, stomach-clenching mess—god, it hurts so much to laugh like this—and Dave *almost* looks as if he's enjoying himself too.

As I lean back into the headrest, he reaches for the car key, cutting both the engine and music.

I wave at the boring adults and laugh again, my head bobbing in Dave's direction. "Your so-called 'calming' playlist might have just done that for me. I needed that, thank you."

There's an awkward moment that passes between us, both waiting for the other to speak. I don't wait for his reply and bound out of the car instead.

Chapter Seven

THE FIRST TIME I RAN AWAY FROM HOME—AND NOT THE 'five-year-old going off to find a pony' kind of running away —I was fourteen and discovering that farm life wasn't what I wanted. All I wanted was to be free of the endless dusty fields and constant diesel fumes from the tractors.

I wanted to be with my new boyfriend on my own terms and even more than anything else, the lure of a city with more than one stoplight called to me.

It's all so vivid in my memory.

That night, moonlight bathed the fields in a silvery glow as I snuck through my window, not even bothering to shut it on the way out. We lived miles from anything resembling human life and I don't even know how I expected to get very far. Even if someone was kind enough to stop and offer a ride, the odds on them knowing me were high. And I didn't even stop for a moment to think about the risk of allowing some stranger to take me away.

Of course, growing up on the farm I knew how to drive the trucks and tractors, but if I cranked up an engine at two in the morning, I would awaken the house, Dad would soon be out, and my escape foiled. With that option out, I sprinted down our gravel driveway to the road with a backpack of full of clothes until my lungs gave out.

Then I walked the dirt road leading to the frontage road that fed to the main highway. I planned to hitchhike the sixty or so miles to Boise, figuring the rest out from there.

What other choice did I have? My freedom was at stake.

When the first set of headlights came over the hill behind me, I stuck my thumb out in the hope it would stop. The engine revs dropped as it coasted to a stop. Without even bothering to look inside the stationary vehicle, I lifted the handle to open the door.

"Where you going, Rache?"

Dad gave me a simple tilt of his chin and I deflated, swinging the squeaking door wider, falling into the bench seat and tossing my runaway bag to the floorboard as he put the truck into gear.

We drove off, my head tucked between my knees that were pulled up to my chest. The work truck was the only vehicle Dad didn't care if my feet were on the seat, so I used the position like a shelter to protect me from whatever he had planned for my punishment.

"I don't want to be a farmer," I divulged, keeping my head between my knees. "I want to travel, to see more than dirt roads and rusty trucks. I hate it here." To drive my point home, I flicked at the mechanical window lever that was missing half of its brittle plastic handle and it swung in a loop twice before returning to its steady rocking from the truck driving down the bumpy road.

"Someday, you might like it out here."

"Unlikely," I muttered.

"Then I guess there's only one thing left to do. Where do you want me to drop you off?"

His question drew my head off my knees. "Really?"

He met my eyes and nodded. "You're going to go no matter what I say, so why don't I get you there safe? As long as you call your mom later in the morning. She'll be upset, you know."

I remember sitting there as he burned precious fuel into our small town and beyond to the next. When he pulled up to a twenty-four-hour diner next to the truck stop, he turned off the pickup and put his hands on the thighs of dirty jeans.

He waited for my direction.

And waited.

And I never moved.

He had offered to recognize my right to choose. He offered my freedom with no conditions. It was not what I had expected.

After a while, I shook my head. "I think I want to go home, Dad."

There was no gloating from him, no I-told-you-so's or hours long lecture, he just left me in the truck and strolled into the diner. A few minutes later, he came back out and handed me a cup of coffee in a paper cup and sipped on one for himself. Tears came to my eyes and a hitch to my throat.

My loving, non-judgmental dad. I had taken it all for granted. I had taken him for granted.

"Thanks Dad," I squeaked out, hardly able to speak, the guilt eating into me alive and biting at my selfishness.

That morning, we drove for an hour around town and among the various farm plots.

He didn't talk during the drive, but as twilight started to paint shades of pastels across the sky, he pulled off the road and faced the truck toward the approaching sunrise, cutting the engine.

I sipped on my coffee, the first real black coffee I'd ever had, and I hated the bitterness. But I drank it as if I enjoyed every drop, because he had gifted it to me.

As the sun pierced our eyes, he set his cup into a holder and rotated toward me.

"Today's a new day, Rachel. All I ask is that it's worth whatever decisions you make. You only have one perfect life to live. Might as well make it count. Otherwise, what's the point?" He started the truck and drove me home without my response and without pushing for one.

When we pulled into the driveway of the farmhouse, Mom was waiting on the porch with her arms crossed and forehead wrinkled, begging for information, but Dad only shook his head as I brushed past her and retreated into my room.

I have no doubt he told her what happened as he never kept anything from Mom, but we never spoke about it again. There was no need. We had a tacit understanding now, an agreement that needed no conversation—and no doubt he knew that a heavy discussion might push me away.

So, I disappeared into my room and at breakfast later that morning I sat next to my younger sister. We fought over the last piece of bacon, the same as we did every morning. And for that moment, and for a little while after, it was all I needed.

Chapter Eight

Dad's studying me now in the same way he did that morning at breakfast, not quite sure what to do with me. There must be a thousand solutions running around the cogs in his brain, but he's happy that we are back together, and even happier that everything's okay.

I'm sure he fretted the entire time I was in Dave's car.

I laugh at him, at the concern etched in every wrinkle on his face, and he scowls more. "Sorry Dad, we were jamming out to music you and Mom would hate. We did you all a favor." I take his arm as he leads us up into a castle over five thousand miles from the dusty back roads of Hammett, Idaho.

The path is dotted with loose cobblestones, and we traverse the incline with caution. For what feels like forever, we climb as a group up the hill to a castle perched overlooking a European village, whitewashed and baked by the heat of the sun.

Teetering precariously on one stone halfway up, the graze of a strong hand rests at my back, steadying the wobble of my body.

When I expect to find my dad, he's turned away, chatting with Mom and Helen.

My head snaps the other direction to find Dave right there, ready to catch me if I tumble. Taking a miscalculated step away from him, I do exactly what I was avoiding. My arms pinwheel, attempting to balance myself, but Dave is faster, wrapping an arm around my middle and leveling me upright on steadier stones.

He's saved me from a fall but hell—who gives him permission to grab me like this? To hold me flush to the upper part of his body. He's lucky I don't elbow him straight in the gut.

Of course, I can't elbow him or say anything, and I don't bother to push back for one very obvious reason. Our parents are watching us with more than mild curiosity. From their perspective, Dave's wrapped around me, my arm draped over his shoulder. It almost looks natural, as if something's developing between us and we're being flirty.

As much as I want to, there's no recoil from his hold, not wanting to give Dad any more reasons to worry that this stranger is holding me against my will. The black scowl must be obvious, even to one as thick-skinned as Dave. My gaze goes over my brows, pinning itself to Dave's, letting him see that the 'helpless little woman' is not okay with being rescued.

Dave just grins. A stupid shit-eating grin. It's the first time I've seen the pristine row of white teeth beaming my way and I should be grateful to be privy to such a rare, genuine occurrence, but I'm not.

"Want me to punch that smile off your face?" I sneer quietly.

His mouth is right near my ear all of a sudden while his arms brace tighter.

"Oh, come on. Most people would say thank you for not letting them eat ancient cobblestones. I was doing you a favor and you know it. Just admit it."

The warmth of his breath against my skin stirs something, a sensation my mind shoves further away than where it would like to shove him.

"Let me go." And he does. No thanks comes from me.

My steps don't falter anymore up to the top of the castle, but every breath grows tight, coming far heavier than for everyone else. Dave remains glued at my side. "Why do you have to keep hovering next to me? Don't you have anywhere else to be?" I snap at him as we near the top.

His head tilts my way. "You know why. It's not a big deal to have someone nearby if you need anything." While he's trying to be casual about it, this is infuriating. Seeing him staring at me relentlessly like a cat ready to pounce on whatever medical emergency or sudden crisis a dying woman might have. I had everything under control before he came along.

There's one consolation to this interruption in my vacation plans as a peel of laughter comes from our parents while they wait in line for tickets. As irritating as Dave is, there's so much gratitude in me for my parents finding Helen. His mom is a riot and the three of them haven't stopped laughing since we left that little café in Praia da Luz. It's exactly what I wanted this vacation to be for them.

If Dave comes as a package deal with his mom, then I suppose I can force myself to make it work for my parents' sake. This trip needs to be nothing but good memories for them.

"We're going to go on up to the top of those steep rampart walls and head on to the tower lookouts," calls my mom, shouting into the wind, her hand shielding at her eyes. It takes a moment to understand what she's saying against the sound of the wind and the flapping of jackets.

Panic invades my thoughts as my eyes trail up the narrow steps past the entrance. And like Dave keeps graciously reminding me, my parents have no idea of my plight. So why wouldn't they push it to the highest points of the castle?

There's no way I physically can do it, not with the way the walk up zapped all my remaining energy.

At the base of the stairs, Dad's adjusting his small backpack straps after passing bottles of water to everyone. They're gearing up to go and I'm chewing on my lower lip. But once again, someone's intense gawking penetrates me, bringing self-consciousness to my cheeks in a flush of red. Dave continues to study every breath I exhale, every muscle in my legs that moves a little slower than the step before.

As our group moves toward the massive blocks of stairs, hesitation comes, my hand resting on a stone wall at the first of the steps while the familiar peppering of spots enters the peripherals of my vision. My eyes slam shut.

Thoughts and visions mix and merge, dizzying and making me sick. *Don't pass out. I can't pass out, not here. They can't see me like this.* But when you feel like passing out, it's all you can think about, and a long breath escapes me, half a sigh of exasperation, half the emptying of strained lungs.

A familiar hand rests on my shoulder blade, urging my eyes open to a squint. "Are you okay?" Dave asks discreetly, eyeing our parents. One shake of my head and he removes the hand, a rush of his scent breezing past me.

He talks to the group and when eventually my eyes open fully, the two women are already climbing the stairs to the highest viewpoint.

Dave trots back to me like a loyal bodyguard. By now, our families must surely think there's something amiss with me because of his over-zealousness.

Dad looks over his shoulder once and it seems he knows everything in that moment, but he turns back and follows the women anyway.

"I told them you're lightheaded from the altitude."

I grimace at this. "I thought you were smart."

"I'm sorry?" He looks perplexed, put out.

"Well, I'm not a scholarly type like you, Dr. Dave, but the ocean is right beyond that river." I point over the ledge of stone wall. "See that? It's the Guadiana River. Pretty much the same level we're at in this castle."

It's snaking through our view and can't be more than several hundred feet below us at the most.

He lifts a single shoulder in a shrug. "Sorry. It's the best I could do. Anyway, I said we'd meet them in Alte. They don't seem too worried. Are you okay?"

They wouldn't be, would they? People get lightheaded sometimes. "I'm fine, just a little winded from the walk, that's all."

He offers a hand. Instead of taking it, I shoulder past him, my feet stumbling down the cobblestones back toward the parking lot, irritated at him. Irritated at myself. Irritated at everything my life has become.

He jogs up beside me, showing off his ability to breathe so easily. In the moment, it's so clear how much we take for granted. The ability to wake each day. To walk, to see, to hear, to think and to breathe with little effort. In the blind arrogance of life, we're sure nothing will ever steal that ability away...until it does.

I go to sneer at him and my face drops, all indignation wiped clean. He has that same look Dad gives me when he's concerned and not quite sure how to proceed. It's vulnerability at the most basic level and when he rakes a hand through his hair, I finally have an epiphany. Dave's just trying to help—*has* been trying to help—and I'm the biggest asshole in the world.

There's no way I can tell him this of course, so I proceed with the walk to the parking lot and into the tiniest car in the entire country of Portugal and beyond. As he routes out the way to the next stop, I fail to find the words to apologize for everything I've been since the moment I met him.

Navigating out of town, he doesn't attempt to play music and we don't jam out like before. Instead, my head sinks against the window, focusing on the glovebox and ignoring the unbearable silence that neither of us are willing to break.

Sixty-eight minutes of pure torture.

My brain computes each one as it ticks by.

When he whips the car into a parking lot near the center of a village with tight alleys and stark white homes with brightly colored window frames, my seatbelt snaps off with quick hands and I grab my purse ready to put a little distance between my brain and Dave.

It's sweltering outside and I'm cursing at myself for wearing black shorts, marching into the new town, no clue where I'm going.

"Rachel," he calls after me, and on turning, he's tucking a thumb behind his shoulder in the opposite direction from which I'm heading. "Go that way. I'll meet you there."

"What, where?"

"You'll figure it out," he promises, taking off to the left down a street littered with tourists and trinket stores without an explanation. He disappears into the meandering crowd, leaving me half-tempted to follow, but I go exactly where he pointed.

It's not a long walk and Dave was right—I couldn't miss it.

A small river cuts through the town and Lord only knows how many years ago someone framed the banks with hand-laid stone bricks, taming a wild—albeit lazy—river into a canal.

An arching pedestrian bridge out of the same rock connects both sides.

Families with little children dangle their legs over the stone ledge, some leaping into the shallow clear waters, splashing with all the fun that summer weather in a river brings.

Next to the ledges, untamed grass fans out and groups of people have colorful blankets spread out and are taking naps while others are feasting on homemade picnics. Very few tourists are here, probably because they all headed in the direction I was going initially.

Dave finds me shoeless there a while later, pink painted toes dipping in the cool spring-fed water, my fingers gripping the rough stone steps leading down into the river, afraid if I dip too far, I'll plunge the whopping eight inches to the water that almost looks emerald with the sun scattering rays of light under the surface.

He has a grocery bag clasped in one hand as an eyebrow slants my way. "Didn't think you knew how to relax. Wow. This is truly a revelation."

I'm saying nothing, only hanging out, keeping the peace, loosening my grip on the wall, hoping he doesn't notice the true level of tension in me. "What's in the bag?" I ask, pushing my sunglasses to the top of my head while a rogue cloud snuffs out the harsh sun rays.

He takes a seat in the grass and opens the sack to reveal a bottle of white wine stippled with condensation, a loaf of crusty bread, some type of pale white cheese, and a bunch of purple grapes. All I can do is gawk.

He chuckles at me. "What?"

"But *Dr. Trenton,*" I tease, fluttering my lashes at him. "You said I shouldn't drink alcohol."

A ghost of a smile floats across his face.

"Actually, I only asked *whether* you drank alcohol or not. You were the one who swore you didn't. Seeing as I've now seen you drink a beer, a rather large strong coffee this morning, and probably will finish half this bottle in one gulp with the way you're ogling it, I'm going to go out on a limb and say it wouldn't matter what your doctor advised. You'll do what you want anyway. I seriously doubt I'm corrupting your so-called squeaky-clean track record."

My face flushes, my focus now on my hands plucking a grape from its stem. "Well, you're horribly misguided. I would never waste wine in such a foolish way." The flavor of the grape coats my tongue. Delicious. Closing my eyes for the briefest moment, a moan escapes. "You must have read my innermost thoughts. Do they teach telepathy at medical school? Did you ace that class, doc? This is my perfect lunch."

The timbre of his laugh charges the air between us. It makes my belly flutter, far preferring these over the palpitations in my decaying heart. "It's *everyone's* perfect lunch," he adds, looking around to the other picnickers. "We only have one problem."

I drag my toes out of the water and tuck them under my leg. "Oh no, it's bad, isn't it?"

Why am I teasing him now? It's a little too flirtatious for not even speaking the last hour.

Sixty-eight minutes to be exact.

He tilts his chin toward me and shakes his head. "I made a mistake. I'm so sorry." His face is serious again, but before my heart sinks at his words, a tick of a smile pulls on his left side. "I forgot to buy a corkscrew."

My attention darts to the bottle, praying for a twist off, but we're in Portugal, land of cork trees. It would be a national sin for there to be a locally produced wine with a twist cap. A sinister smile creeps up my face, and I stick my hand out.

"I can fix this."

His eyes narrow and I can only imagine what he's thinking. Will I be the mad American woman running from group to group, begging for them to open the bottle? Will I smash the neck of the bottle with no regard to glass shards? I'm not that desperate. Not yet anyway.

Dave drops the chilled bottle into my hand with a touch of reluctance.

"See, you have to have a skillset of a desperate woman." My nails try to peel the foil seal. When that doesn't work, my teeth come into play. Despite the wide eyes he's sending me upon my spitting a sliver of foil into the air, I get the seal removed and stick out my hand. "Give me your shoe," I command.

His brows pull together, but he takes off a leather loafer and hands it to me. "I'm beginning to understand what a desperate woman might look like."

"Are these expensive?" It has a Made in Italy seal on the underside. He shakes his head. "Of course, they are," I decide. "They might not make it, fair warning. But I'll try my best."

"Guess that bottle of wine better be worth it then."

I place the bottom of the bottle inside the heel of the shoe and raise it up high into the air.

Dave's about to protest, but I slam the heel incased bottle into the stone ledge once before he can say anything. I look over to him to make sure he's breathing, but he looks alarmed and perplexed as he comes to his knees in an instant.

"I'll try it again." And I do, as if squishing the biggest bug ever seen.

Maybe dashing around like a mad American woman to the other people enjoying the park would have been less traumatic for Dave. On the third smash, his hands cover over mine, stopping me, the horror of it all written across his confused face.

Tipping back until I slam on my butt, I clutch at my belly to try and assuage the fit of giggles. My lungs are breathless, so much that he thinks I've lost my mind.

He sets the bottle aside. "Okay, I think that's enough of whatever—"

"Look!" I point to the bottle neck where half an inch of cork has unseated itself. His head whips from the bottle then back to me. His mouth falls open as though he might laugh. Or cry. Or take me to a mental institution.

But then he grabs the shoe and wine bottle from between us and repeats what I did with a lot more muscle. With two solid whacks, he's able to rock the cork out between his fingers.

He stares at me, a grin extending a mile wide across his face. "I don't think I have the words to properly convey my awe," he says, offering the open bottle to me for the first sip. "Where did you learn that?"

"I grew up on a farm and my best friend's family owned a winery. Azzy and I snuck into the cellar a lot.

You learn how to use what you've got. Azzy always had a sturdy pair of combat boots. Is there a glass to drink from?"

Dave shakes his head, so I take a swig instead.

The crispness hits the back of my throat, and its effervescence is unlike any other wine I've ever drunk. The label catches my eye.

"Vinho Verde," he says in an almost authentic accent. "It's green wine and only produced in country. Most people get the white version like this one, but there's also a rosé and red version too. The green referenced is not the color of the skin, but the age of the harvested grape."

Dr. Dave knows his wines. Impressive.

Passing the bottle to him, he takes a long pull and I'm honestly feeling a little jealous of the bottle pressed to his lips right now. This almost feels normal. It feels ridiculous to assert that I'm dying and find myself here with this cardiologist who can't do anything for my diseased heart.

It feels as if he is just someone I chose to spend time with. Almost.

Dave must sense the moment my mood shifts, but doesn't say anything, as he unwraps the bread and spreads the paper out, putting cheese and fruit on it like anchors. He breaks off some of the bread and a hunk of cheese and leans back on his elbows into the grass, still only wearing one shoe. The sun is blocked out again but this time, it's by a massive tree. The shadow lengthens across us and its coolness is a welcome visitor.

"Your mom mentioned you have a sister. Why isn't she here?" he asks. I know what he's doing. He wants me to talk about *it*, but I'm in no mood.

"You first, tell me about yours."

He stiffens, the piece of bread that was sailing straight

into his mouth stops, and he brings it back down to the paper.

"What do you want to know?" His voice has changed, tinged with something darker.

Maybe there's a reason he doesn't want to talk about it. It makes me feel bad for a split second. But then I change my mind. He asked me first.

"Why isn't she here with you? Why is your mom the only one here? And where's your dad?"

His jaw tightens as he pushes himself up, brushing the crumbs off his fingers when fully upright.

"For what it's worth, my dad left us when I was four and we haven't seen him since, so no real loss there. And my sister—" He makes sure to make eye contact with me. My insides tighten and I cringe at what he's about to say, knowing he's been pushed to say the next four words. "My sister is dead."

There are two million thoughts running simultaneously through my head, but an apology seems the hardest to get out. Sputtering, the words won't come. "I-I—"

"It's fine," he says with a wave, reclining to his former position on his elbows.

Before I can ask any more terrible questions, he pops the bread and cheese into his mouth and closes his eyes, taking an overexaggerated breath through his nose.

Embarrassment makes me wish to die in this moment, but that'll have to wait for five more months. A blur of two teenage boys in bright red shorts races down to the canal drawing my focus away from Dave.

They launch themselves over the ledge and their splash sprinkles droplets of water on us, but it's not enough to be upset.

With a hefty dose of reluctance, I glance over to test the

murky water between us. Dave's chewing slowly, but his eyes remain closed. It's as if every muscle in his jaw is making a concerted effort to grind the piece of bread into pulp.

Finding my voice, I offer a truce. "My sister followed the tradition of women in farm country."

His eyes lift open and there might be a sheen coating them, making me feel even worse. He clears his throat. "And what's that?" he asks.

A frown escapes, but at him and not for my sister. "To get married to a farmer straight out of high school and pop out as many kids as you can before you're thirty, so the farm has plenty of free labor." I reach over to the cheese and break off a piece. "She's pregnant with number three and can't travel. And honestly"— I look out to the emerald waters being churned up by the teens—"I'd rather her not be here at all." I pull my knees to my chest and take a bite of the cheese. "That probably makes me sound like a terrible sister."

"Sounds like you two have issues to work through. Don't you think it's a bit extreme to say something like that about your own sister? Again, I'm in no way telling you how you should run your life, but maybe it's time to bury the hatchet."

I scoff and hate sounding so dismissive. "Five months won't change anything. We are tolerable toward each other, but on two different planes. We always have been. We've reconciled in a lot of ways the past few years. I mean, I love her, and she loves me, and we share the same DNA, but often it seems like that's where the similarities end."

He takes a swig of the wine and doesn't say anything. Neither do I. What can be said when someone is dying, and they don't want to fully mend fractured relationships?

We sit in silence for a while and it's more comfortable this time around. Eventually, I sprawl out and copy Dave's position after eating a little more cheese. My toes are tickled by the blades of grass, and my body falls back to the soft earth until parallel with the sky, tucking an arm under my head and scanning the cloudy puffs of white drifting by as shadows shift around us.

I don't realize I'm crying until Dave's thumb swipes a rogue tear rolling off the side of my cheek.

He hasn't really moved, but his arm is extended over to me and when I turn to look at him, one cheek rises, but not something you might say is a smile, more like sympathy.

Or maybe understanding.

"Why are you being so nice to me? You barely know me." My own words crackle in my ears as I use the back of my hands in an attempt to clean up more tears.

His whole body shifts, resting on a hip and in one swift motion, he drags me into his arms. This man is still a stranger, yet he is oddly allowed to comfort me for the second time.

My tears are staining his button-up shirt under the shade of an oak tree probably planted hundreds of years ago.

"I know enough about you to know that you need this," he whispers as his hold tightens.

"You know my chart and my scans. You don't really know me. I've not always been a good person. I've done terrible things and I'm not worth your pity."

"What I am offering you is certainly not pity, Rachel." Dave touches my cheek, turning it toward him. "I may not know you well, but so far what I've seen is enough for me to stick around to get to know you better. I'd like to think the feeling is mutual."

My phone starts to vibrate in my purse and in a snap of fingers, I jump back from Dave, trying to not seem so... desperate. Swiping at my cheeks with one hand, the other digs through my purse until I find it and answer.

Mom is on the other end, not taking a breath as she goes into the grand details of the adventure of our parents, droning on about gift shops and churches in some small village not far from where they are currently exploring. She's rambling, sounding happy enough that I swallow away my remaining tears. Dad's grumbling in the background, but not out of frustration.

He's hungry, of course, desperately wanting to find a place to eat and Helen's offering suggestions. "Mom, get to the point!" I finally snap.

"Rache, where are you guys at? Still in Alte? Would it be terrible of us to meet you back in Luz? We found a couple more places to go. There's a church in this one village that was built in 900 A.D. Can you believe something can be *that* old? We want to take a quick side—"

"Mom." My eyes make contact with Dave's. "We're fine. See you back at the hotel for dinner."

And she's off on another tangent, instructing Dad where to drive. Helen is in the background calling out all the road signs. They're giggling again. I hang up and shake my head.

Dave's watching me but offering no words. My mascara must be a mess.

I don't even care.

I wipe the rings around my eyes and slip on my sandals. "We don't need to hang around. We can go back to the hotel. They're taking their time and said they'll meet us for dinner."

He nods but doesn't budge, and I notice the wet splotch of tears marking his shirt.

It makes me want to grimace. I want to be back in my hotel room, under my comforter, curled up in a ball and away from him and the emotions that he draws out of me.

"Rachel." I want to ignore him, but can't, his voice calls to me like a drug. He wiggles his fingers of an outstretched arm and I look between them and his face. "Let me be someone you can trust."

But my purse is already over my shoulder. I'm ready to get the hell out of Alte.

My body disagrees with me, feeling myself leaning toward him, collapsing in his strong arms as if I was meant to fit there. He pulls my purse off and sets it to the side, then reclines all the way back, bringing me with him. My head takes position on his rising chest. No tears come this time as his fingers smooth the tangled waves of my hair.

I've only ever been held like this once before by one other man and it's intoxicating, something so much more than one human comforting another.

It feels like something undeserved.

Chapter Nine

The second time I ran away from the farm, I was sixteen. Two years was a lot of time to figure my shit out and become a happy farmer's daughter in the middle of nowhere, USA.

Or not.

Boyfriends had changed several times and all I wanted more than a perfect edgy boyfriend and perfect boobs, was to cure the incessant need to be free of the grasp of all things Idaho.

So Azzy and I came up with The Plan.

Both standing out like anomalies in our strangling town, Azzy suffered from the same need. Our independence clawed away at us like a ravenous lion. Freedom was anywhere outside of the county limits and past the boring highways of sagebrush and silted dirt.

We bided our time, waiting until harvest where everyone was so engrossed in their work, they wouldn't notice we'd slipped out in the middle of the night. Harvest hours ran all night some seasons and as luck would have it that year, the crops were being cut up until sunrise.

Dad and Mom would be running themselves into the ground while expecting Chloe and me to take care of ourselves.

Chloe... my perfect little sister never did a single bad thing growing up. By the book, straight-A student, class president, and well on her way to head cheerleader with perfect glistening auburn curled hair to boot. Even though she was a grade behind me, she seemed leaps and bounds ahead with her life's ambition to marry the star quarterback and most eligible farmer's son that put Hammett on the map for the entire swath of southern Idaho football teams.

If Chloe was yin, I was yang, but without the balancing each other out principle. Total opposites in every regard and with zero stability to our relationship. We may have been only a year apart, but we were universes away, acting more like a seesaw. We fought over who went up and when the other went down, we'd jump free just to piss the other off.

We fought daily, hourly, and at any other time the other was breathing or existing too close.

She would surely tattle on me to our parents for any infraction. It wasn't always out of spite, but out of 'the right thing to do' mentality beaten into her at church. As we got older, she ate up everything the church sold her and that included trying to make her sister see the celestial light.

Fat chance of that ever happening. I never fell for that bullshit Catholic guilt served up in heaping doses of holy water and rosaries. Saving my soul seemed like a far stretch when I shared a black heart with Azzy. It was never for me.

I could care less about divinity, making my position well known from a young age.

Mom, obviously the devoted woman of Christ, was appalled by my self-proclaimed atheism, but Dad knew better. Just like when I'd gone missing from home that first time, he saw the wisdom of letting me figure out my own errors and understood that if he let me figure this out on my own again, I might come around. So, he overrode my mother —an extreme rarity in my childhood—allowing me to forgo church and all the depressing, damning things that came with it.

But it wasn't enough, and Dad probably understood that as well. I think he always felt as though he was barely holding onto my pinky, and I was pulling as hard as I could to be released. More than once he told me that my spirit was freer than the wild mustangs once occupying the valley.

That wild spirit is what drove Azzy and I to plan our escape so well, waiting until Chloe went over to a friend's house so she couldn't rat us out. Like our parents, others in the community were busy in the fields, leaving us with a rare free pass all the way to the highway without the possibility of being spotted by a nosy neighbor. I didn't want a repeat of Dad picking us up a few miles down the road, especially now that Azzy would be with me too.

That evening, while Dad donned his faded John Deere hat and Mom followed him out to the fields with the dump truck riding next to his combine tractor, I grabbed my backpack and snacks and ran into my parents' room, knowing where they kept their savings.

Mom was paranoid about banks stealing their hard-earned cash so half of it went to the banks and the other to the safe in their closet, the combination of which was easy to crack: Chloe's and my birthdates.

Once the safe was open, I took half the stack of bills, ramming them into my bag without a second thought. The guilt about stealing their money didn't manifest until years later, and then it would eat at my soul, but at the time of our escape, I couldn't care less. We planned on never coming back.

Azzy arrived on time with a cloud of dust encircling her electric blue Acura with its cracked windshield and death metal blaring from blown-out speakers. We both had licenses and Azzy had bought a car a few months prior.

She rolled down her window with a spiked leather choker wrapped tightly around her throat, a white painted face, and neon pink hair striped over jet-black braids pulled so tight on her scalp, her eyebrows couldn't move. She stuck her tongue out.

"Let's get the hell out of this town!" She screamed it so loud over the riffs of a bass guitar. I laughed and responded with something equally poetic.

"Fuck yeah!"

We were teens, what can I say? Our vocabulary only came in the form of cussing, otherwise we weren't worth our age. She squealed tires and spun gravel out of the farmhouse driveway, and I think I even flipped the bird to the dusty pit.

We drove hours and hours that first night, lingering at a few truck stops for bathroom breaks and nice truckers to whom Azzy would flutter her spider eyelashes and pucker black lips in order to get us free gas.

Looking back at it all now, we were so lucky no one ever messed with us.

Stopping along the way at a seedy hotel and several twenty-four-hour diners, the liberating feeling of making our own decisions pushed us south. We made it to the Bay Area at sunset two days later and purposely went the long way into the city so we could cruise across the Golden Gate Bridge.

There was magic in that moment.

Untapped freedom about to let loose.

It was fall and the fog crawled underneath the bridge in a bowl of mist, but we cranked all the windows down anyway and screamed to the music playing on her stereo, excited for a new start of our adult life. At sixteen. We'd finally made it out of Idaho and into the big wide world beyond.

For Azzy, the freedom was backed by a different motivation than my own. She didn't come from a household like mine.

Her parents were Mormon and stricter than any other family I knew. She was required to attend religious classes weekly, speak in front of her church about her sins, and was expected to marry a good Mormon boy from her ward, someone vetted through the elders of her church.

Her parents weren't lenient like mine either. Well, my dad in particular. They'd berate her clothing choices and she rebelled. Hard. She loved calling herself a jack-Mormon and toasted herself with plenty of coffee and beer whenever we could score some. There was a weird irony that her parents owned the largest winery in the valley but were Mormon, strictly enforcing the 'never drink alcohol' policy. Maybe in their own way they were jacked too, but I supposed that as long as they donated their obligatory tithings, the church probably looked the other way.

At least that's what my sixteen-year-old self thought.

Her reasons for breaking out of Hammett were vastly different from mine and she even tried to discourage me from joining her, citing the fact that my parents seemed to actually like me. However, it didn't do much to change my mind. I needed my freedom from them. From everyone.

I was suffocating and needed to breathe for once in my life.

Even though I craved freedom, I cared enough to leave a note for my parents. It was simple and to the point, some-

thing along the lines of 'I hate it here and need to find myself anywhere other than Idaho. Will call at some point.' As if that would be enough to appease them and not cause worry, but at sixteen, I didn't really think of the consequences that square piece of paper would cause. There was no considering the chasm that would divide our family for years to come by my misguided decisions.

I wanted what I wanted and along with Azzy, we were achieving precisely that.

As my mom would say, by the grace and mercy of His holiness, we survived five days in San Francisco without any incidents. It's funny, with enough cash, the hotel we stayed at seemed not to even care about our age. No one did, which should have been concerning, but it helped us secure our perceived future.

Immediately, Azzy and I fell in love with the city. There was a vibrancy that lacked in Idaho.

People moved with a purpose, and it didn't involve alfalfa or wheat. Some even dressed like Azzy, and I could see her melt into the city life effortlessly. She partied in the Castro District with the drag queens and in the bumping clubs, while I found my peace hiking up and down the hilly city streets, bright eyed and eager to make my mark on the world with my exploration.

On day six, things took a nasty turn when someone spiked one of Azzy's drinks at a club we snuck into, and she became violently ill after we got back to our room. I managed to half-carry, half-drag her from our shambles of a hotel to the nearest urgent care where they called an ambulance, and we were at the hospital within minutes. When the doctor came out, his wrinkles deepened as he scanned around the waiting room noticing I was the only one there for Azzy.

"Where are her parents?" he asked me.

"In Idaho, is she okay?"

He narrowed his eyes and looked down at me through gold wire-rimmed glasses. "Are you runaways?"

"No," I lied. "They know we're here. We're just taking a vacation."

I'm not sure if it was my matter-of-fact attitude or if he didn't want to have to call the cops, but he bought it. "You need to call them. Your friend is extremely ill, and I need to know what they'd like me to do."

"It was just a spiked drink." I can still feel the tremble in my voice.

He nodded and tapped the chart. "There's more I can't discuss with you. Please call her family. There's a phone at the nurse's station, over there."

It took me a whole ten minutes to muster up the courage and when I dialed her parents' landline, it was answered on the half-ring, as if they were waiting for the call.

They flew in on the next flight out of Boise and must have called my parents too, because as Azzy's parents busted through the hospital doors, my dad was trailing behind them still wearing his faded John Deere cap and dirt-stained jeans. He stared at me for a long moment, then collapsed in the chair next to me in the empty surgical waiting room. He had offered me no welcoming embrace. That withholding was worse than any yelling or endless lecture.

While Azzy's drink had been spiked, a bigger issue was found during her examination. She'd also suffered from an epileptic seizure during the incident. Scans showed a lesion on her brain that the doctors wanted to remove in hopes that it would stop any further episodes from occurring.

My best friend almost died during that surgery. In fact, she did. She coded for thirty seconds. Thirty solid seconds *they couldn't bring her back. And it was all because we ran away.*

When her parents told us what was happening, they didn't make accusations, didn't even send me one nasty glance. Instead, her mother, a pudgy lady the exact opposite of her daughter, gave me a simple thanks while her father patted my shoulder.

Dad still didn't speak to me through any of it. He sat next to me, stoic and contemplative, waiting for me to break the silence that stretched a mile wide. After her parents returned to Azzy's bedside, I remember turning to my dad, full of excuses and accusations at the ready, but the pain and disappointment on his face halted me before I even spoke.

I broke down, full meltdown mode that required me to tuck my head between my knees to control the sucking breaths that wouldn't stop. And he had no reason to even look in my direction or acknowledge that distress.

What he did have was every reason to sneer and cross his arms and count off every misstep I had taken over the last week. But Dad didn't do that. He yanked on my hoody tilting my trembling body into his arms, keeping me against his chest until I couldn't cry anymore, then he held me even tighter.

I fell asleep in his arms in the waiting room of a major metropolitan hospital hundreds of miles away from the loss he was taking on not harvesting his crops in time, and he never said a word about any of it. Not about the crops that didn't get harvested, not about my running away, not even about the stack of money he and Mom had spent years saving and I had blown through in days.

He held me as though I was worthy of his love. As though I deserved it.

Chapter Ten

I awaken to dappled sunlight dancing over my eyelids, and it's almost as though someone is shining a light in circles around me. A chest rises and falls under my cheek, while the giggles and squeals of delighted children splashing in the canal reach our peaceful retreat.

There's a smell of clean laundry, crusty bread, and mildly stinky cheese.

My arm is slung across Dave's stomach. The muscles under my limb are surprisingly firm, especially given he seems to be relaxed under my weight. His arm, the one snaked under my middle, strokes my spine through the tank top, a feather-light touch, soothing and unhurried.

So much so that I pretend to sleep a few minutes longer to absorb the moment into my memories.

His other arm reaches over, and he brushes a piece of my hair away from my face with the pad of his thumb. "You're not a good faker," he murmurs, but it sounds louder against the shell of my ear cupped against his body.

As I squint one eye up at him, his body rumbles out a chuckle. "I just woke up," I lie.

He smiles. It's an easy smile, a knowing pull of muscles upwards until a small depression hints at where I think a rogue dimple may hide.

"And I'm a cardiologist that's been monitoring your heart rate for the last hour. It started increasing quite significantly, might I add, about five minutes ago."

"I'm sorry. I shouldn't have fallen asleep on you. I..." I trail off, examining the spot where our bodies indented the grass.

He holds up a hand to pause me. "Don't apologize for something we both needed." My ears warm and I sit up, pulling myself away from his grip, but he doesn't seem put off by this. Instead, Dave slips on his makeshift wine opener —the shoe—and collects the food into the grocery bag. "We should head back," he suggests. "Our parents will be worried if we aren't there by dinnertime, especially since I had to lie and tell them about needing to return early."

He's talking while popping another grape into his mouth. He grins at me and tosses another one in my direction, and it falls into my cleavage.

"You're kidding. You did that on purpose!" I smirk at him and fish it out while he laughs. My eyes lock on his as I crunch it between my molars. "You don't really have work to get back to, do you?"

He shrugs. "A little, but this seemed more fun and gave us a chance to listen to some music and get to know each other. Know something? It's actually a relief to be able to crank up the volume and sing out loud along with someone in the car. You might not believe this, but my mom is not really into my jam sessions. Makes for quiet road trips."

I giggle at the thought of Helen trying to rock out. "No? She struck me as someone that is into the real deep hardcore death metal stuff. Headbanging and all that. But your playlist did surprise me. Not complaining by the way, just found it a little out of character for who I thought you were. Thought the concert might have been a fluke."

His head tilts. "And who exactly did you think I was?"

There's no hesitation. "A studious doctor that has little to no time for anything as menial as fun music in his life. Given the emptiness of your office, my theory seemed to be confirmed." My lashes flit toward him. "But I stand corrected."

A raucous laughter erupts from him. "My office? You're judging me based off *that*?"

"There's more decorating in a padded cell."

"Well, you're right about one thing. I don't have a lot of time. Especially for decorating. Doesn't really take priority when I work twelve-hour days. Hmm..." His hand caresses his jawline. "Maybe your assessment *is* correct."

"Get used to it. I'm never wrong when it comes to judging people." My smile is wide, looking up into the sky as if telling the time by how low the sun is hanging, but it's no use. I've no idea how to read the sun, so I grab my purse and pull out my phone.

There's a missed call from Chloe and a string of text messages from Azzy. My clock reads 15:25 and it takes a moment to realize I switched it to the European twenty-four-hour clock to really immerse myself. A purportedly uncomplicated math calculation runs in my head.

Dave's watching me as I switch from my head to my fingers to count down the time.

"It's 3:26," he says as if he knows I'm struggling. "Subtract twelve from the first two numbers."

"I know." I push past and he grabs my upper arm, not a firm grab, just enough to get my attention.

"Thank you for today," he says, and I have no clue what

he's talking about. "I think I needed that." And I still have no idea what he's referencing, but I nod once as he releases me, and we head to the car.

The drive back to Praia da Luz is uneventful, but at least Dave has enough sense to play some music in the background while we cruise down the coastline, taking in the jagged rocks that swim within the waves, caves popping out with tourists lining up to take a peek inside such glorious works of Mother Nature. It's an impressive sight as the tiny car handles the road with ease.

The ride is silent other than the music, but it isn't loud enough to rock out and even if it was, I'm honestly a little too tired to give it my all.

After what must be an hour, he pulls up to the hotel at which my parents and I are staying, and it occurs to me I've no clue which hotel Helen and Dave have booked.

"You're staying here too?" I point to the three-story whitewashed building with its fire engine red shutters and pretty terracotta tiled roof.

He points next door and I roll my eyes. Sure, it's a hotel, but with one more tourism star than mine and modernly posh. They probably offer turn-down service and a chocolate on the pillow, given the caliber of hotel guests filling the umbrellaed chaise lounge chairs out front.

"What time do you think they'll be back?" I ask.

He whips out his phone, pressing the call button and holding it up to his ear. "Let's find out."

He speaks to someone, likely his mother, and I like the way they banter and tease. It's fun and lighthearted. A longing for the same relationship with my own mother overcomes me.

The phone drops into his pocket and a lopsided grin forms on his mouth.

"They're already here."

Sure enough, a quick glance around reveals Dad's rental in the cobblestone lot. "Where are they?"

The answer is clear before he speaks it. Mom's laughter drifts over the warm breeze of the Atlantic.

His eyes shift to his right, toward a restaurant on the opposite side of my hotel.

"Sure you're willing to cross into this seedy side of the neighborhood?" I tease as we walk through the parking lot. "That one star makes a difference, you know."

A dimple appears in his left cheek, catching me off guard because it's so new to me. When he sees me staring, he waves to no avail. With a shake of my head, I move ahead and cut him off at the three stairs leading to the restaurant. The chuckle coming from behind me has me grinning as we spot our parents.

An empty bottle of Vinho Verde and another half-empty one sits on the table. Helen and my mom are leaning into one another like old friends telling secrets. Dad is watching us approach, a brandy swirling in his grip. It's weird to see Dad drink. He only does so on rare occasions and only when super relaxed, when most comfortable to let down his guard.

The brandy in his hand makes my heart sing. He's having a good time despite the deadpan face he gives us both when the women shriek out laughs.

It's going to be heartbreaking when they finally learn I only have months before the inevitable. I doubt neither of them will ever look this relaxed again, but right now... it's enough.

Dave pulls out a chair for me next to my dad.

"Miss Heltin," Dave teases, urging me to sit before taking one on the other side. Dad's noticing, studying Dave and me to see if he can crack whatever secret code we have.

Not yet, Dad. It's not going to be that easy.

Helen pours Dave and me a glass of wine, emptying the bottle before gesturing at the bowl of olives in the middle of the table. "There's something in there that I can't figure out. Any guesses?"

My mom chimes in. "I think it's parsley." She looks at Helen and takes another olive, chewing it slow. "Yes, I can definitely taste parsley."

After taking a long sip of wine, I reach into the oil-covered olives, plucking one out and examine the herbs dotting the slick black flesh. Mom may be right. It might be parsley. I pop it into my mouth and quickly dislodge the pit, putting it into the little bowl meant for such things.

The olive is otherworldly. Salty and firm to an almost unyielding crunch, the oil gives a little nuttiness and then there's that extra something they're debating. After tasting it, I decide it can't be parsley. It seems too simple for such a complex menagerie of flavors.

"It's cilantro," Dr. Dave declares, pulling a pit from his mouth and depositing it in the growing pile in the cute blue bowl.

I grumble because he's right and both moms are praising him for being the greatest human alive. Between his apparent impeccable palette and ability to decipher the 24-hour clock, what hope have I got? I'm trying not to be annoyed and Dave's not trying to soak in their praise, but it takes solid effort not to give him a sarcastic and playful eyeroll.

My phone buzzes in my purse and I debate pulling it out but decide to check it after taking another sip of wine. It's Chloe calling again, so I take it and put it up to my ear.

"Yes, my dear sister?" I say while looking at Dad and he perks one brow up.

"Hey, I tried to call you earlier. I'm about to leave Dad and Mom's. We just finished up for the day, but a rather thick envelope came in the mail for you from UCSF Medical Center and it has urgent stamped all over it. It looks important," Chloe says.

The blood drains from my face and although Helen and Mom don't notice, I sense the scrutiny of both men flanking me. I have no clue why a letter would come there, but then realize I forwarded all my mail to the farm, knowing I wouldn't be coming back to my apartment in San Francisco.

There's no way to know definitively what's inside that envelope, but I have no intention of it being opened until we get home. "Don't open it," I snap loudly. And in my peripheral, Dave turns fully to me.

"What's the big deal?" she asks, the sound of paper rustling in her hands.

"Don't you fucking dare open it!" I slam my glass on the table, surprising even myself that it doesn't shatter. The whole table falls silent and I chance a glance at the others. Helen's frowning and Mom might as well be clutching her pearls. The men both look confused, brows identically pinched inward. But I don't care, pushing back out of the chair and screeching it across the patio to stand up. "Chloe, for the love of god, don't open it. Don't touch it. It's not yours."

"Well now I'm really curious," she jokes.

I hate her so much in this moment, so much that clawing her eyes out through an international phone call crosses my mind.

If I could jump through the line and tackle her, there

would be no hesitation because whatever's in that envelope will say too much, and she'll never keep her mouth shut.

I am not about to let Chloe ruin the last good month of my life.

"Leave it alone!" I shriek, knowing I'm only making it worse, but she can't ruin this trip. Almost in tears, my voice cracks. "Please don't." Every syllable teeters as I resort to begging. "Please, Chloe."

"Whatever," she says, and the rustling of the envelope ends with a thud on a table. "I was only joking. Geez Rachel, you're so uptight. Isn't Portugal supposed to be relaxing? Anyway, it'll be here when you get back and I can always pry it out of you then. Ted's having trouble getting Cayden into the truck. I gotta go."

I'm pinching the bridge of my nose and squeezing my eyes shut, trying to calm my breathing as Chloe ends the call. My hand with the phone drops to my side, and I don't want to open my eyes. I'm only feet from the table and it's dead silent. I dread what I'll meet when I ultimately face them. There's no explanation I can offer that would make sense.

Taking a two-step approach, I lift my eyelids open and focus on the water, turning only after a few seconds of forced breathing passes. As predicted, four sets of eyes gawk at me and I want to scream, but I must fix this.

But I can't.

I can't fix *any* of this.

Offering nothing more than deflated shoulders and a quivering chin, I toss my phone on the table and retreat to the beach. Heading toward the escape of the ocean for the second frustrating time in one day, I'm not surprised to feel someone approaching from behind. I'm not in the mood for this and start speaking with exasperation before I've even fully spun around to Dave.

"Can you seriously just leave me alone for—oh, Dad."

My whole body droops at his familiar presence. He has no idea why I'm angry at my sister or why I've brought him and Mom out to Portugal. He also has no idea why I've been a jerk to Dave, but it doesn't even matter. He gives me a pointed look then turns his attention to the breaking waves.

A few moments pass as I rage inside trying to lock down the torrent of emotions. I only let a little of the way I'm feeling boil over. "Why does she have to piss me off? Why can't she stay out of my business?"

"One day, you two will get along. You might even like each other to the point that you'll be friends. Look at how far you've already come over the past couple years." He says this as if he almost believes it himself. Little does he know, time is short and what he hopes for will *never* happen. "What's your sister done this time?"

This time. He knows she's not as pious and innocent as she acts, and I appreciate this tiny admission. "She's going through my things." I shake my head because Dad must think my reaction is way over the top for a sister being nosy.

"What's up with this Dave guy?" Dad asks, still watching the waves roll in.

His question floors me because it's out of left field and Dad never—*never*—talks about guys with me. My mouth drops, but I recover it quickly. "What do you mean? There's nothing—"

"We just met him and Helen, but I get the impression you already knew him before today. Maybe I'm wrong, and I'm sure you'll correct me, but you seem too familiar for a couple who've just met."

"Whoa, stop right there. We're not a couple, Dad."

"I didn't mean it in that way," he says, a sigh behind it as if he's about to give up.

Struggling to understand, I take in a deep breath even though I'm still spun up over Chloe and not ready for this conversation. I maneuver the best way I can. "No, you're right, Dad. I met him at a concert a few weeks ago. He's nice and a little irritating, but no, there's nothing there. I think we were both caught off guard about being here at the same time." I force a half-smile. "I'll tell you this much—he's better than Chloe at the moment."

For extra measure, I roll my eyes and Dad barks out a laugh.

"Your sister and you have always been complete opposites. Did you know that I knew she was going to take over the farm before you two were even in high school?"

This surprises me. "Really? What if I'd wanted it? Or what if I still want it?"

He laughs harder and the lines crinkle around his eyes more than I've noticed before. "I think you and I both know that you belong as far away from Idaho as you can get. You were never meant to stay there. It's not your place. You seem happy in San Francisco."

I gulp in the salty air. "I *have* been much happier." It comes out in a whisper. "You know I never wanted to hurt you and Mom when I lived at home. I just...I couldn't stay, Dad. I don't fit there."

His gaze rolls up and down the beach. "Don't worry about it. We're fine and you never were a bad kid, not really. I was always proud of you. Loved you the same no matter where you wanted to live. I'll always love you no matter what choices you make even if I don't agree with them."

A lump comes to my throat, eyes stinging. It might be

better if he didn't say such nice things. I definitely don't deserve them.

But he's not finished yet. "It's nice to see you in your element here. To see you enjoy a different country. If I didn't like the snow and wind in Idaho so much, I would almost think about living in some place like this," he says it with a hint of sarcasm, but there's a shred of truth in those words.

"Dad, you would never leave Idaho. We both know it. Don't be silly."

We laugh but it doesn't last.

He exhales and glances over his shoulder at my mom back at the restaurant. "She really likes it here. You know, I'd go anywhere she wants." He rests a hand on the back of my neck, yanking me into his side and kisses the top of my head. "My girls are the world to me."

Wrapping my arms around him, I hug him tight, not sure anything has been resolved, but to have a man in my life who loves so deep and true gives me hope for the rest of the world. My time might be ticking down, but if men on this planet were half the man my dad is and has been, this world would be a great place.

The only problem is that men like my dad are rarer than the cancer in my heart.

My outburst sucks the remaining energy out of me and by the time Dad and I make it back to the table, the edges of black come seeping into my vision. I don't bother looking in Dave's direction—can't—afraid he'll scoop me up and have a stethoscope to my heart before I can blink.

Instead, I grab my purse and excuse myself from the table, retreating into the hotel and the privacy of my room. I shower off the day and try to not think about Chloe and the envelope, the chat with Dad, and the many wandering thoughts of Dr. Dave.

Sitting in my pj's with the night settling over the ocean out my window—its red shutters that up close look faded and chipped with time—I grab my phone and read all the missed text messages from Azzy.

Azzy: Umm... hellllloooo bestie! Where's my pictures?

Azzy: LC says she walked by your apartment and there's a rent sign in the window. WTF?!

Azzy: Have you run away with a cute boy saying that you're with your parents? That would be a lame excuse, but believable given your track record.

Azzy: It's okay bestie, it's been thirteen hours since I last heard from you and nothing... not worrying... okay, a little.

Azzy: It's official. Now I'm worrying. What's 911 in Portugal? Do I need to dial the country code before calling it?

I giggle and call her, flipping onto my stomach on the bed like a teenager while facing the window, ivory sheer floor-length curtains blowing in the breeze.

Azzy answers without a greeting. "Holy shit, I thought you might've been murdered or taken. Do I need to practice my Liam Neeson voice?" Her voice deepens. "'What I do have are a very particular set of skills.'"

Another giggle rises out of me again. "Sorry, it's been a whirlwind since we got here. Do you remember the man who helped me home when I was woozy at the concert?"

"The *doctor* that you kept hidden from me until I had to force out the reason why you left early? The one I still can't believe didn't go inside your place? Well, if it's *that man*, then yes, I remember. What about him?"

I cringe at my white lie. It was the only thing I could

think of at the time. "Yeah, the very same one. Well... he's here. He's here in Portugal with his mom and staying at the hotel next door."

There's shifting around her apartment and after a moment her voice sounds closer to the phone. "What do you mean he's *there*?"

"As I said, he's here with his mom. Apparently, his mother and mine are new best friends, met at breakfast and now I can't shake them."

Azzy laughs hysterically and shouts into her apartment. "LC! LC! Remember I told you about Rachel's doctor hero man? Well, he's in Portugal and their moms are best friends." I can't hear LC's response, but Azzy's breathing into the phone again. "And?" She draws the word out.

"And what?" I flip off the bed and saunter to the window. "He's nice—"

"And incredibly good looking—that's what you said when I forced it out of you. So..."

"So, nothing." I dip myself in front of the sheer curtains and lean forward on the windowsill. The beach is quiet, my parents and the other tourists having all gone to bed. There's only one person walking in the sand toward the water.

"I smell an opportunity, Rache. Oh hey, why is there a 'For Rent' sign on your place? Is Mr. Chen tired of your loud music at last? Can't say I'm surprised. He's been great all these years, but I bet he wants more money, doesn't he? Fucking gentrification's taking up all the cheap places and ruining the city. We have an extra room, but I know you were wanting to keep your own place."

I'm not listening anymore, perplexed by the lone figure on the beach. "Azzy, I have to go."

"Send me pics!" she shouts before I get the chance to end the call. "And good luck with the doctor."

I squint to make sure it's him, but I'd recognize his tall form anywhere, even in the curtain of nightfall. What's Dr. Dave up to so late?

Not bothering to change out of my PJ's, I find a beach towel and cocoon myself into it, slipping on my sandals before heading out of the hotel.

The night clerk gives me an odd look, but I ignore her and trudge out the main entrance.

Dave is near the edge of the water, and I come across his loafers left in the sand and can't believe how irresponsible he is for leaving such expensive shoes out in the open.

But regardless, I kick off mine and leave them with his.

He doesn't know I'm sneaking up behind him, wrapping myself tighter in my bright orange and pink speckled wrap. The foam is coasting up to his toes before retreating back into the depths of inky ocean.

The breeze isn't as strong as earlier, but it's still tousling his dark hair around. His hands are buried in his pockets, and he's frozen in place, looking toward wherever Morocco and Africa sit across the sea.

There's a jetty to his left, a few fishermen wandering along the outer ledge, finding a spot to drop their lines for a little night fishing. To the right are rocks—cliff edges broken free from the jagged shore and dotting the entire coastline. Even in the blackness, I can make out the bright green growth on the top, unsure whether it's bushes or grass or even moss, but it still glows in the moonless night.

A hand comes out of his pocket, and drags across his face, settling on his chin and jaw as he works the skin with his fingertips.

He's lost in thought. What's keeping him up tonight?

Something crawls over my toe, and I don't even care what it is, a crab, a bird—a fucking monster from the deep—but it makes me squeal and hop on one foot, sending Dave spinning to see me shuddering and hopping around in the sand, flinging my hands and towel in disgust like a bird doing a weird mating dance.

He doesn't offer an ounce of assistance, just lets me flounder.

He's not laughing, but he isn't upset I'm here either. It's somewhere in between with one raised brow. "Are you finished now? It's an unusual dance, admittedly, but I'm flattered you choreographed it for me."

"Haha. Very funny. Something gross crawled over my foot." I shudder one final time before repositioning the towel over my shoulders. "I saw you out my window." I signal back to the hotel, trying not to make it seem as though I'm stalking him. "I was curious what you're doing out here so late. So...um...here I am."

His head bobs and he peeks over his shoulder at the ocean. "I was thinking about my sister," he says in a way that makes my heart sting. "She loved the ocean. Said it made her feel alive to hear the waves crash on the shore. She wanted to come here so bad, but never made it."

"Is that why you brought your mom here?"

"Partly," he admits and does this thing where he looks down toward my feet then up to my eyes and it seems as though he wants to add something.

"What're the other reasons?" I'm not sure where I get off being so nosy.

"What happened with your own sister earlier?" His question is his way of ending my interrogation. And it works. I chew on my bottom lip, thinking back to the conversation.

"A thick envelope was sent to my parents' house for me, from UCSF. She tried to open it. Thought it was funny, so you can understand why I was pissed."

He nods. And seems unsurprised. "I'm sorry to hear that. I should have mentioned that at your appointment. It's your end-of-life treatment plan and resources for everything from DNR's to hospice care."

The nonchalant way he says the last sentence might as well be a slap across my face because I recoil, tripping backwards into the sand, collapsing into a heap.

Dave's beside me, pulling my hands away from my face, tipping my chin up. But I can't look at him, can't see past the blurriness in my eyes.

"Rachel, maybe it's time to end this and tell—"

"No!" I slap his hands away from me. "Not yet. Now is not the right time." A sob bubbles up. I try to push it down, sinking my face into my hands again. "Why do you even care what I do?" I cry it out through the muffle of my fingers, my voice deteriorating into a visceral cry of pain, the agony of a wounded animal giving a vent to its injured soul.

He sits back and away from me, and we are both in the same position we were this morning on the beach. When he speaks, I have to tilt my ear to hear.

"I don't know why we've crossed paths," he ventures when my sniffles lessen. "But we have, Rachel, and we crossed paths again here in Praia de Luz and now that we're here, it feels like we are supposed to figure this out together. Something brought us back together to sort this all out."

"This?" I sneer. "*This*, as in my death?"

His chin rests on his bicep as he faces me. "This, as in us."

"There is no us. I barely know you," I tell him a little too harshly and he nods on his arm before looking away.

"That's not what I mean. I..." He's scowling and if thunder clouds were to roll in right now, I'd think they'd be caused by the storm brewing from within Dave. "My sister, Kim, died from a cardiac sarcoma too."

My blood runs cold in my veins. *How is this seriously possible? Aren't they rare?*

The pieces snap together and like a switch, it hits me. "You can't save me." I don't know why, but those words really hurt to say aloud as they tumble out. "You made that pretty clear at my appointment." There's a feeling that blooms within... maybe because he could not save his sister, his sense of guilt makes him desire to save me. For forgiveness. From whom, I am unsure.

His mouth is drawn tight. "I'm not trying to, Rachel. I was actually hoping we could be friends and enjoy the time in Portugal and that I may have a little more understanding of what my sister went through from your perspective."

"Friends?" The word disappoints me.

"Maybe I can be there for you more than I was for Kim."

"You're using me?" Is all I can manage.

"Not at all." He rakes a hand through his hair. "Maybe at first," he corrects. "But not now. Now, I want to spend time with you because... well, I want to spend time with you. I like you. I also like being with you. Take it however you will."

"Friends," I repeat. It's not a question or a statement. I'm not really sure what it means, uncertain what I really want from this.

He scoots closer to me and flexes out his palm and fingers in front of me. "May I?" His eyes flicker to my chest and normally if a guy did this, I'd be appalled and punch them, but I only nod as his entire palm rests against my breastbone.

There's no sexual tension behind the move or his touch. It's somewhere between a doctor and a superhero, as though trying to extract the cancer using 'the force'. His palm remains there as I watch the waves roll in. There's only one certainty—they don't teach this technique in medical school.

When he glances up at me, the mood shifts and a simple touch over my heart is now fluttering other areas of my body. I want to lean into him. I want him to kiss me, but all I can think about is the cancer leaching from my black heart, the heart that will cease to beat in five short months.

I reach up for his hand and remove it from my chest, our fingers intertwining for only a moment until I pull mine away. "I should be going," I say.

His mouth is closed, but his tongue runs across his teeth. "Can I show you something before you leave?"

I don't move when Dave grabs my hand again and moves it under his shirt and I'm about to protest, but I'm not sure what's happening. I secretly don't mind feeling his heated skin against my palms, the light scatter of chest hair tickling my fingers. He presses my palm flat and forces my fingers to spread out in the same spot in which his rested on my chest.

He's watching me and I, him. He doesn't speak at first, but the muscle under his breastbone is thumping palpably in its cage. Dave lowers his voice. "Do you feel that, Rachel?"

Mouth dry, I can only nod. Words are becoming difficult to form.

"That's life." He reaches over to my chest with his free hand, splaying it identical to the one under his shirt, the warmth of his skin on mine. His voices wobbles. "This is your life." He presses my chest enough that it's clear he's talking about my heart. "It still beats. It hasn't stopped yet. You are *still* here. Maybe it's time to start acting like it."

I'm rendered speechless under Dr. Dave's hands—and my own.

Chapter Eleven

Azzy stayed in San Francisco for over a month after her surgery, her parents returning to Hammett a few days after Dad and I flew home. They had chaperones from the local church look in on her from day to day until she was well enough to come back.

There was something about being caught doing what I knew I shouldn't be doing that made me feel as though I had the 'dead man walking' sign plastered on my back for months. I did my chores, didn't bother fighting with Chloe and generally tried to stay out of everyone's way.

At least for a while.

Mom was at a loss with my behavior as it had evolved into a nasty cloud of angst hovering over the family those final years spent under their roof. She constantly talked about how her eldest daughter should have been doing this or should've been doing that and neither of those options involved running away and stealing from my parents, or repeatedly fighting with a sister who was at least helping out on the family farm.

Just like the first time though, Dad never spoke of the

incident again. I think in his mind, we had worked it all out and that was in the past, even if Mom couldn't quite let it go.

I struggled through my eleventh-grade year. Even when Azzy came back to school, things had changed within me and as much as my parents hoped that I would be scared out of running away again, the entire ordeal in San Francisco only made me crave my independence more.

The chasm created with my parents only grew wider and by the time graduation came a year after that, it might as well have been as wide as the Grand Canyon.

Sure, we smiled for the cameras and I'm sure Mom was even shocked to find out my diploma was indeed real and not printed off of our inkjet printer, but the relationship was fractured regardless. It healed incorrectly, making everything disjointed and painful.

My impending freedom simmered under the surface those last years at home until two days after graduation. I had three duffel bags loaded down with everything I owned.

I wasn't surprised that Dad stayed on the porch while Mom forced an obligatory hug out of me. I loaded everything up in Azzy's car and slammed the trunk, giving a half-hearted wave to them.

It wasn't a declared running away from home, but the sadness in Dad's eyes and the worry in my mother's was enough to make me feel not-so-sweet sixteen all over again.

And once again, I didn't really care or fully understand why they cared so much. I just wanted out.

Azzy and I stopped at the only stoplight in town, her Acura with its same unfixed cracked windshield and blown-out speakers revving as we clasped hands. She gunned it all the way out to the highway. And without so much as a glance in the rearview mirror, we went back to the city that had almost killed her.

It was my twenty-third birthday when my mom and Chloe came out to the city for the first time, towing my dad along for his second visit.

I remember kicking beer cans out of the hallway of our second-story apartment in a slender rowhouse in Chinatown, making room for their luggage. How Azzy scored such a shitty place, I'll never know, but it was cheap and that was rare in the Bay Area.

Weirdly enough, the neighborhood was a perfect match for us both.

College was a pipe dream, another disappointment to my parents, I'm sure, but Azzy and I made our lifestyles work. She took a position in a locally owned coffee shop until she finally landed her dream job as a developer for a startup that designed research apps.

I had no clue what any of that meant when she first told me, but the bump in pay was great for her and the office was within walking distance from our place.

Putting it mildly, my career was a bit bumpier. I was a fulltime cashier at a health food store and part-time dog walker, but neither paid great and I jumped into more odd jobs the first few years in San Francisco than most people would in their entire life.

But everything changed for me when I read an article online about travel blogging.

Hooked by the promise of traveling the world on someone else's dime, I spent all my free time designing a website and social media pages and with Azzy's expertise, it grew over the years. I wouldn't say I made it to a status most would be proud of, but my bills were usually paid on time, and I didn't have to work seven dead-end crappy jobs at once just to buy groceries.

And if there were any negatives, the perks of traveling for reviews made up for them.

My moderate success still didn't matter when my family arrived to our rowhouse. I ushered them inside, knowing the silent judgement had begun. Mom eyeballed every inch of the sparse apartment, her brows disappearing into her bangs of a new shorter cut.

Music posters lined every free space on the walls, empty alcohol bottles decorating the fridge top, and Chinese takeout containers were overflowing in the garbage—the ones that had made it all the way there, anyway.

Chloe rolled her eyes the entire three-day visit and kept her nose in her phone, texting her boyfriend and top student in Boise State's Agricultural Department, Ted. They'd been dating since high school and Chloe had followed him to college, claiming her degree in Liberal Arts could be used for many purposes. If only they'd offered Home Economics as a major and Over Eager Housewife as a minor.

She'd proudly thrust her hand in my face before I'd even set the luggage down, a sad excuse for a diamond wiggling near my nose.

Dad only sighed and plopped down into a plaid and dingy thrift store find of a couch while Chloe spewed out all the wedding details for their post-graduation nuptials. Mom was eating it up too, talking on and on until I gave up and joined my dad.

"It's been like this since he asked her at Christmas. I wish you could have seen that spectacle," he mumbled over their chatter. A pang of guilt exposed my choice to travel overseas rather than spend the holidays in Idaho. "I like the guy, I really do." Dad continued on oblivious to my shame. "I just don't know how he'll ever live up to your sister's expecta-

tions. But I don't need to explain that to you. Know what I mean?"

I snorted and Chloe sent me a look of disgust before returning to her phone and pulling up Pinterest to show Mom what she wanted for a bouquet.

"Something tells me he already knows what's in store for his future. It's all there," I said, pointing at the Pinterest app she was scrolling through. "All planned out for the rest of their lives."

This had Dad snickering, drawing the ire of Mom's sneer this time. Ignoring her, he patted me on the leg. "You doing okay, sweetheart? I'll be honest, it's not my cup of tea, this city."

"Not enough wind and snow?" I guessed.

He leaned into me and muttered, "There's that, but more importantly, there's too many damn Californians."

I adjusted my Stanford sweatshirt—a parting gift from a short-term boyfriend, but I liked the way people looked at me whenever I wore it. "I'm doing okay. The pay's crap half of the time, but who knows where I'll get to go this year?"

"How many countries have you visited now?"

I started to tally them in my head but pulled out my phone and counted them on a list I'd made. "Fourteen."

Dad whistled low. "Fourteen. I haven't even been to that many states. Where should we all go together someday? Where would you recommend for your uncultured parents?"

I pinched my brows. "You don't want to travel, Dad. You don't even like Californians, remember?"

"That's true but sometimes, it's okay to branch out and try something scary." Dad leaned in closer and lowered his voice. "Why do you think I married your mother?"

"I heard that." Mom tossed a half-earnest glance over her shoulder and Dad's face turned beet red.

"How does she do that?" he asked me in a hushed tone.

I shrugged, stifling a laugh. "I've read that Portugal is a great place for people your"—he gave me a warning of a look—"people who haven't left America. Definitely wasn't going to say you were old," I corrected. "Not that old anyway."

He pinched my arm.

Chloe spun around to us. "I don't ever want to leave this country and I won't. I don't even like it here in California. Too many people. I'll be glad to be back home in the country."

"Well, you don't have to come, then," I happily said, looking back to my dad. "Portugal, but let's wait until I can pay for us to go. It's going to happen one day."

"I'm sure it will, sweetheart," he said, squeezing my knee.

Chapter Twelve

When I found out about my diagnosis, I had to speed up the plan, of course. I'd been living by myself since Azzy moved in with LC, but I'd been saving to move into a better place. Through the odd freelance writing gigs and the moderate but growing success of my blog, I had enough to fund the entire trip with some penny pinching and complete draining of my savings.

There was a little vindication in paying for their trip. It almost felt as though I was repaying them for the money I had stolen, even if the price of their trip and stay was probably a mere fraction of what I blew through. I hate that I lied to my parents about my job paying for it and not telling them the truth, but how else would I have convinced them? I needed them to move fast.

They didn't even have time to process the trip details or ask too many questions.

I rush ordered their passports and we were flying across the pond sans Chloe within two weeks on the premise that I had to get there quickly before peak travel season began.

And now it's been a week since we first arrived, and

Dad and Mom seem happier than I have ever seen them. Equally important, it's been four days since Dave touched my heart on the beach, and I his.

Mom and Helen are the best of friends now and Dad's become their willing third wheel. I get the distinct impression he doesn't mind playing chauffeur to a gaggle of girls... and to Dave, even though he always seems to have a suspicious eye on him. But I guess that's normal for any good dad.

The days have been spent lazily strolling the few villages along the bus route, exploring trinkets shops, and discovering forts built for maritime defense. On one free day, we followed a rough trail to a cliff edge, picnicking on the local delicacy of brined and dried cod prepared in several ways that Helen and Mom found in a local grocery store. The real find was the custard tarts Dad attempted to hide for himself. I devoured three in a row to wash away the lingering and overwhelming fishy taste of the cod.

We've laughed over meals together and I even snorted at the table, trying octopus and instantly spitting it out. The wine is always flowing, and the company really makes me not want to leave, ever. Dad even shared embarrassing stories about me growing up and I didn't mind for once.

He's in the middle of telling them about my first trip abroad when I beg him to stop.

"They don't want to hear this! It's too early. We haven't even finished coffee yet. Come on, Dad. At least let them wake up before you mortify me."

It's been a lazy morning and Dad's hazel eyes dazzle in the rising sun when Helen nods rapidly for him to continue. I lean in Dave's direction.

"Dave, help me out. You agree, don't you?"

But he merely smiles and holds up his hands. With a

roll of eyes and a hefty groan, my forehead connects with the metal table as Dad begins.

"Big shot Rachel gets this invitation to Athens from some workout person wanting her to feature their friend's resort—"

"Yoga instructor, Dad," I correct him from my faceplant.

"Whatever. *Fitness* guru from some fancy neighborhood in San Francisco."

"The Marina," I tell no one in particular.

"Anyway, she flies all the way to Athens, passport in hand, bright-eyed and ready to conquer the world on her first major overseas trip. Her mother and I are worried sick the entire time, tracking the flights, trying to follow her route, and I get this call at two in the morning when she should be over the middle of the Mediterranean..." He starts to choke on a laugh, and I groan into the metal table. "She's in Athens all right. *Athens, Georgia.*"

Everyone's laughing at me. Hell, I'm trying not to laugh at myself as I sit back up to sip my Galão, trying to test my own personal theory that caffeine can ease the sting of embarrassment.

There're tears escaping out of the side of Dad's eyes, and he can't catch his breath because every time he tries to deliver the punchline, he thinks about it again and cracks himself up until he's wheezing.

Finally, he takes a big sobering breath. "She's—she's in Athens, Georgia and it's a place where they do *goat* yoga." He's cry laughing again, face turning redder than my cheeks. "You know, yoga with goats. She thought she was going to be doing sunrise yoga with Greek gods at the Parthenon and she gets goats!"

Looking around the table, everyone's chuckling, even Dave. I narrow my eyes at the group. "Come on, it's an easy mistake and anyway, goat yoga has proven extremely therapeutic. I wrote a whole piece about it. Science backs it. What say you, Dr. Dave?" I cup one hand to shield my face and mouth from the others, "Help me!"

He waves me away, taking a sip of his coffee. "Don't think I've read those studies."

"Traitor," I mutter.

Mom touches Helen's arm when she giggles, and Dad swipes at the stray tears. Dave's smirking at me over his coffee cup. This moment makes me almost complete. This is what I wanted. There was no way of knowing two strangers would be factored into this trip, but I'm glad they're here for them. Maybe even for me too.

There haven't been any more naps in the shade. Dave's kept his distance since the night on the beach. Sure, he's laughing and cordial now, even pulls my chair out for me when I sit, but at times, he seems a little disconnected, and I wonder if there's a way to fix that final thread to make this trip perfect.

We haven't been able to talk since that night, not really, but today we'll be spending the entire day all crammed up in Dad's car on another escapade our mother's have schemed up, so that should be interesting.

Once all the coffee is consumed and we've made it to the parking lot, Dad, Mom, and Helen go straight for their seats from their first adventure. Mom's riding shotgun and Helen sits behind Dad, so she has direct line of sight to Mom. I roll my eyes and take the puny middle seat.

I shouldn't be surprised at that since I'm the tiniest person here, but I'll miss having my window to lean against. The back seat of the car is tight, and I mean *tight*. To buckle our seatbelts is a masterclass in gymnastics, although it has much more room than the sardine box Dave rented.

Helen pats my leg and gives me a smile once we've settled in, then launches into the itinerary planned for the day while Mom is busy highlighting everything Helen mentions in her travel guidebook.

Dave is squashed into the door, and a mild sense of guilt comes over me. I try not to giggle at the way he looks with his hands clasped in his lap, shoulders rolling forward slightly while attempting to fit his large frame into a tiny box and not encroach on my small seat.

"How long is this car ride?" I ask, scootching a little forward.

"Thirty minutes to an hour," Helen says, tapping Dad on the shoulder to turn on the highway.

Mom shifts her body in the seat so she's facing the back. "Any idea where we're going, Trout? Have you done any research for your blog on the town of Silves?"

I squirm as Dave's amused face glows at me. "No," I grit out. "I haven't."

"Wait, *Trout*?" Dave says and now I'm certain they should move up my expiration date to today.

Mom claps her hands and erupts in laughter at my reddening face, almost completely facing backwards to talk to Dave. "Oh, I'm sorry. Let me explain. When she was three or four, she caught a fish in the Snake River. It was so small, more like a minnow, but she insisted it was the world record trout she'd seen Randy reading about in the paper. She went on and on for days about that teensy trout. Isn't that right, Randy?"

Dad grunts out his confirmation.

"The nickname stuck after that," Mom explains.

"Do you want to trade places so you can tell more embarrassing stories without straining your back?" I snip at her. "Or you could pull over the car and let me walk the rest of the way in peace."

"No, that's it for now, and we're almost there. No need to be dramatic, dear." She turns back facing forward and side eyes Dad's lame attempt to not chuckle, her own giggling barely contained.

"Well, Trout," Dave says, straightening his back. "Looks like you're stuck with me back here in the live well."

I roll my eyes and scoff. "That's the best you can do?"

"I'm not one to *fish* for compliments."

I groan and Dad's laughing now. He can't resist. Puns and dads are like two magnets that can't be pulled apart.

"I'd make him walk the plankton for that, Rachel. He has no sole," Dad says, cracking up. Helen and Mom don't seem to get the jokes which only makes it all the funnier.

"Wow, Trout, he really put you in your plaice," quips Dave.

Dad replies with a quick point to the rearview mirror and a gleam in his eye, "That makes me eel, young man. And here I thought you were a sturgeon."

"What's wrong?" Dave asks, finally looking at me with such conviction. "You're blushing like a catfish that's just seen the bottom of the river."

"Stop it." I nudge him, but now I'm laughing too, watching both men's cogs turning in their heads.

Finally, nineteen puns later, we arrive at our destination. My stomach hurts from laughing and the other two women even found several bad puns to be worthy of their own giggles.

Dave gets out and holds the door for me. "Trout, out," he says with a dramatic bow as I exit. I elbow him in the abs, and he mocks a serious injury and a cough. "Ooh, don't pout, little Trout."

I point up at his scrunched nose. "You better leave that nickname right here, right now, Dr. Dave."

"Or what?" he dares, leaning down to cage me against the open car door.

My nose raises up to meet his challenge. "Or I'll tell my dad you had your hands all over my chest the other night."

Dave's face drops, his mouth falling open, and he starts to form a smile, but that drops too, his ears turning bright pink. His reaction is exactly what I wanted, but he's not looking *at* me. He's looking *over* me. I don't want to turn around, but my head swivels anyway.

Dad's halfway through the motion of closing his door on the other side of the car, but it's as if he's frozen in time. I've seen that look once before. It's only a flash across his eyes and not nearly as intense, but I am instantly seventeen all over again, and Dad is fuming.

Mom and I had been fighting about something I can't even remember, but I called her a bitch and stormed out, slamming the screen door of the porch, the squeaky hinges screaming.

A few seconds later, they screeched again, and I spun around, ready to fight. But it was Dad.

I never feared my father until that day. A man built on compassion and calm, I'd never known him to yell. He never hit us, never slapped or spanked us as children.

He never even raised a hand in anger or curled a fist at his side. But that day, his face contorted, and he barreled toward me at full speed. He skidded to a stop mere millimeters from my face as he gripped the railing with white knuckles.

A burning expression consumed him, enflaming him from the collar of his worn yellow CAT Diesel T-shirt collar to above the point where his eyebrows gnashed together.

His pupils dilated under the narrow slits of his eyelids, the hazel not so calming, but churning dangerously as he stayed close to me, mouth drawn tight.

He spoke no words, but his message was loud and clear. If I ever called my mother anything other than a saint again, it would be over for me. That was the gist of his silent warning to me. And I believed him to be true to his unspoken word.

Dad's face is shading red like that day and mine flushes too. Even good men have their limits and Dave and I found his. Dad knows I date and have had boyfriends in the past, but I have never brought any home and never talked about them touching me.

I'm seeing this for the first time and even though there is nothing between Dave and me, a part of me is living for the discomfort growing between them.

Helen and Mom come back to collect us. They look between the three of us, no doubt able to sense this awkward standoff. "Come on you guys. Lots to do," Mom says, pushing at Dad and he shuffles away with her and Helen.

I spin back to Dave and when our eyes meet, we both burst out laughing and by the quick glance Dave shoots over my shoulder, he sees my dad is looking back at us. But we're out of control and I'm laughing so hard I hold onto his arm to stop myself from tipping over.

"You're in so much trouble, Dr. Dave," I choke out.

He slings his arm over my shoulder for a brief moment. "The path to hell..." he says as we follow the three parents up to another castle.

For thirty minutes while we wait in line for tickets, Dad shoots daggers at Dave and to his credit, as each one heads his way, Dave acts as if embarrassed, as if he's done something wrong. By the time we get inside the grounds of what my pamphlet reads as 'Castelo De Silves', Dad has become preoccupied with Mom tasking him to take pictures of all the various possible angles of ramparts stained with red clay and time.

Helen is adjusting a straw hat, oddly similar to the one my mother wears and with her oversized sunglasses, she looks like a movie star trying to go incognito. Dave helps her adjust it and she hugs him around the waist, while looking up at him and talking quietly.

I wander the interior courtyard solo, happy to have the time for my own thoughts. The last week has been wonderful, generally speaking, except for the lack of time alone.

The intrusive thoughts in my head have been buried willfully, leaving me afraid of what they might produce, but now seems like a great time to sit and contemplate about the next five months.

Swallowing away the forming lump, I think about the contents in that envelope waiting on the kitchen table at the farm. It sits five thousand miles away, but the weight of it is with me now.

My apartment was the first step and that's done.

All my personal effects went into storage the week before thanks to a moving company. Azzy can take what she wants and donate the rest, not that there's much there.

I figure that I will spend the last months in Idaho, even though I wish I could stay in my new home state, but I have no intention of having Azzy take care of me. I'm already worried enough by the thought of how my best friend will recover after our shared heart separates and rips apart one fibrous frayed piece after another. Putting it on her to watch me die? No, thanks.

The hardest part will be those true end-of-life considerations. Arrangements I shouldn't have to make. Things I don't want to decide. I watch from my bench as the green and red Portuguese flag flies over the tallest tower, wishing that same gust could blow away all the responsibilities weighing on me.

Clueless, Dad and Mom wave to me from the upper battlement walls as I sit in a little square vignette of benches, red brick, and lime-green bushes trimmed to perfection.

Dad is probably still concerned about Dave, but he's smiling as Mom prods him along and they hold hands as they explore the perimeter of the castle walls.

Helen finds me and drops to the bench in a theatrical sigh.

Her chin tilts up to me though nothing is visible under her brimmed hat except for giant black sunglasses and the bob of salt and pepper hair sweeping her jaw.

"My daughter would've liked it here," she says.

Is she directing it at me or the universe? I only nod.

"Dave and I try to go away once a year to somewhere we can feel her presence. Somewhere to remember her for more than a tombstone. So far, we just keep returning to Portugal." Her chest inflates and then deflates, and she rests a hand on my knee. "Kim would've loved you."

The last part catches me off guard and my head whips to her. "I'm sorry?"

She pats my leg then tugs on the brim of her straw hat. "I see the way he looks at you. A mother sees these things. He's had a lot of bad in his life and you seem to bring out the good."

My heart is crumbling, and every cell in me wishes to cry, but I gulp it down and shake my head. "Helen, there's nothing between your son and me."

"Sure, dear. I also see the way you look at him too. If you honestly think there's nothing there, there ought to be."

There ought to be so many things, I think, saltwater threatening to cascade from my eyes.

Without another word she lifts from the bench and floats to another area of the castle grounds.

Across the courtyard, Dave inclines against a half wall of ancient stones with one arm folded across his chest and the other using it for leverage to bite the pad of his thumb. He doesn't know what passed between his mom and me, but from how he's studying me it appears as if his mother may have told him the same thing.

In my quiet moment of contemplation, two freight trains have clotheslined me from opposite directions. I don't want feelings for Dave, even though they're already there. I want to spend my days around people who can move on from this with minimal impact. Bringing someone else into the mix is not only unfair, it's downright cruel.

So as Dave wanders around the courtyard, pretending not to glance my way, I've decided it's time to part ways with Helen and Dave before too much time makes it hurt even worse.

Chapter Thirteen

Healing is not an easy task. After a heart is broken, it creates scar tissue to fill in the voids and cracks. That's what Dad and Mom surely must have done over the years to repair all the damage from my choices. Every time I hurt them another crack would form. Some would mend with minimal scarring, but others—like running away at sixteen—would have been filled with so much scar tissue, it's surprising the muscle underneath would even function properly. Perhaps it didn't.

Twenty-five should be an age where you finally get your shit together and start acting like an adult, fixing all the rifts you have caused to those who love you.

Yeah.

Right.

Chloe invited me to her baby shower a year after she married Ted Conner, local god of all things farming. They were expecting their first, a boy, and I'm half-convinced that Chloe might have even figured out the science to plan that as well. Who knows, maybe Pinterest had a board about it.

John Deere cupcakes and green and yellow balloons

lined the porch at the farmhouse, tables decorated in the same colors with little paper tractors. Against the red, white, and blue flag that stood proudly at the front door, the bright colors really popped into something straight from Americana roots.

Mom and Chloe had spent days planning and decorating, and I was truly excited for them and the future of our family. It was what Chloe always wanted, which was more than could be said for me. Kids and me? Not so much, but I vowed to my dad to at least pretend to be a little interested as a good aunt. All I really promised was to corrupt them with rock and roll and—gasp—thinking more of life than small town Hammett.

Which is why my gift to the first born of my dear sister was luggage.

She thought it was a diaper bag, but I knew better. The kid would need an escape route and while Aunt Rachel might not be the best role model, I would sure as hell take in a refugee from the Conner Clan and its controlling matriarch.

Chloe was about to burst, her belly so swollen and round, she had to waddle everywhere she went. Dad caught me chuckling behind her back and frowned at me with his displeasure, but I couldn't help it, seeing my perfect little sister looking like a penguin trying to hold a football between her knees was hilarious.

And the complaining. My god, Ted was a saint to listen to her rant and rave about everything from the balloons not being hung the right way to the strip of grass not mowed at the right angle.

Surely, he understood what he signed up for. Good 'ol Ted jumped at her every demand. I didn't know if he was scared of her wrath or loved her more than his dignity, but he ran around the hours leading up the party like a man on a mission.

I, on the other hand, wouldn't give an ounce. I may have been the older, wiser, more mature sister, but I still had a nasty streak of rebellion running through me. My dear sister Chloe had a way of extracting it from me with minimal effort. Or often, with none at all.

When she asked me to move a chair from one side of the porch to the other because 'the sun might come out later and if it does, there's a slight chance the person in that chair will receive a sliver of sunlight on their kneecap', I barked out a laugh and shook my head.

Then I plucked a cupcake she had spent twenty minutes getting into the perfect formation on the table and devoured it in one bite, tossing the little plastic tractor decoration into the trash.

It sounds like I was being an asshole and petty—I was—but Chloe knew how to push my buttons, and I knew how to push hers. I suppose that's what sisters do, and I took my role seriously, pushing her as far as possible.

She waddled up the table, sending a scorned look my way as she fixed the spot I left empty.

"Don't be jealous," she said, adjusting the last cupcake in the row, licking a finger that had lightly skimmed the overly sweet green icing. "Just because you'll never have any of this. Unless you marry Azzy, of course. I guess that's acceptable in California, but don't expect anyone here to welcome you both with open arms. That's all sinful."

"You're a real bitch when you're pregnant, you know that?" I said, kicking my feet up on an adjacent chair. "Azzy doesn't deserve that. For whatever reasons I can't fathom, she likes you so leave her out of your witch hunt. Say what you

want to me, I'm used to it, but leave others, especially my best friend, out of it."

She backed her butt into the largest chair on the porch and it strained under her weight. "Why don't you go back to California? You don't even want to be here. Do what you do best and run away and leave us alone. You've always been rude to Mom and Dad, and ungrateful for all they've done. You don't deserve us."

Normally, Chloe wouldn't get me worked up, but those words stung. I put my feet down and braced on my knees. "Is that a suggestion or wishful thinking? At least I didn't settle."

"Settle?" She cackled as she rubbed her belly. "You think I settled? I have a perfect husband, a perfect farm, a perfect baby growing in my belly. I'm happy, other than having an ungrateful brat of a sister who only shows up for obligatory family functions. Why do you even bother coming home anymore?"

I clenched my teeth together. "Because I keep hoping that one day you and I will actually get along. Until then, I come out here for Mom and Dad. Never you. But you're right. I won't pretend to like you anymore. You can have your perfect life here in Hammett and I'll never bother you again."

She jiggled out a laugh as I stood. "It's about time. I wasn't even sure I wanted your negative influence around my child." Her eyes grew big, brows creeping up her forehead. "What are you waiting for? No one wants you here. Just leave and go back to California where anything goes. Somewhere you obviously fit in." She waved perfect manicured nails at me.

I'd never hated anyone in my life, but in that moment, I came really close to hating Chloe.

"Is this pregnancy hormones? Because once you cast me out of your life, I won't come back begging to be in it."

Chloe stood—well, tried to twice before pushing to her feet. "Good. It's about time you figure out that we don't want you here. You're a black spot on this family. Even Mom and Dad are tired of you and your ways. We all will be so much better off without you here. You're not welcome anymore."

"Chloe!" Mom yelled from the front door, and I wasn't sure how much she heard, but it was enough for her to plant her hands on her hips and come between us. "What on earth is going on between you two? This is supposed to be a day of celebration."

I locked onto Chloe's sullen face. "Nothing. She's politely asked me out of her life, and I have agreed." I turned to my confused mom. "Sorry for the abrupt departure, but don't worry, I'll make any future visits minimal."

I stormed into the house and gathered my things and was back in my rental car before anyone could stop me, not that they even tried. Chloe smirked as I slammed my car door shut.

On my way out of the driveway, Dad's farm truck was pulling in. I rolled down my window and waited for him to crank his open as the dust settled around us, attacking the streaks of tears rolling down my face with a layer of fine particles. His face pinched at the sight of me.

"Sorry, Dad. I made a scene. Sorry you'll be the one stuck with the aftermath yet again. Seems like that's what I'm best at, hurting them." I choked. "Hurting you. You deserve a better daughter than me."

Without giving him time to react, I punched the gas and left him and my family in a trail of dust.

Chapter Fourteen

THAT SCAR TISSUE THAT FORMED A FEW YEARS BACK still aches as I think about the way Dad watched me leave, and I'm rubbing the soreness in my chest when Dave finally settles next to me on the bench. My body is rigid and tense, knowing I'm about to be cruel once again, and he doesn't deserve any of this. He just walked into the wrong patient's room one month ago. The pinprick of tears stings, and I don't understand why a man I barely know is causing such a visceral reaction in me.

"I know what you're going to say," he says before I formulate a sentence.

My head bobs in his direction, heavy and full of impending tears and thoughts. "And what's that, Dave? Because I have a feeling you have no idea what I'm thinking."

A pained smile sweeps across his mouth. "You're about to say that you're going to take your parents and go your separate way from us. You're ready to leave Portugal and my mother and me." He pauses. "You're scared."

Okay, maybe he does know what I'm going to say.

"Your mom thinks you're interested in me," I tell him. "She's certain of it." He doesn't argue with this. "You're not."

"I'm not?"

"Interested. Interested in *me*."

"Rachel."

My breath catches. "You can't be. It's been a week."

He tips his head backwards on the bench and crosses his arms. I don't know whether he's focusing on the few stray clouds or staring right past them and into the space beyond. "Is that what you want? For my mom and me to leave you and your parents alone? To take Mom and distance ourselves from you and your parents permanently? If that's what you want, then..."

Giggling erupts on one of the tallest ramparts and draws my gaze. Mom has an arm wrapped around Dad, and Helen is taking a picture of them. Mom runs to Helen and checks the phone to make sure it's perfect, then drags Helen by the arm, thrusting the phone at Dad so the two women can have a picture together. They hold each other like sisters, adjusting their floppy hats to bend in half against their chins as they pucker their lips.

Well, sisters that like each other, not ones that despise one another.

I fold my body in half and groan, resting my head on my crossed forearms, my face buried in my lap, and I groan again louder.

"We discussed this the other day," he's reminding me, but it still sounds as though he's looking skyward. "I want to stick by you. Friends. Remember? I thought we'd been through this already?"

I sit up and turn my head to him, my eyes rolling in the process. "Dave..."

His eyes roll in an identical fashion toward me. "Rachel..."

I let out too big of a breath and my lips purse at the pressure. "That's all you want? Truthfully? Nothing more than being friends?"

"What do you want?" He's deflecting. My nickname may be Trout, but I don't bite.

"Uh-uh." I wag a finger at him. "Answer my question first."

"One day." My brows come together, and he clarifies. "I want one day with you without anyone else. I understand your time and days are precious and I will respect it if you say no, but I'm asking for one day. That's what I want. So, there you go. My cards are on the table."

"Why though? Why do you want to spend time with me alone?"

He looks back to the sky. "I want to tell—no—I want to *show* you why I'm lingering, why I want to be a part of Rachel Heltin's world."

I take another deep breath. He's still not looking my way, but I stare at him. "When do you want this day? Here in Portugal?"

He turns his head, dark blue eyes locking to mine. "Whenever you'll gift it to me, but I was thinking sooner rather than later."

I almost snorted. *There won't be a later, Dr. Dave.*

"What will our parents do? What will they think? It will seem a bit odd if we tell them we want to spend the day alone."

"Your dad already thinks a lot of bad things about me, I'm afraid. So, I'm not really concerned about it, to be honest. But I understand what you're saying. We're not children though. We should do what works for us. Let them think whatever they want."

I snort at this. "You're entirely right, and that's my fault how my dad's behaving."

He nods at me. "Yes, it is."

My parents and Helen are walking down the stairs toward us, and it feels like this decision needs to be made now. "Okay," I finally say. "One day. Then you'll leave me alone?"

His mouth turns down enough for him to catch it and smooth it back out. "If that's what you want, I'll respect your decision. And to be clear, a day is twenty-four hours."

I pop up from the bench, whipping my body toward him. "But that means"—I look to see where the parents are then lower my voice to a whisper—"You want me to go with you somewhere *overnight*?"

He tucks his lips over his teeth, trying not to smile. "I promise to be a complete gentleman. Separate beds. I promise."

I narrow my eyes at him, but our parents are almost here. "As friends." I reach my hand out.

"Sure," he says, taking my hand and shaking it. "If that's what you decide you want."

In the car ride home, Dad gets lost thanks to Mom and Helen telling him to go the wrong way down the highway for almost thirty minutes. They're arguing about which exit they should take to turn around. I'm growing tired and Dave is getting antsy in his corner of the tight backseat.

He finally untucks his arms and stretches one across the back of the headrests. His arms are so long that the one freed limb sails right past me. His hand rests on Helen's shoulder near the door.

She pats and squeezes it as though it's something they do a lot.

Exhausted, my eyes are growing heavy, my head bobbing violently as I fall into a clunky sleep. The jerking motion alerts Dave, and he removes the arm from his mother's shoulder and curls it around mine, pulling me to the side of his chest.

If I had the energy to fight him, I might, but I don't. I sink into the comfort of his body and the space between his shoulder and torso and fall into a deep sleep as we bump along the highway.

The sun is dipping into the ocean when Dad pulls into a sandy cobblestone parking lot, and I come to.

I don't immediately move off Dave, but instead open my eyes with a perfect line of sight to the rearview mirror. I have a feeling by the glances Dad's shooting back that he's not liking me sleeping in another man's arms. I've only ever let Dad hold me this way—not even boyfriends earned that privilege.

They never held me like this when comforting me when I cried, never holding me so close as I slept. Never protecting me. And Dave's done it twice now and to be honest, I might be on my dad's side with this whole situation.

I'm not sure I like it either, and I'm beginning to feel things in my scarred black heart that shouldn't be growing there.

Dave's running a single finger up and down my arm, causing Dad's eye to twitch. It's by no means sexual at all, just comforting and reassuring. That's it.

There's also the fact that Dave's not trying to hide it while I start to rise away from him. Dad's final glance in the mirror holds a glimpse of that flare from when I was seventeen.

Why is he so worked up? This all seems so benign. Then I remember that he knows two things—the first, that Dave's hands have been on my chest. The second, that no one messes with his girls.

We unfold ourselves out of the car and mom takes my arm.

"What's the plan for tomorrow, Mom?" I ask, still groggy. Helen is at our side too, and they begin discussing and debating doing another exhausting day of traveling to all the villages.

I give an exaggerated sidelong glance to Dave and that dimple that has only made an appearance once, shows itself with a vengeance.

Bringing their conversation to a halt, I manage to get out our request. "If you guys are okay with it, Dave and I might stay back tomorrow."

This catches Dad's attention and he's quick to join the group, flicking his worried gaze between Dave and me. "What will you two do?" he asks.

A slight flush creeps up my neck. I've never been more grateful the sunset is smearing streaks of bright oranges and pinks, so it looks as though my neck is reflecting glorious light.

Dave moves beside Dad and they're walking in step. He's standing straighter now, as if his height might have Dad backing down.

"I want to take Rachel to a spot my sister wanted to visit years ago." This is news to me, and I watch Helen's head turn sharply toward her son, but she doesn't frown. She smiles.

Dad's huffing, grumbling, "We'll meet for dinner tomorrow night, then?"

Even Dave's not immune from the same flush I'm trying to fan away and like the worst contagion, it spreads up to his cheeks. "No, sir," he says, and I want to facepalm myself.

Dad is no idiot. Any man addressing a father with 'sir' is asking for something more than just a day out. "We will be staying overnight there," he adds.

Yup. The flush is definitely contagious, all five of us now feeling the burn and discomfort of the entire ordeal, but no one more than Dad. He's beet red and can't look at Dave. Or me.

He stares straight ahead, locked onto something beyond this planet while the women look at each other with great big round eyes.

Dave doesn't even try to tell him we'll be in separate beds, and neither do I and in the awkwardness of the moment, all logic has run away with the sun.

Dave's head bows, not in shame, but probably so he doesn't have to look at my dad. "We're leaving at ten and will be back the next morning." There's finality there. No challenge will be accepted. Dave is telling the group—my dad specifically—in not so many words that I'm thirty years old and can make my own decisions and this is what I want. Part of me wants to hug him for putting his foot down, but the other more mortified part is still in full recovery mode.

No one speaks, but Dave gives me a nod and a pained half smile before taking his mom by the arm and heading to their hotel, leaving me with two parents word slapped into silence.

"Rachel," Dad finally manages to get out, and he motions for me to remain outside on the patio of the main floor. Mom glances back at us but thinks better of joining.

She's in an elevator within seconds. Whatever happened to girl code?

He's nervous, both adorable and humiliating in the same breath. Here stands one of the toughest men I know, a farmer by trade, one who has determination and grit pumping through his veins.

He doesn't cower and doesn't scare easily. Then there's that added special bond between a farmer and his daughter, that same grit and perseverance bleeding through into our relationship.

So does the tenderness and patience that it takes to bring life into the world and nurture it into something wonderful. But he's shuffling his feet awkwardly. This impending conversation might be better said if he had a brandy in his hand... and if I had a large one too.

Night is in full bloom, the patio ablaze with tiny white lights that jiggle up and down in the air. There's a film of sea spray on the railing I lean against, waiting for Dad to speak his piece. Part of this is hilarious that he's reduced to sputtering and unease, but then I keep remembering he might want to talk about my sex life. It washes away any humor in the moment.

He tries to speak. The second I rush to place my fingers on his lips, he shuts up, saving my embarrassment.

"Dad, I love and respect you, but I'm an adult. There's nothing going on between Dave and me anyway. We're just friends."

His jaw works back and forth—he doesn't believe me. "You're my little girl," he utters in a weak voice, and a splinter of scar tissue rips away from my heart. "No matter how old you are, I'll always worry."

Brushing the salt from the railing off my arms, I wrap them around his middle, resting my head against one hell of a steady heartbeat. "And you're the best dad in the world. Your concern is heard. But really Dad, there is nothing going on for you to even worry about."

He squeezes me. "I love you, Trout."

I hate—*hate*—that nickname, but when Dad says it, I want to cry because the thought of never hearing it again crushes me.

Instead, I hold myself together. "I love you too," I squeak out. I look up to him and catch a whiff of the same spicy aftershave he's worn for at least thirty years. "Is Mom going to freak out about her daughter running away again, but this time with a man?"

Dad laughs and it rumbles deep in his chest.

"Your mother might have conservative views, but she"—he smirks at me—"*and I* figured out a long time ago that we can't control you. You're a wild mustang, not meant to be caged."

His smile grows when I frown at this. "It's not a bad thing. It's refreshing to see you with such passion. Seeing you here, in Portugal, you seem happier than you ever were in Idaho. If that *boy* has anything to do with that, then neither I nor your mother have the right to stick our nose into it. I only want you to be careful with your heart. I'm sure you understand."

"Dad, he's a cardiologist, the perfect person to know how to look after hearts. And he's anything but a boy," I remind him, but a collection of tears hits the back of my eyes. The words sound stupid to me. There is nothing anyone can do to protect my heart at this point. Not even Dad.

"Even so."

Dad kisses the top of my head and urges us back into the hotel and we go our separate ways.

I'm exhausted back in my room, but don't know if it's the events of the last twenty minutes or the nap in the car, but sleep is going to come quick, so I pack with the last remaining flicker of energy. Why my bag is busting at the seams for one night seems a little odd. Nevertheless, I fall back into the bed, worrying a whole lot about the next day and not enough about my overpacking.

Chapter Fifteen

Azzy's descent into the goth lifestyle turned her family's world upside down. Hammett, Idaho wasn't prepared for my best friend to be born into their conservative world, and I'm sure her dad and mom would have preferred that she was more like me, square on the outside, raging metalhead on the inside, at least attempting something akin to a normal way through their world.

But that wasn't Azzy, and it never would be.

My best friend reveled in all things noir, not just the color black. It was the entire lifestyle of finding beauty within the darkness toward which she gravitated the most.

Sometimes, I believed she even embraced her namesake, the Angel of Death aka Azrael, the one who separated souls from bodies. And with her perceived dark soul came a severe societal disadvantage.

I never gave the downfalls to her darkness any thought until we were both twenty-seven and I found her one morning passed out on the same gross plaid couch that'd served and cured one too many hangovers.

On her stomach, she was still in her knee-high platform

combat boots and torn fishnets, but her face was smushed against the cushion and her makeup smeared from a white-washing of foundation and black eyeliner.

An arm hung to the floor, fingertips grazing the scratched faux wood grain. She'd recently started growing out her bangs and they were in that awkward in-between phase. The inky strands fell in front of her eyes and a half an inch past her nose, limp and plastered to her skin.

This wasn't an unusual sight in our apartment. We often rotated turns on that dingy old couch, so it was understandable that I thought she was asleep and hungover. I walked past her to make a cup of coffee and reached up on my tippy toes into the cabinet for my favorite cup.

Fingering the handle and trying to scoot it closer to me so I could fully grab it, I angled my head back to her, working the cup free between my fingers.

Something about the way she was lying didn't seem natural. I watched for a breath to raise her back.

One second.

Two seconds.

Three seconds.

Her bangs weren't moving in front of her nose. They were limp.

On the fourth second, I was halfway across the room, blood running cold as my coffee cup crashed to the ground, shattering into porcelain dust.

Shaking her violently while screaming at her to wake up, I begged her to breathe, but she didn't move. I flipped her off the couch and she landed on her back with such a loud sickening thud, I'm surprised we didn't go through Mr. Chen's ceiling. My fingers searched her neck for a pulse but couldn't find one. When I pried open her eyelids, only a third of her lifeless pupils were exposed, the rest rolled into the back of her head.

Azzy's cell phone was the closest and I grabbed it, my hands shaking so much I could barely hit the Emergency button hard enough to activate the call. Everything became a blur of panic and disorder and within minutes that stretched on like hours, EMT's were overtaking the apartment, poking plastic tubes and liquid bags into the near corpse of my friend. One female medic straddled Azzy as they pushed her out on a stretcher, pumping too hard to be normal against her chest wall.

They didn't have time to even consider letting me ride along, instead shouting which hospital they were taking her to so I could follow. The doors of the ambulance were slammed shut in front of my face and the wail of the siren ripped through the deserted Saturday morning streets of Chinatown.

I stood in disbelief in the middle of the road long after I could no longer hear the whine of the siren, hands clasped over my head. It took a car coming over a hill and a solid honk for me to snap out of it. Racing inside, I grabbed my things and called a taxi to take me over to the hospital.

Azzy's only flaw was the common misconception with people dressing and living the goth lifestyle like she did. Everyone assumed all the black came with an extra helping of depression and suicide attempts, and drugs—lots of drugs. They assumed no one willingly gave their life over to that kind of darkness unless something had gone haywire in their brain.

People didn't understand that someone like Azzy could be more straight-edge, highly intelligent, and happier than most 'normal' people. Other than the spiked drink when we were sixteen, Azzy's body had never ingested recreational drugs. Never.

Even when I made it to the hospital a mile away from our home and found a nurse to give me an update, they spiraled down the 'we're testing her for whatever she's overdosed on' and 'we've given her NARCAN' and 'they'll figure out what she took' route.

No one asked about her medical history.

No one knew that she'd had a history of epilepsy from a lesion in her brain. They knew my best friend had to be a suicide case or a drug user based on her makeup and clothes, letting her sit in the ER, trying to stabilize her without giving any more thought to her medical history.

More worrying still, no one would listen to me as I pleaded to anyone that would look my way.

I paced for an hour as they ignored me in the waiting room, begging to speak to the on-call doctor. When the doors unlocked to let in another patient from the waiting room, I bolted inside and lost my mind on a team of doctors huddling around the nurse's station. Actually, I think they were interns, supervised by some ass clown of a physician. The woman in charge had a severe bun of auburn hair tucked at the nape of her neck and a clipboard plastered to her chest.

She carried herself with her chin pointing up, unwilling to look down on any of the interns that hung on her every word. When I marched into the center of their lecture yelling, the woman rolled her eyes at me and side-eyed a nurse behind the desk.

The nurse picked up a phone and spoke quietly into the receiver.

I pointed with my entire hand back to where I could see Azzy's lifeless form surrounded by a variety of machines. "What the hell are you doing about her?"

"Ma'am." The woman looked down at me over her nose. "We are giving your friend the best care we can until we get the results back of what she took. This is our third overdose in an hour. We will get her stabilized, but you need to wait out in the waiting room until we figure it all out."

My hands went to my hair, and I thought about ripping out every last follicle.

"Are you fucking crazy?"

I've since learned that telling anyone this, especially a doctor treating your friend, would have one of two possible outcomes. One, I'd get thrown out of the hospital by two very large men in security uniforms. Two, the doctor would stare back with curious round eyes and wait as I peppered them with Azzy's epileptic history. Actually, there was a third option. Both things might occur.

The doctor jotted down my ranting and sent several interns scrambling to Azzy's bedside, then she nodded security over and had me thrown to the curb.

I remained there for four awful, agonizing hours.

I spent the time calling Azzy's parents and giving them the complete details—at least what I knew. They couldn't get a flight until the following day, but I'd promised I would tear down the hospital brick by brick if that meant getting Azzy the proper care.

Deflated and folded over my legs on the curb, a white coat settled next to me. She smelled nice over the scent of rubbing alcohol, like cinnamon and nutmeg. When I twisted my body toward her, I could tell her arrogance had been knocked down several pegs.

"How is she?" I asked Dr. Kragen, according to the name stitched on her coat.

"Not well." She pinched the bridge of her nose, closing

her eyes and I wondered if her head hurt due to how tight her bun pulled. "I owe you an apology."

I shook my head, my jaw locking. "Not me. You owe my best friend the proper care."

She nodded, looking over to me. "If you hadn't been there to tell us that, it might have been too late. As it stands, she is prepped for surgery right now. Part of the lesion they attempted to remove years ago has returned or maybe it wasn't fully resected, but either way, we'll get it all this time. We have a great neurosurgery team." She messed with the laces on her sneakers with worn soles and for some reason, I thought about how many miles the doctor walked a day inside the hospital corridors. "You are welcome back inside. Again, I'm sorry."

Frustrated at the stupidity of doctors and hating the thought of going back inside a hospital, I remained on the curb for another hour until the fog inundated the city enough to make my jacket damp. When I finally went into the hospital, I made my way straight to the surgical waiting room and slept in the most uncomfortable chair of my life. When I woke again, no one had any updates and I sat through the remainder of the day drained and ready to break Azzy out and take her back home.

Finally, thirteen hours after I had found her on the couch, Dr. Kragen herself appeared, looking not too dissimilar to how I felt. She ushered me back to the ICU.

"Azzy's surgery went well, but she'll have a long road to recovery."

She left me at Azzy's bedside with a parting reminder.

"Your friend is lucky to have you. And I'm sure you feel the same way." I didn't see Dr. Kragen again and that was a relief because once I regained some strength, I probably would have gone full crazy on her for the trauma she put us

through. At the time though, I just wanted to be with my friend.

Azzy looked so helpless and frail, machines beeping around her while gauze wrapped around her head, the contrast between her dyed hair and the layers of wrapped white gauze startling under fluorescent lights. I got a chuckle at how much more alive she looked with all her makeup wiped clean, yet she was the sickest she'd ever been.

I met LC when the night shift rotated in that evening. She was assigned as Azzy's RN. It's funny how I could see a connection between the two of them even while Azzy slept.

LC obviously cared for Azzy like a nurse should, but there was constant lingering in the room. Questions were asked to me about Azzy and by the end of LC's shift, she was sitting across from me, wanting to learn more about my best friend.

I didn't know she was into the goth lifestyle at that point. Her scrubs were hiding the truth about the tattoos, and all the piercings that covered her body were concealed by clear plugs and makeup.

I didn't see LC return for a few days and in between Azzy's parents visiting and trying not to lose my mind on the hospital, I was surprised to find the nurse with an awake Azzy one evening.

They were talking quietly, the sterile room light dimmed down to a soft ambient glow and LC sitting on the edge of the bed. Azzy was rolling her eyes and snickering as she mimicked something. The sleeves of LC's undershirt were pulled back, exposing forearms covered in tattoos.

Azzy was touching one of them, studying it intently.

Azzy lit up when I came into the room and LC jumped back as though she'd been caught, sliding her sleeves down and dropping her head as she gathered herself.

"I won't tell," I told her, not even sure who or what I would tell, but LC excused herself anyway as my friend smiled up at me, doped up not on the drugs, but on something even stronger.

I shook my head at my friend's lopsided shit-eating grin. "Oh, Azzy, you've got it bad."

"Bad," she dragged the word out, falling into her pillow, grinning. "She's amazing, Rache." She patted the spot LC had just left and I sat. "I hear you went full psycho on some doctor."

"I hear you're alive because of it."

"Ha! Those assholes always think goths have a constant razor blade to their wrists." She shook her head. "They don't get us, which I kinda like."

I forced a smile and squeezed her hand. "I'm glad you're okay."

"Me too. I guess this means I owe you one."

I frowned. "You owe me a crazy meltdown at my hospital bedside someday?"

"At the very least."

"Deal."

"At least we won't really have to worry about death."

"Why is that?" I asked.

"Besides me being the Angel of Death herself? Rachel," she said so seriously, grasping and sandwiching my hand with her other one. "Black hearts can never truly die."

The next day, I went to the hospital with Azzy's parents. As we entered the room, LC jumped back from holding Azzy's hand and retreated into the hall without looking up from the bleached vinyl floor. Her parents seemed a little uncomfortable, but nothing that warranted what happened next. There wasn't really a reason given, but it had to be a combination of LC's presence and the fact that they probably had no clue their daughter was gay until that moment.

Her parents edged into the room, her mother wringing her hands and her dad staying near the door, unable to even make eye contact. They informed her that they had suffered enough of Azzy's plight. They were done.

They made their peace, disowning their own daughter in a hospital room four days after a major life-changing surgery, washing their hands clean of their daughter and her lifestyle.

The kicker was that I'd have been willing to put money on the fact that Azzy's lifestyle was congenital. She'd been a goth since the moment she came out of the womb and her parents sealed that fate with her name. They probably assumed she'd been diseased from birth, that her mind and personality were so peculiar and offbeat from everyone else in a small town like Hammett that there couldn't be another explanation for her behavior, even with all their prayers.

Acceptance was never an option for them. Never. Seeing her and LC must have given them some consolation, knowing they couldn't save her because she was already a lost gay goth soul. They simply gave up.

I always found it interesting that her family treated me like a sigh of relief, as if I was any better, as if I was the only hope for Azzy to be a respectable citizen. That maybe one day, she would be more 'normal' like me. But they didn't realize that I suffered from the very same disease as their daughter and that was the thing truly cementing our bond from the beginning.

Being gay or straight, goth or straight edge, mattered little. Those were facts, demographics. They weren't what defined us as souls bonded together, best friends fused by one shared black heart.

Azzy tried to let her family's disapproval roll off her

shoulders, but the abrupt banishment crushed her, even if her parents had treated her poorly anyway. Not to have parents, not to belong, hurt and cut her deeply.

I spent days curled up next to my best friend, trying to convince her that her family didn't deserve someone as wonderful as her and that she was better off. It had to be soul draining.

One night, a few days after we had returned home and she was free of the head wrap of gauze, she laid her head on my lap while we stared at a paused movie on TV.

I combed her raven hair with my fingers, staring down at an incredible and beautiful soul, at the most amazing best friend a woman could ever have.

"You know I will always be your family, right?"

She nodded in my lap, and I could feel the moisture of tears absorbing into my leggings. Her voice was muffled and fragile. "I don't even like them. I should be grateful. Had they actually cared about me, I probably would have been sent to a conversion therapy camp. I don't even know why I care so much."

I thought about Chloe and all the emotions that I tried to wish away, the way that no matter how much I wanted to hate her, I couldn't. "Because despite how shitty they are, you still love them."

She turned her head in my lap toward the watermarked ceiling and pressed the heels of her hands into her eyes. "But they don't love me. I don't think they ever have."

"It's their loss, Az. You're worthy of more than they've ever given you."

"You'll probably leave me one day too. I'll become too much."

"Never, ever," I promised.

Chapter Sixteen

Dave drops a leather duffle bag next to the chair at the café below our hotels. Dad won't look at him, but Mom and Helen have already moved on with their lives, ready to embark on another arduous day of travel adventures. They stand to start their morning packing away their travel books into cork purses then both pull out similar oversized sunglasses. Dad hesitates, giving us a parting glance, but I just wave at him as he trails his wife and Helen to the parking lot.

The whole exchange doesn't get past Dave. "You're sure he's okay with this?"

I snort. "Not in the least bit. I'm sure he's wishing he could slash your tires or something to stop us from leaving."

Dave cranes his neck toward the parking lot. "He still has time."

"He's protective," I offer.

"If I had a daughter and were in his shoes, I'd be locking you up in the hotel room and would never let you leave with me."

My mouth falls open. "I thought you said you're a complete gentleman?"

He sends me a knowing glance. "I am, but I'm more worried about *your* intentions, Miss Heltin." He eyes the bulging suitcase on the other side of my chair. "It's only one night."

I shrug. "Can never be too prepared."

"For what? How many outfits does one woman need?"

"Maybe I'm trying to help you stay in shape by lugging my suitcase around."

"Who says I'm carrying any of your crap? You seem like the headstrong, independent female type. I wouldn't want to insult you by assuming my manners and chivalry are welcome."

I'm laughing now and I nudge his shoulder with my own. "Okay, Dr. Dave, I'll haul my own luggage, but don't blame me when my heart gives out."

His face drops. "I really don't like those jokes."

"Well," I say, reaching out to expand the handle on my luggage. "Then don't threaten me with manual labor if you can't stomach my twisted death jokes."

"Fair enough," he snips, prying my fingers from my luggage and handing off his jacket for me to hold instead. "But don't for a minute think I don't realize you are scamming me with a guilt trip, so I'll carry your crap."

We aren't on the road for more than five minutes when my phone rings. It's Azzy. I turn the screen with her face on it, tongue sticking out of a ring of deep purple painted lips, to Dave as if he knows her and understands I must take the call. Pressing the phone to cup my ear, I brace for the incoming barrage of words from my best friend.

"Hey lovely, what are you doing up this early? Isn't it

like—" I'm searching the car for the clock and counting backwards on my fingers.

Dave whispers over to me, "It's 2:15 in the morning in California."

"2:15!" I exclaim, mouthing a thank you to him.

"LC got home from her shift an hour ago and I was working late. Thought I'd catch you before you went off on another adventure. What's Mom got planned for today?"

I like that she still refers to my parents as her own.

"Well," I say, eyeing Dave, "they're on their way to another village with a church she and Helen want to see."

"Helen?" It sounds as though she's far from the phone and I'm on her speaker as she moves around.

"Dave's mom." His eyes coast my way, but when I look over, he goes back to concentrating on driving.

"Dave..." She taps her nails on a table. "Right, so where is Dave relative to where you are?"

Why was she so frustratingly observant? "We are going to explore a different area of the coast."

"Mm-hm, I bet you are going to explore."

"Azzy!" I squeal.

"Oh, shit!" She's putting the phone up to her ear, no doubt tucking herself into a ball at the table, eager for more information. Her knees are probably up to her chin, even if she's wearing platforms. "He's there isn't he? Can he hear me?"

"No," I say, and it sounds like a whisper.

"Put him on speaker."

"I will not."

"Rachel, put your dreamy doctor on speaker, please."

I groan into the phone. "Be nice," I warn, and she just scoffs. I turn to Dave. "My best friend would like to say hi, but I promise"—I put my mouth against the speaker so

Azzy has no doubt—"she'll be nice." A giggle filters over the line.

Dave raises a shoulder and wiggles two fingers from the steering wheel at me and I pray she's not going to make this awkward.

Clicking the speaker button, I take a deep breath. "He can hear you. Azzy, meet Dave."

Azzy doesn't even give Dave a chance to say hi. She's been holding a breath for what seems like ten minutes, and she spews out everything building in her head.

"Hi there, Dave. I've heard not enough about you. Apparently, my best friend lacks the proper communication skills to call her best friend and tell her that she's traversing the entire country of Portugal with some random doctor she met at a concert."

Dave sends an eyebrow my way, but I shake my head, while Azzy continues ranting.

"Did you know that she thinks you're hot? And although I can't confirm this, if you so much as look at her the wrong way with your dreamy doctor eyes—" I cut the speaker off.

"That's enough," I tell her, but Dave's pulling my phone away from my ear and moves it against his.

"Azzy? Yes." He looks over at me. "I see. I haven't been told my voice is as deep as the Mariana Trench before. Well did you—sure, but—hold on." He's suppressing a laugh as he hands me back the phone. "She wants you to put it back on speaker."

I do, and I hesitate to even say her name. "Azzy... you're back on speaker."

"You were right, he does have a sexy voice." I slap my palm to my face. "Anyway," she says it as if she might actually have something important to say. "Dr. Dave?"

"Mmm?" he responds.

"Do you know what trigeminal neuralgia is?" The term rolls off her tongue as though she knows what she's talking about.

His brows furrow and it looks as if he's racking through his memory of medical ailments. "Yes."

"How about Complex Regional Pain Syndrome?"

"I do."

"And Shingles?"

"Of course." He's perplexed and it's cute to see him not sure about what's happening.

"All those, but a million times worse if you so much as blink wrong at my best friend. Anyway, gotta get to bed. Love you, Rache." The phone goes silent.

So do we.

"So that was Azzy," I say after a minute.

Dave's adjusting his grip around the steering wheel. "She's..."

"Intense?" I suggest.

"I was going to say a breath of fresh air." When he sees the surprise filling my eyes, he explains. "It's nice to know someone is that protective over you. And different than your dad. How does she know what trigeminal neuralgia is? It's not a condition most people even know exists unless they have it."

I laugh sharply. "My guess is she googled 'most painful conditions' and picked the ones that sounded the most intense."

"Yeah, I like her a lot, if that's the case." His gaze drifts my way. "She doesn't *know*, I'm assuming, seeing that she thinks we met at the concert?"

All the humor drains from my face. "I almost told her before I came out here but couldn't. She's not going to take it well." I focus on the coastline blurring past as a flutter of anxiety seeps into my skin. "Can we not talk about this right now?"

It's supposed to be a nice day out. I don't want to get into deep talk before we even get to where we are going. To be honest, I don't want to get into any deep soul-sucking talks at all.

He nods once, reaching down for his phone and tossing it to me. "Remember the pass code? Let's cruise to the second playlist."

I glance at him, chewing the corner of my mouth and I want to hug him for respecting my decision not to talk about *it*.

Reenergized, I plug in the numbers I didn't think I memorized, scrolling into his playlist on a search for 'Pump Me Up'.

As the music plays, I giggle as I scroll through the songs. "It's literally the same songs as the first list. That's the weirdest thing."

His bottom lip sticks out, his head tilting toward me.

"What can I say? Years of meticulous research has led me to the same conclusion."

"Really?" I tease.

"Yup," he grins wide. "Went to med school for the sole purpose of finding out if two identical playlists with different names can affect a person differently. My investigation has shown that the effect, is indeed different depending on which one I listen to."

Spreading my fingers across my chest, I swoon into the seat. "I think I'm in love," I say while laughing. Then I realize what I've said, quickly adding, "With your playlist."

He stalls for that moment too and the heat comes

creeping up again in my cheeks, so I crank the music and look out my window.

We get to Lagoa before lunch and Dave has us seated at a little family-owned restaurant cut into the side wall of a trinket shop one block from the beach. It's not ideal. My view is of the bathroom and his is of the kitchen, but that becomes irrelevant when the waiter pours us both large glasses of red wine, tossing a plate of oil-seared crusty bread and a bowl of green olives on the crisp ivory scalloped tablecloth. We soon forget about the scenery around us.

"Why did you say your sister wanted to come here?" I ask.

He's about to put another piece of bread in his mouth, but his fist comes to a rest on the table. "Kim wanted to travel the world, but she wasn't like you or me." He studies the bread between his fingers. "She suffered from more than a tumor. She was also schizophrenic and like many schizophrenics, didn't take her medicine, even though we jumped through hoops to get her to stay on a schedule. Traveling wasn't easy, even if we could afford to go, which at the time we couldn't."

I want to say that I'm sorry for all the obvious trauma he's been through but stay quiet while he collects his thoughts instead.

"She had a picture in her room in high school that she had ripped out of a travel magazine, a photo of this beach with red-painted cliffs and caves surrounding turquoise water. Anytime Kim would get upset, she'd run over to that picture and point at it. Sometimes, she'd jab at it so hard I thought she'd punch a hole in it. She'd yell at Mom or me that if we took her there, she'd be okay. That it would heal her. She thought that beach was her cure-all."

"That's here in Lagoa, isn't it?"

He nods. "Right below the rental we'll be staying in. Maybe we'll even kayak to the best spot from the photo if we have time so you can really see it. Listen Rachel, I'm not into crystals, or voodoo, or weird special healing powers, but she really believed there was something magical about this beach. I figured it was worth a shot for you."

I sit back in my chair, swirling the large glass of wine in my hand. "You think the beach can heal me? Is that why you brought me here?"

He shakes his head, his mouth pulling into a tight line at the same time. "No, of course not. That would be silly. I don't believe that a beach heals all ailments. Believe it or not, modern medicine has come leaps and bounds from the Victorian-era. I think your fate is quite sealed. Miracles happen, but not with what you have going on in there."

I wish I hadn't bothered asking. I have to remember he's a doctor. I can't turn him into a normal man who won't weigh and measure every tiny thing I do against the balance of my sick heart and his medical training. He will always be who he is, always have the knowledge he possesses about my condition.

Dave's words weren't meant to provoke me, but tears threaten my lash line regardless.

He leans forward, not drawing any attention to me trying to blink back the blurring. "In all the places in the world, you and I end up in Portugal together," he ventures. "And not just the country, not just the city—at the same restaurant after our mothers meet. I've never believed in divine intervention or fate—until now." He sighs and puts the bread back on the plate and takes his wine, drinking a big gulp. "That beach is only water and sand, but maybe you'll find peace there. Maybe I might even find a little too."

Chapter Seventeen

Healing should be step number six in the stages of grief.

It took Azzy's last hospital stay to elicit a change from within, to finally see the importance of family—even annoying monsters disguised as little sisters. Which is why, after two years of avoiding Hammett, Idaho, I took a short one-and-a-half-hour flight into Boise and met my dad as he leaned against his 'ol faithful rust bucket of a truck in the arrivals pick-up lane.

He hugged me and held tight for a long minute but didn't say anything before letting go. Then he tossed my two-hundred-dollar carry-on into the back with the dirt and seeds and shovels as if it was a sack of grain.

The bright green bill of his John Deere ballcap was pushed up high on his forehead as he started the old beast, rolling a cloud of coal into the airport arrivals. In California, this act would probably be a fineable offense, but in Idaho, he got a fist pump from a guy dressed head to toe in hunting camo coming out of the terminal with a rifle case tucked under one arm.

The ride to Hammett was never entertaining once out of the capital city and I stayed quiet as his truck sputtered along the sagebrush-lined road after we exited the highway. But then I caught sight of Azzy's family winery passing by, a large red sign proudly displayed.

Dad scoffed as I plastered myself to the window. "They sold it last month to some yuppies from Seattle. They're already gone," he said in disbelief.

I spun to him. "What do you mean gone? Where? I don't think Azzy knows this."

He rolled the truck to a stop at a single flashing light, looking both ways before going again. "Somewhere in southern Utah. Guess they've got family there. Honestly, everyone's selling."

"And our farm?" I grimaced at the use of 'our' because I definitely didn't have a stake in the family business. The last of Azzy's childhood home disappeared from the window and into the sideview mirror.

"Nah, your sister and Ted are taking it over for us. I'll help out during this harvest, but I plan to be fully retired in a couple of months."

"You sure you're ready for that?" Then I giggled. "Is Mom?"

A smile tugged at the corners of his mouth. "I often wonder what that woman has seen in me all these years because it sure ain't money or good looks."

He snorted. But while my family may not have been rich, we were comfortable, and Dad wasn't a bad-looking man—in fact, my father was classically handsome.

"I think she's the one who got lucky," I said, feeling a little twinge of guilt for putting my dad over my mom.

"We've missed you," he muttered as we passed a dairy, his words searing me like the brands on the dairy cows' hide.

As he turned onto the last road before the farm, I kept watch out the window, unable to meet my father's eyes. "I've missed you too."

Our chitchatting ended there and when we pulled up to the farmhouse, my pulse quickened, but not from nostalgia, more from my sister with one baby on her hip, another one running around her ankles and tugging at her legs. Chloe waved while grinning so wide I thought she might have been high.

I unclipped the seatbelt and gave Dad a confused look. He laughed as he jumped out, scraping my bag across the bed of his truck to free it.

"Aunt Rachel, these little terrors can't wait to meet you," Chloe came up to me with excitement etched over her features.

She thrust the baby on her hip at me and I held him at arm's length, unsure what the little creature was looking at while a string of saliva dribbled from his mouth to the deck between us. Chloe chuckled and Dad grabbed the baby from me in one swoop of a hand, my luggage in the other, and he disappeared inside.

Chloe swallowed as she approached me.

I was frozen by her expression, the entire way her body seemed lighter, almost friendly. Then she did something so unexpected and cruel to my senses that I thought I might punch her in those perfect homecoming queen teeth.

She hugged me.

Stiff as a board, I wasn't sure how to react, but Chloe sensed my bewilderment and dislodged my arms from my sides, forcing them around her. And as awkward as it was to hug a woman I hadn't seen in years, it was even more awkward to hug my little sister.

"I'm an asshole and so incredibly sorry for the way I acted. You deserved better than that," she whispered in my ear. "But if you cuss or play your devil music in front of my children, I'll come unhinged." She squeezed me tighter. "I've really missed you."

Then, as if nothing happened at all, she released me and walked into the farmhouse, steering a little dark headed boy in overalls by the mop of his messy hair.

Yup, she had to be on drugs.

My unpleasant, repellant, self-serving, narcissistic, self-congratulatory, smug sister had somehow metamorphosed into something tolerable. Someone I might actually like rather than loathe.

Dumbstruck, I stayed on the porch until Mom came to the screen door, wiping her flour-covered hands on a denim apron. "Get in here and give me a hug," she hollered from the doorway.

When she embraced me, I asked, "Why is Chloe being nice? I'm a little worried. Is she planning on an exorcism tonight? Is this an intervention?"

She squeezed my body tighter, her laugher shaking us. "She's been teaching a Sunday School class to the little ones about the power of forgiveness. Guess she's trying to practice what she preaches. So far it's been a positive change."

"Aunt Wachel?" The little one in overalls emerged at Mom's side and yanked on the hem of my threadbare Rancid shirt. "Why don't you visit? We got to make lots of cookies when you're coming here."

"Sorry about that," I said, eyeing my mom as the little boy ducked back inside.

"That's Ted Jr., but we all call him Junior. Eats anything, but mostly things with sugar in them." Mom pointed in the

house. "The other one is Cayden. And between you and me," she said, pulling on my arm to come closer, "they're so much better behaved than you two girls ever were."

"That, I don't doubt," I said.

I only intended to be in Hammett for two days, enough to get my obligatory fill, but on the second day, I changed my ticket. That visit lasted nine days in total, and for the first time in twenty-seven years, I felt a part of the family, as though I was wanted there, and as though I enjoyed being there. Because I did.

Chloe still grated on my nerves from time to time during that week, but she was so caught up with the kids and daily farm chores, her energy wasn't focused on me.

Dad and I spent the mornings drinking black coffee and running the perimeter of the original 200-acre farm while he pointed out all the improvements over the years and the new land they recently leased. I didn't know much about pipe irrigation versus sprinklers, but I enjoyed watching Dad light up about it as we trudged through the muddy ditches while he checked on the crops.

When he'd head to the recliner for a mandatory afternoon nap, I'd sit on the porch swing and listen to the robins squabble in the weeping birch tree that spilled long green tendrils of vines over the corner roof of the house. Mom often joined me, and I caught myself napping on her lap more than once, her loving hands weaving through my hair the way only a mother could.

There were no serious conversations. No major bickering. A perfect, textbook visit. And when I boarded my plane back to San Francisco, I was surprised to shed more than a few tears for leaving them and already missing their love.

My heart called to my family after that trip, and I made a vow to be present for every major milestone. Even if I had a travel trip coming up, family events would take priority, and little by little, visit after visit, the scar tissue on all our hearts began to fade to something not as noticeable, not so painful.

Chapter Eighteen

It's funny to look back at that trip and the subsequent ones, especially as I'm sitting in Lagoa, Portugal on a lounge chair overlooking one of the most incredible beaches of my life. I sit here, wondering how a farmer's daughter ever made it halfway across the world.

"Do you even want to see the inside?" Dave asks while sliding an entire panel of glass doors apart, allowing the inside to merge with the fresh sea air.

"I don't know if it can get better than this," I say on an exhale, unable to take my eyes away from the cliffs.

We finished our early lunch an hour ago and drove the five minutes to what I thought was a resort. Turns out it's a rental. *Our* rental. I'm loving that Dave's a doctor right now.

Prying myself away from the view, I jump up from the lounger and strut past him and into the rental home.

"Dave..." I turn back, my hand resting on the black fabric of the T-shirt covering his stomach. I jerk it back, not sure why I did that and turn away quickly, looking over the living space, trying to not facepalm myself. "This is incredible."

I explore inside without him as he heads out to the patio, adjusting the sliding doors to lock them in place. The house is only one level, palatial, but somehow intimate with cozy leather chairs and piles of folded blankets in the living room. The master bathroom makes me squeal at the tub, certain I would find a way to use it. The bedroom is equally pleasant with whites and creams decorating the bed and a loveseat facing a view of the cliffs and ocean beyond.

"The view is almost better from here, isn't it?" he says from the doorway.

"I can't imagine how amazing it must be, having a cup of coffee in the morning and watching the sunrise. It's got to be incredible." I shake my head, not peeling my eyes away from the ocean.

"Well, you'll see it tomorrow."

I run my hands across the back of the loveseat, glancing at him over my shoulder and squint. He looks relaxed, barefoot, and leaning a shoulder against the door frame.

"Where's my room?"

He tips his chin to the massive bed. "Here."

I narrow my eyes more as I spin toward him. "Where's *your* bed, Dave?"

His cheeks twitch in sync and he nods to the bed. "Here." Then he throws up his hands defensively. "I swear I told them twin beds. It's a European thing, I'm sure."

"Yeah, I bet. But seriously, where's the other bedroom?"

"So, here's what happened," he starts. I can't help rolling my eyes. "There are two other bedrooms upstairs."

"Upstairs? Where's that?"

"*Exactly*," he says with purpose. "It's only accessible from the outside and I guess when you rent here, you have to specify access to the other part."

"And let me guess"—I splay my hands over my hips—"you didn't?"

"Innocent oversight."

"I didn't think doctors were allowed to have oversights."

"This is hard to believe, but doctors are still human, Rachel." He smirks, moving toward me and the way he prowls with such confidence has my breath hitching. "The other half can be unlocked. I'll message the host right now if the idea of being so close to me repulses you."

He's almost to my toes, tipping his head down to me, leaning in enough for me to feel the warmth of his body heat radiating against mine and I almost reach out to him.

Oh, he's *good*.

"Whatever," I demur, taking a step back to slow my pulse. "If you snore though..." I glance out the window briefly. "Why don't you seem as impressed as I am? Is this the type of place UCSF doctors have in San Francisco?"

"Actually, I live by Ocean Beach."

I scoff, my snobbery of the city coming out in full force. "Well, excuse me, your mailing address still says San Francisco."

He looks around the room at nothing in particular. "This is my third time here. We've been coming every year since Kim died."

"Then why isn't your mom here? Why are you staying at a hotel?"

"It was booked except for tonight and she knows spending this time with you is important to me."

I want to ask him what he means, but also don't want to know, I'm not ready for *that* conversation. "How did you know I'd agree to come here tonight? How did you swing that?" I didn't even know I would be agreeing to an overnight trip with him, let alone planning for it to be today.

"I didn't."

His words remind me of his talk at lunch about divine intervention and fate.

Is there any truth in that? Is it possible that the great beyond manifested this into one entirely unbelievable, but true coincidence?

Is it possible that divine intervention arranged for my cardiologist to be Dave?

Did Dave and Helen happened to book a hotel right next to ours out of pure coincidence? Did fate know Helen and Mom would sit next each other at the perfect time and become fast friends?

How is it that this rental only had availability for one night, tonight? The one night I only agreed to yesterday? Did fate also think it was funny to throw one bed into the mix and see what happens?

My head whips back to him.

"You say you've rented here three times? Then how did you have an oversight with the other rooms?" I take a calculated step toward him. "You knew you'd have to request those rooms!"

"I'll never tell." He pretends to zip his mouth and throw away the key. I can't help but shake my head and nudge him out of my way, trying to suppress the grin I shouldn't have.

I head back out on the patio and lean over the glass railing, watching people migrating to the sand below. There are umbrellas striped with blue and white fabric, and beach towels in all shades of the rainbow being spread into the breeze.

A few kids are racing into the water as parents chase them down to slather on sunscreen.

The air carries a hint of coconut in their spray lotions and also a little bit of the marine air which doesn't seem as briny and fishy as that of Luz. Another scent whirls around me, smelling almost like blooming peonies. I'm searching for the source, my eyes darting down the cliffs, to the line where the waves are casting foam into the sand.

They track back up the cliff face and over the ledge.

Plants are tucked all along there, and even some growing directly under the balcony, tempting me to lean over the railing more to take a closer look. Like succulents, their wildflowers sprouting from finger-like greens vary in off white, baby pink, and neon purple blooms. They sway in the air, mingling with the sea spray, and the mixture it produces intoxicates me. Not peonies at all, I realize.

The fragrance reminds me more of night-blooming jasmine and I'm certain I've smelled it before. There's a comfort in the fragrance, a sweet familiarity bringing a smile to my face.

"They're my sister's favorite." Dave walks up to the balcony and points to the spreading plants. "The purple ones, specifically."

"But she's never been here."

He leans his hip into the glass, peering over the ledge. A long arm stretches down until his fingertips skims the top of one of the purple blooms, plucking it.

"You haven't seen these before back home?"

I shake my head as I watch him twist the bloom in his grip. He lets it drop between his fingers and we both watch as it floats back to the rocky ledge, settling on another plant.

"They're called ice plants. When Mom and I came out here, we didn't know that they're invasive species. We thought it was a sign that Kim was happy we were here celebrating her life and showing up where we celebrated her life." He laughs softly. "We never really disproved the theory so we could keep coming back in her honor, but they're everywhere in California. You won't miss them now that you know."

"They smell so familiar."

Dave leans over even more, scrunching his nose and sniffs. "Really? I don't think they smell at all."

I pull away from the railing to face him. "Is Kim the reason why you became a cardiologist?"

"I always wanted to be a doctor." Dave pushes away from the glass railing and brushes the soil off his hands. "If I'm going to give you my life story, could we at least sit?" he asks, retreating to a lounge chair meant for two. I sink down beside him, kicking off my sandals. He isn't even sitting in it properly. I'm lounging all the way back, like a normal human, but Dave is sitting in the middle of his side, legs crossed under him, and one knee touching my thigh.

The position makes him appear younger, like a teenager eager to share a secret. It also makes me feel like one. The minimal contact point is heating me up, making it difficult to concentrate on anything other than his skin pressing on mine.

I try to cover my eyes from the sun, but he's already up, fixing the pop-up shade on the lounger to cover me. "Thanks," I say as he resumes his prior position.

"Anyway, I busted my ass through high school in an accelerated program and graduated with my associate's. I was two years ahead when I made it to college and then med school. Getting accepted into UCSF was the easy part if you can believe that.

"Mom worked for this old crotchety executive who treated her like garbage for thirty-four years and she put up with him, but the pay wasn't enough to even put me through public college. I did everything I could to not become a financial burden to her. Getting a scholarship was like winning the lottery." He rakes a hand through his hair and the hand drops to his knee—and to the edge of my hip. "Kim was living on the streets. She was a heavy drug user and didn't care that she was homeless. Mom still has a lot of guilt about that. Not doing enough, finding that fine line between enabling her habit and setting limitations to protect us. But my sister was a loose cannon."

"How old were you when she left home?"

"Which time?" He half-laughs and a twinge of guilt floods me about my runaway attempts. His sister had real issues. I had silly teenage angst.

"It happened a lot?"

"I think through my high-school years she was in and out weekly, but by the time I went off to college, Mom had enough and drew a hard line. Partly to protect me, but also to protect her own boundaries."

His thumb traces the pocket seam along my shorts and I'm trying not to focus on the sensation it's causing across my skin. "I mean it got to the point that we didn't know if we'd get a random knock on the door from the police that she was in jail or dead. It became that bad."

"I can't even imagine."

"Long story short, I got through college and med school on scholarships and entered my residency a couple years before most doctors. Surprisingly, when Mom's bastard of a boss kicked the bucket, he left her everything. I'm talking the woman never has to work another day in her life and could pay someone to carry her around if she wanted. It was so unexpected and a huge sum."

"And she made me pay for her gelato the other day?" I gasp in mock horror. "The audacity of those snobby rich people. I've heard about people like that. What a cheapskate!"

He chuckles at this. "Yeah, it's so well deserved though. I'm not even sure it was worth what he put her through, but I'm glad she can finally not worry."

"And your sister?"

"Oh yeah." His thumb stops moving and he readjusts so his legs go the same direction as mine. When he leans back, he tucks his hands under his head and stares at the shaded covering above us. "I was a resident trying to dial in what I wanted to declare as my specialty. I was working the night-shift in the ER and was almost off going. Think there was an hour or so left."

"Oh no," I say involuntarily.

His brow jumps up, but he doesn't look at me. "Yeah. One moment I'm treating an OD—overdose—shaking my head at the physician in charge so she can call the time of death and then someone moves out of the way, and it hits me—the chest I'm slamming my hands into is none other than Kim's. I lose my shit, pumping on her heart for well past what is considered survivable. I brought her back. Then they kicked me out."

"What do you mean they kicked you out? Why?" I'm up on an elbow turning toward him and he drops one arm, his head turning toward me.

"Out of the hospital, out of her treatment plan, out of the intern program. I violated a lot of rules, but the biggest was that I ordered the staff to keep working on her. I used every resource I could, but it went against all the rules and protocols including treating a family member."

"But you saved her." I was puzzled. "Why would they kick you out for saving a life?"

"Yeah, I saved her for a month. But there's more to it than saving a life."

He closes his eyes as though replaying that entire time,

agony consuming his features. "Kim's scans came back, and I did a real number on her in that panic. I cracked her sternum," he tells me, opening his eyes and pressing a fingertip to my chest. "And almost all her ribs were broken here." He drags a finger down the centerline of my breastbone, and it may seem odd, but shivers run down to my toes.

Dave retracts his touch. "They also showed the tumor. I begged the cardiac surgeon to remove it, but he refused, saying it was too far gone, too dangerous. The cancer had already spread into her lungs and bones. He said that it wouldn't matter because she'd be lucky to live through the recovery of what I'd put her through when I did things my way and broke all the protocols. It's my own personal Catch-22."

"But. But that's not your fault. That guy sounds like a douche."

He coughs out a laugh. "Yeah, that guy is now one of my best friends and became my mentor. He taught me everything I know. Remember Juan Santos?"

"*Doctor* Santos?" I balk. "How, after all that, could you look up to him?"

"Because he was right. Sometimes, tough things happen, and you have to let them. I had to realize I was in the wrong, that I only did what I did because this was Kim. But there was also a reason *why* it was Kim. Because Kim's condition was not survivable so I'd brought her back so she could suffer a world of pain." He winces. "I'm sorry. I shouldn't even be saying that. It doesn't mean you will be in that same level of pain."

"It's all right." And it really is.

He splays his hand, hovering it over my chest and waiting for me to nod for him to touch me. His hand covers the entirety of my breastbone, and it feels almost normal to feel him this way on me. His eyes flicker up to mine. "The heart is one tough muscle, but it has limits—it can only handle so much trauma. My aggressiveness made an already terrible situation much worse.

"It sped some things up and slowed others down in the worst way. Kim would have died from the overdose or tumor either way, but if I hadn't saved her from the overdose, she would have died relatively peacefully and pain free. Instead, she suffered for thirty-two days. A slow, excruciating death. My mom and I had to watch it unfold in slow motion. We were the definition of helpless."

"God, Dave, that's terrible, but you still don't know that you're responsible for her pain." My hand rests on top of the one over my own heart. "And now? Am I some sort of redemption for you to clear your conscience?"

His eyes never leave mine. "No, Rachel. You're my worst nightmare."

Chapter Nineteen

Repulsed, I try to pry his hand off me, but Dave doesn't let go. "Let me explain," he says way too calm as I stumble up to my feet, wrenching his fingers away.

"Yeah, I don't think there's any way you can come back from that. Was it a Freudian slip? Or are you just a jerk?" I toss on my sandals, looking for the quickest exit, wondering if hitchhiking in Portugal is safe.

His arm snakes around my middle and he drags me onto his lap. I'm fighting him, but he's stronger, holding me while I struggle. "Let me explain, please." He's breathing hard as I fight against him, but there's an eerie quietness to his voice.

"What is there to explain? You just said I'm your worst nightmare!"

I'm still thrashing to break free, and he grabs my wrists and crosses them over my waist, pinning my back against his front, effectively locked down.

His nose grazes my cheek, then his lips ghost across my ear. "Listen to me, *please.*" I stop fighting, but only because I'm winded. I snap my head to him, his face incredibly close to mine. "You are perfect, Rachel. You are everything I want. And that utterly terrifies me."

"And I'm about to die!" I spit out the words, his jaw clenching against the side of my face. "And that's why I am such a nightmare for you to spend time with!"

"That's not what I'm trying to say. You terrify me *not* because of your diagnosis. You terrify me because you're the first person I've ever felt anything for. Felt like *this*. It's scary and new and I'm all control and textbooks and statistics. You are wild and unpredictable. Please just hear me out before you try to leave. Please."

It's the desperation that has me deflating in his hold. "You're not the first to tell me that I'm a lot to handle."

"You're not listening to me, Rachel. I can't get you out of my head. I flew to *fucking* Portugal to get you as far away from me as possible, but you've shown up here. *I'm* here. With you. There's a reason for that. A big reason." Letting go of my wrists, he pulls me impossibly closer to him by twisting me by the waist.

I'm paralyzed in his arms as he brushes hair away from my cheek.

I don't want him to say it. He *can't*. I've only known him a month at most. It can't happen this quick. It *can't*. "Please don't finish what you want to say."

He studies my profile, allowing his fingers to trace my cheekbones. "Tell me why. Is it because there's no truth to my words or is it because you're afraid to hear the truth in them? Or maybe—*maybe* it's possible that you might feel the same?"

A tear slips from one eye. I'm so mad at that stupid tear because more are coming. My voice shakes. "I'm already losing so much."

"I know you are," he says while swiping the tear, but another replaces it, racing faster to the ground. He's turning me to face him fully while pulling me tighter to his body and I'm holding on as if my life depends on him, curling into him and clutching at his shirt.

"I don't want to die," I choke out, burying my head. "I'm not ready. I'm too young to die."

Dave caresses the side of my face with his fingers, pushing back more loose strands that the wind keeps blowing across my jaw.

"I know, Rache. I can't imagine anyone would be ready."

A sob rocks through me as I cry out, into his chest. "I'm just getting my shit together. It's too soon." I look up at him. "Why can't this be fixed? Why can't *you* fix me?"

His blue eyes are glossing, and he blinks several times to clear the sheen. "God, I wish I could. I spent the last four weeks racking through studies and journals trying to find anything... something I missed. Anything."

This dries up some of my tears and I sit back. "You spent weeks researching my case?" He nods.

"I mean, I've been looking into cardiac sarcomas ever since Kim died, but with you—it changed things." He collects the moisture on my cheek with the heel of his palm.

"But you didn't even know me then."

"That's what I've been trying to say. It's what I was trying to say at lunch." He pauses when I shake my head, begging him not to say it. "I won't say it—*yet*—but that's why."

"The books in the backseat of your car? You brought them to Portugal to research?"

He nods slowly, brows raised high.

"Your mom said you took a sabbatical because of a difficult case."

"You," he admits.

"I'm so sorry." I bury my head in his chest again.

Dave finds my chin and tilts me back to him. "Why in the world are you apologizing?"

"Because I'm about to *really* complicate things."

His brows pinch together, but I'm already moving, sitting up higher in his lap, pressing my lips against his. Every muscle in his body freezes and I may have stunned him.

I draw back, threading my fingers into his ruffled hair, studying the way he's watching me as if he can't quite figure out what to do or what I'll do next. Just when I start regretting the kiss and thinking I made the wrong move, his hand betrays him, moving to my waist. The tips of his fingers press into the flesh there.

Dave parts his lips, chest heaving. Mine too.

We're staring into each other's souls as though seeing one another for the first time. It hurts—there's pain in those endless depths of the other, but there's an ember of light in there too.

And it sparks to life when he drops his gaze to my mouth.

He's on my lips this time. That hand on my waist is drawing me into him and I let it, wanting nothing but his touch on my skin, craving the way he moves over my lips like I've tasted them thousands of times. But my drive is of a mad frenzied woman getting her fix for the first time.

I'm practically forcing myself onto him. But he's doing it right back.

I part my lips, finding his tongue joining mine as my hands grip the nape of his neck, begging for more, needing him closer. As the kiss deepens, the gnawing in my belly grows and so do the flutters in my chest, but they can't be from a damaged heart. No, these flutters are new and they're breath snatching in the best way possible, and I can't get enough of how my body is reacting to the feel of him.

His touch. His lips on mine. Claiming me. Wanting me. Needing me.

I've decided as he's kissing me that if I'm going to die anytime soon, I want this to be the only way I go. I want him. All or nothing because there is no way I can go back to a life without him now. I'm hooked.

He withdraws first, but he's still against my mouth so that when he speaks, our lips brush against each other and he's almost in a pant. "I think—I think we should go to the beach, otherwise we will never leave this house."

I hum out an acknowledgment on the damp flesh of his mouth, but neither of us moves. Somehow, I'm straddling him, and have no clue when that happened. His lips curve against my mouth but then they're moving again along my jawline, to my neck.

I lengthen it for him to taste me and the delicate skin there. He does so briefly, but then he's relocated my body to the lounger and he's a foot away from me, jumping up to his feet, breathing harder than I've ever seen him.

He's running a hand through his hair, mouth parted open with swollen lips. "We *really* need to go to the beach."

I like the power I have, knowing I'm the one who's created whatever is happening to him and I want to revel in it, but he's right. Things are about to get way out of hand if we don't get into a public space. I stand and strut over to him and he licks his lips.

I press a palm to his contracting stomach, looking up at him. Everything seems on the verge of coming out. All those emotions that were all twisted and tangled are now exposed and threatening to fray in a thousand directions.

I clear my throat. "I need a few minutes to get ready." Then I head inside, leaving him backed against the glass railing, watching me leave to the bedroom.

For some reason when I unzip my suitcase on the ivory duvet, my hands tremble.

I don't think it's from being sick, more likely the nerves and adrenaline that my heart is so unused to, and I take a steadying breath before digging into the jungle of clothes, pulling out my neon pink bikini and cutoff denim shorts.

Dave's in the kitchen drinking a glass of water upon my emergence from the bedroom, and he's mid drink when he spots me over the rim. He sputters and coughs out the liquid, spinning to the sink to spit out whatever water is working its way out of his lungs.

He smacks his chest as he coughs, eyes watering as I stare, blank faced. He holds up a finger as he coughs one more time, wheezing when he finally speaks. "Dammit, Rachel."

My head retreats back on my shoulders. "What did I do?" I place a hand on my hip.

His eyes travel the length of my body and when he's completed his inspection, he's shaking his head, coughing one last time. "Can I put a blanket over you or something because it's becoming increasingly difficult to force myself out of this house. Especially," he says, looking me over again, "when you're wearing *that*. What are you trying to do to me?"

I look down at my outfit and frown. "It's shorts and a bathing suit. And if I'm not mistaken, we're headed to the beach. You know—swimming, beach? See a connection?"

He nods slowly and walks around the island to circle

past me, giving me wide berth as though I might lure him in, as though I have a magnetic force. "Yeah, you keep telling yourself that's all that is." He disappears into the bedroom, leaving me trying not to laugh.

A few minutes later, we walk out of the rental with towels tucked under our arms and a beach bag slung over Dave's shoulder, filled with all the essentials for a day in the sun, including an umbrella strapped to the bottom of the bag. Dave's still in what I'm beginning to think is his signature black T-shirt, but he's changed into swim trunks and their aquamarine and electric blue wave design seems to blend in with the local surroundings.

Neither of us bothers to put shoes on since only wooden stairs lead from the house to the sand. Soon, my toes finally hit the golden-hued blanket of warmth, and I have to resist the temptation to run straight into the water. Waves are crashing, but they aren't big enough to ward off the small children jumping into the gentle rolling swells.

We walk along the edge of the same tawny and ivory layered painted cliffs above which our rental is perched, keeping watch. The rock face is jagged, little divots and holes poking through the stone, some bigger than others. As we approach a calmer area of the beach where the waves are only lapping up the shore, I see it from the corner of my eye.

I latch myself to Dave's arm, trying to catch my breath at the site revealed before us. "Oh my god," is all I can breathe out.

Dave grins down at me, watching me take in everything. We've stopped walking. "Impressive, eh? I told you this beach was special."

Along the edge of the rock face where the sand begins, a hole has been cut through. Hundreds of years of waves created a cave that eventually hollowed out, pushing through the cliff and to another beach. It's an archway of shadows and cold stones, leading into a secluded stretch of sand, sunshine, and sparkling water.

He urges me forward and we walk through the tunnel of sand and stone. I swivel my head around to take in everything, feeling Dave take my hand so I can wander on a tether in complete awe of what the forces of nature can do, my palm and fingers skimming along the rock's surface.

I don't let go of him once we've made it through the cutout and to the hidden beach until we agree on a spot far enough away from the few other people, the ones who've discovered what's on the opposite side of that massive cliff.

Dave throws our towels out across the sand, driving the umbrella into the ground, opening up the same blue and white striped shade everyone else seems to have. I toss my hair into a messy knot of tangled strands and unbutton my shorts, noting that even as he's applying sunscreen to his face, the hand smearing it across his cheeks is moving at a glacial pace because he's staring again.

He might be wearing dark sunglasses, but his eyes are lasered in on me.

I ignore him, shimmying the shorts down and stealing the sunscreen. He pulls off his shirt in one quick grab of the back of his collar and now it's become my turn to reciprocate a stare.

Dr. Dave is ripped.

Not that I didn't feel those firm ridges when he forced my hands into second base and had me feel his bare chest the other day. Nor did I not feel them from pressing up against him earlier on the lounge chair... But the lines and coiled muscles still catches me off guard.

Mr. June, indeed.

He's tan and trim and my mouth is agape, and I don't give one single shit.

"You know you're not wearing sunglasses. I can see you ogling."

A grin is plastered across his face.

"As if wearing sunglasses hides anything," I say, picking my jaw off the beach and swiping at the glasses resting on my head. "You must work out all the time." I might be drooling.

He's liking my appreciation, sinking to the towel and leaning back on his elbows. His muscles throughout his core tighten and I don't know whether he did that on purpose or not, but I'm not upset about it at all. I search the other random people on the beach.

Are they far enough away that I can do inappropriate things in public to him? That kiss still has my mind swimming with all the other delicious things he might be capable of doing to me.

"Want to go for a swim?" He pushes his glasses down his nose.

"No." It's a whisper. "Not that at all."

"If I knew all I had to do was take off my shirt, I would have done it a long time ago."

"If I knew objectifying you would feel so good, I would have insisted."

He laughs and pops up, grabbing my hand. "You need to cool down, so let's go for a swim."

Obviously, Dr. Dave's intense medical training hasn't prepared him for me if he thinks that a swim in the calm Atlantic jewel-hued waters with him holding onto me is going to cool me down. Things are beginning to heat up, and I struggle to figure out how to rope that in—or even if I want to.

The breaker on the opposite sunburnt cliff deflects so much of the turbulent waves that we wade into more of a lake than an ocean.

The swells are minimal and I'm so happy I don't have to expend energy trying to stay afloat.

I'm up to my neck and he's up to his shoulders in delightful bath-like water, Dave circling me like a hungry shark. He wears a devilish grin that makes me think he's about to strike.

"The ocean agrees with you," he tells me, moving a little bit closer as his slick leg grazes mine.

I'm thinking about how slippery his abs must feel under the water's surface, unable to figure out when I became so shallow, but I step into him, not giving one damn about anybody else on the beach.

"Rachel," he says, looping a finger in the strap connecting the two halves of my bikini bottoms.

A sensation rolls up my spine as I look at him, but my thumbs find his shorts and are running the inside of the waistband from both his hips to below his belly button and then back.

"Hmm," I breathe out.

He leans in, about to kiss me again. His free hand cups my chin and he feathers his mouth across my lips. "You stop that right now."

My cheek pushes up against his hand, trying to get closer to his lips that seem so close but so far away. "Or what?"

"Or I'm not going to be able to walk out of the water."

"Because you'll scare the children?"

He nods into my forehead, his hands going to mine teasing at his waist, drawing them up to his mouth. He presses his lips to the wet briny surface of my knuckles. "Behave."

I bite the flesh of my cheek. "You started it."

"And I'm ending it right now." His forehead is still against mine. "I want to suggest tapping into the bottle of wine in that bag, but as I've already told you, I'm terrified of you. I'm not sure adding alcohol and us is a great idea."

"Is there cheese in that bag too?"

He chuckles and nods. "And bread made fresh this morning, from a local bakery."

I leap backwards and out of his hold with a splash of water. "Why didn't you say so? I thought I had to earn my snacks around here." And I dash to the beach, leaving Dave stunned in the shallows.

By the time he walks up to our spot, I already have the wine opened and two plastic glasses filled. I'm still soaked, the towel doing little, and there's sand up to my elbows and calves. I don't mind as I give a sopping Dave a cup.

"Did you find the wine key or were you attacking the neighbors for their shoes?" He digs into the bag to pull out the bread and cheese, water dripping everywhere.

"Neighbors, of course," I say, trying to hide my amusement as I toss him the towel I was using as a pillow. "Who calls a corkscrew a wine key? That's almost as bad as someone who says soda over pop."

He deadpans midway through drying off his hair. "What's pop besides a verb? Sounds like you're from the sticks."

I sit up proud. "I am."

"They're two different things." He nods at the bottle of wine, "A wine key and corkscrew. You'd think that someone who has a best friend with a winery would know that."

"The only thing I know about wine and wineries is that

I didn't like the taste much at sixteen, but that's probably because we usually stole raw wine before it went into barrels, and—"

"That's called grape juice," he interjects.

"Well, we thought we were drinking wine."

"What else does your limited knowledge of wine cover?" He takes a sip and refills our glasses.

"A shoe makes a great opener. The more expensive the better."

Dave clinks his plastic glass to mine. "It was a lifesaver the other day. Bet you didn't think you'd ever use it that way."

"In Portugal?" A laugh bubbles out of me. "No. And I definitely didn't think it would be with you, and under these circumstances."

"Same." A sadness lingers over us like a black cloud, and he senses it too. He takes another sip then tips the cup in my direction. "Can we not talk about anything medical related or sad or anything other than how fucking good this wine is?"

My chest flutters and I almost feel like crying or singing or both. "That is the best thing you've said all day." I clink his plastic glass in agreement and grab some cheese. "Can we add goat's cheese to the approved list of topics?"

"As long as we can add this to it as well." A finger pops the side band of my bikini top.

"Agreed, but only if I can stare at your stomach and wonder how the hell you have the time to get *that* body."

He laughs at this. We joke and tease for a while longer and I have no clue how long we've been on the beach and frankly, neither of us care. It's long enough for us to be sun dried and the sand that once clung to our arms and legs to have been swept away in the breeze. The bright star above is starting its arch over us and into late afternoon when my eyes grow heavy from wine and laughter.

Dave grabs a blanket from the bag and beckons with a seductive finger. Without hesitation, I'm curled against the length of his body and he's tucking the sun-heated blanket around us, dragging fingers up and down my arm that's flung over him.

I drift off in the shade of our umbrella, listening to the steady beat of his heart.

Chapter Twenty

My first symptom began a few months before meeting Dave in the cardiology department of the university's medical center. I'd been jogging through Golden Gate Park on my usual route when suddenly, everything around me blurred. The grass and the path were coming up to meet me, and the earth spun. The unexpected lightheadedness was enough to freak me out, making me pull off the asphalt path and to the nearest bench I could find to brace myself.

It was so scary and abrupt that I called Azzy to come and get me, but by the time she arrived in her severely beaten-down blue beast of a car, I was already feeling better.

Low blood sugar, I unknowingly assumed.

I hopped inside anyway for the ten-minute ride home.

"What happened?" she asked, casting a side glance my way as she steered out of the park.

Scrolling through my phone, the events that led me to her car were almost long gone. "I don't know. Just felt weird. Anyway, I'm fine now—crisis averted. Were you at home?"

She pulled her lips over her teeth and gave me the guiltiest of looks.

"Azzy! That's the third time this week you've spent at LC's. It's serious, isn't it?" With her sheepish grin, I slapped my hands to the sides of my face, squishing my lips. "Oh my god, you're going to leave me."

If a goth could blush, Azzy would have been the same color as the Chinese lanterns stringing across the street of our rowhouse.

"I really, really like her, Rache. And I've said that about others, but this time is different."

The sting of abandonment pierced me, but Azzy and I had lived together for almost twelve years. Eventually, one of us would be leaving the other. It was as inevitable as our need to leave Idaho.

"Can we brunch and at least talk about it?" I asked her.

Azzy shrank her shoulders into her steering wheel, her nose squishing. "Eww Rachel, honestly you're starting to sound more and more like all these hipster influencer types that are trying to be different."

"Says the goth."

"Whatever. Where d'you want to go??"

I pointed her to our favorite diner little used by tourists or locals because it was in a seedy area, but they served awesome pancakes, and cheap. We toasted our bottom-of-the-pot sludge coffee and dug into a shared stack of greasy pancakes.

"What is it about LC that makes her The One?" I shoved too big of a bite in my mouth while Azzy looked at me in disgust.

"There's a reason you're still single and I'm observing it right now."

I pointed my fork dripping syrup at her. "I'll have you know that I have quite a few matches on Bumble."

"That's because they haven't seen you eat yet. Maybe if

you post a video of this monstrosity on your profile, they would withdraw and save themselves the trouble." She sliced off a respectable amount and chewed it like a dainty lady, and only when she dabbed her mouth with a paper napkin did she answer my question. "You know that first night in the hospital? I knew she was it."

I almost had a bite three stacks high in my mouth but stopped short. "How? You only knew her for minutes at the most." I shoveled in the food and tucked it into my cheek. "You sure it's not lust at first sight?"

Azzy shook her head at my full pancake and maple syrup-rimmed mouth. "I just knew. Everyone always talks about love at first sight and having some aha moment and honestly, you know me, I'm the biggest skeptic. But really, there was something about LC."

"That's true, you're practically anti anything cliché," I said chewing through a full mouth then chasing it with a gulp of coffee.

Her eyes drifted to the booth's dingy window and out to the street as someone in ratty clothes pushed a shopping cart past us with one busted wheel. "It's like I've always known her. Really similar to you. Like she's always been a part of my life and the thought of not having her in it makes my heart want to rip in half."

"It's too black to fix if that shit happens."

She laughed. "Why?"

"Because our stupid black hearts can love so much, but once they break, I think there'll be too much darkness to find the edges to sew back together."

"God, Rachel, how are you not one-hundred percent goth? That shit hits me right here." She slammed a fist into her chest with a grunt.

"See? It's because we get each other." Dropping my fork,

I pushed the plate to her. "I'm really happy for you. But if she breaks your heart, I'm coming after her. Because even if I find those edges, I'm not a good seamstress. You won't be the same after I'm done trying to repair you, so she better not hurt you."

"I don't think she will."

I sat back in the booth, glancing toward the bell ringing at the front when a few stragglers make their way to another booth. "I'm going to miss you. I already do."

"Don't make me feel more guilty," she pleaded.

"I don't mean it in a physical sense. This is the natural course of life. We always knew we'd go our own directions, but now it's happening. I'm sad to close this chapter, but excited to see this new one open for you. You deserve to be happy, and I'm really thrilled for you. I'll even help you move." I pursed my lips, tapping them with a finger. "No, I don't know why I said that because I don't want to walk up and down stairs all day dragging your crap out. So, I'm afraid you're on your own for moving, but I'll bring you beer and pizza afterwards. How about that?"

Azzy tossed her folded napkin at me.

"You know it will happen for you too," she said. "Who knows? Maybe Mr. Right is in San Francisco right now. But I'm gonna be honest with you about one thing."

"What's that?"

"He better have a black heart like us, and he better not be lame like some of those other guys you've dated. He better be all good and not boring. Only the absolute best for you."

"Such a man does not exist. Plus, you said you liked the guys I've dated."

She rolled her eyes. "I have to say that while you're dating them. It's bestie code not to trash the other's romantic interests. Now that you're free of them, I can tell you my true thoughts."

"Well, bestie code aside. I approve of LC and if I ever find a man who meets all your rigorous standards, I'd expect you to give me your honest opinion."

"Done, but you'll have to say the magic words to alert me that he's the one."

I giggled. "I'm not telling you how big he is."

"Gross. If I had another napkin, I'd throw it at you." Azzy's black lined eyes softened, and she leaned into the scuffed table. "Rachel, you'll have to tell me that you're in love with him point blank and with conviction, that's how I'll know."

I matched her lean and narrowed my eyes suspiciously.

"Are you trying to tell me something?"

Her gaze dipped to the side, and she twisted her mouth, big pointy eyelashes swept back over to me. With a sigh, she said, "I'm completely head over in heels in love with LC. Like strap that ball and chain to my ankle and throw away the key because I never want another human to share that part of my heart. I want her there every day until my last breath and even then, there might be a place for us."

Chapter Twenty-One

The sun is setting over the western sky and although I can't see it dip below the horizon, its brilliance scatters across the clear water and sky above. We've been cocooned in the blanket for so long that leaving almost seems cruel.

The blanket is wrapped around us as I watch Dave's arm move underneath. He's been skimming any exposed areas of my skin for hours. My arms, my shoulders, even my stomach, and he's kept it clean, not drifting anywhere that would spark me to life. How his arm isn't sore is beyond me.

But I'm okay with the result. There's a certain peace in our little world we've created, and it feels intimate and secretive, and I like that he's the one I'm sharing it with.

"You slept for a while," he says.

Stretching my torso against his, I pat his bare chest. "It's your fault, you lured me into sleep with wine and a warm body."

"My superpower," he chuckles. "Ready to go back up? I was going to attempt to make dinner."

I roll to my side, rotating my body sideways so that my

head is resting on his bare stomach, looking up at him. "Two questions."

"Can't wait." He props up on his elbows, the muscles of his stomach tightening under me, and I wonder if he did that on purpose. "Be gentle."

"How is there food at the rental, and you say you cook?"

"Rachel, I've been pretty much single for thirty-six years, and while my mother does live in the city, I have to fend for myself most days."

"Guess I assumed it was a strict dietary requirement of vending machines and coffee for all you doctors. Grabbing whatever's available on the go."

"There are those times, but I also cook when I have the time, especially at home. I can guarantee my food will be edible and it might even taste halfway decent. Don't you cook?"

I roll my head off him, tossing my head back laughing.

"Not if you value your life. Azzy kept me alive with her meals when she lived with me, but lately, it's been a steady stream of Chinese food from my landlord who pities me *and* owns a restaurant two blocks from my apartment. Sometimes, Azzy still brings me leftovers."

He shakes his head at me. "That's pitiful."

I shrug. "Azzy says I have a trash compactor for a stomach. Don't watch me eat because it's disturbing how much I shovel in there. I'm prewarning you."

"Another reason you might terrify me, but I've seen you eat, and it isn't all that scary. If that's as bad as it gets, then I can handle that."

"Don't be fooled. You've seen me eat around my parents and in public. I try to act civilized in their presence, but you just wait. You're about to see the real me."

"Should I buy a tarp for an easier cleanup?"

"I like the way you think." I'm pulling on my shorts as I chuckle. "Excuse me, you owe me the answer to my second question. How are there groceries already in the kitchen?"

"I'm still hung up on this trash compactor thing and might have to secretly record you in your natural habitat."

I throw my sunscreen at him, and he ducks out of the way, tossing the bottle back to me after digging it out of the sand.

"Okay, fine. I contacted the owner of the place and he offered to pick up groceries."

My eyes narrow. "You rich cardiologists get all the perks. Cliffside homes, shoppers for food, five-star hotels. You could have made more of an effort with the car though." I wag a finger at him. "Be careful, Dr. Trenton, I might get used to all of this."

"I sure as hell hope so." His face grows pink under the setting sun, as though he didn't mean to say that, but I brush it off and gather our things as we head toward the house. "And there's nothing wrong with the little car. It's practical for Mom and me on these tiny roads."

As soon as we get back into the rental I'm itching to go back out on the patio, but sunscreen and sand are in all my areas and begging me to head the opposite direction where a hot shower awaits.

"You can have the master bath," Dave says, as he trots across the living room with a fluffy white towel slung over his shoulder. "I'm going in the outdoor shower. Take your time and relax. I'll start dinner when I finish."

I didn't even know there *was* an outdoor shower, but he's gone out a side door, only leaving a trail of lights leading outside. I retreat back into the bedroom and gather my things. The bathtub is sitting there, provoking me and

I'm trying to decide whether to take a long-ass bath or a quick shower.

If it weren't for the growl in my stomach, I would already be filling the tub, but I relent and head to the shower after dragging my suitcase into the bathroom.

Thirty minutes later and smelling more like shampoo and bodywash than sunscreen and salt spray, I emerge into the living room in hunter green sweats, my nose instantly aware of something delicious happening in the kitchen.

Dave's standing over a frying pan that's steaming and he's rocking it back and forth.

His hair is still damp at the tips, falling over his forehead, and he's changed into gray joggers and a slim-fitting white T-shirt. I like the change up and I really like that he's barefoot.

He seems comfortable in what he's doing, and I observe his actions while he moves about, unaware I'm spying on him. There's a speaker playing 'Pump Me Up' and I'm sure it's that playlist and not 'Calm Me Down' because—well—it's obvious by the way he's almost dancing as he spins back to the island and catches me standing there watching him.

"What?" He lifts a shoulder in the air with a frying pan in one hand and a crooked grin. "I get in a groove. Come on, help me. You may even learn a thing or two."

I remain planted against the wall by the hallway leading back to the bedroom and cross my arms. "No way, you don't want me in that mess. I'm more than happy to stay here at a safe distance."

"If you want to eat, you're going to have to help me." He tosses a bright blue apron at me from a hook near the stove. "I won't let you cut off your fingers or anything."

Catching the apron, I shake it out but don't budge. "I'm telling you, this is a bad idea."

He comes over to me and spins me away from him, taking the apron out of my hands and tossing it over my head, securing a knot behind my back. He leans into my ear. "Even a trash compactor can learn new tricks." Dave's halfway across the room as I try to smack him.

Sighing out the world's longest signal of defeat, I trudge over to him as if it's the worst thing in the world. "Okay, what are we making?" I say, bested. "Or rather, what are *you* making?"

"Trout." He cracks up and corrects when he catches my glare. "Kidding. Are you okay with a little heat?"

I take the opportunity handed to me. "I'm okay with turning things up a notch."

The humor fades a tad across his features and he blinks. "I meant food-wise. Behave."

"Me too. Tell me, what did you *think* I meant?" My brow quirks at him.

He's stirring something in the frying pan, but pulls out the spatula, pointing it at me rather aggressively. "You are making things complicated, and you better stop it right now."

"Fine then." Opening the fridge, I find a bottle of Vinho Verde, take it out and go to search for a wine opener in the neighboring drawer.

"Uh-uh. You have to earn that wine, sous chef." He nods at the cutting board next to him. "Grab some of those herbs, and you can cut them up."

"Need I say again that this is a very bad idea?"

With a groan, I give the bottle of wine one last forlorn look as it goes back in the fridge.

Several bunches of herbs have been washed and sit next to the cutting board. I pick them all up at once and inhale their fragrance between my fingers. My eyes close and I'm breathing in their scent, trying to lock this in my memory bank for later, quite certain I won't smell anything like it again. When I open my eyes, Dave is watching me with a longing in his face, almost the same way I had just looked when forced to put the bottle of wine back in the fridge.

He blinks once and returns to the pan. In that brief standoff, something shifts between us. It's not as if there wasn't already attraction, heavy flirting, and a wicked toe-curling kiss, but now it seems whatever was brewing deep within us has risen to the surface. As much as I have been pushing back against anything serious—hell against it all—there may not be much of a choice left.

Whatever *it* is, it's here officially.

And Dave knows it too if that glance was any indication.

Half a raw chicken is pieced next to the stovetop and Dave steals half of the herbs I'm trying to figure out how to cut, right from under me. I go to protest, but I'm enjoying the show he's putting on, like a dance, tossing the herbs in an oil-butter-shallot combo and then placing the chicken on top after coating the raw meat with another oil from a black bottle that tinges the skin dark orange.

I haven't even started to chop what's in front of me when he slides the frying pan into the oven. With a snap and a flourish, he grabs a towel from the oven door and wipes his hands, tossing it over his left shoulder.

"You're doing a lot of gawking and not so much chopping," he says, coming over to me, peering from behind to see my fingers wrapped around the knife handle, but nothing is happening.

His chest comes flush to my back and his cheek grazes mine as he takes my hand with the knife, curling his on top.

He's regulating the speed of the blade to the herbs and

although I'm certain he's doing all the work. I almost feel as if I'm chopping like the chefs on all the reality TV shows.

I lean into his frame, not for leverage or to assist me in any way, but because it feels right to be in his warmth. I'm not even watching him and me chop the herbs, my eyes now closed, listening to the music play a slower melody as my head falls backwards into the crook of his neck.

My nose grazes the sun-kissed skin there. He smells like soap and brown-buttered herbs, and I inhale his scent the way I had with the ingredients.

Dave's head points to me, his voice thick and laced with a smokey undertone. "Can we get through one thing today without me having to take a cold shower?" He's stopped chopping and we're standing against the island, motionless against the other.

"Dave?" I say, and he responds with a low growl. "Your chicken."

"Shit!" He lets go of me, spinning back to the oven to peek inside. The door slams shut and he's shaking his head and walking over to the fridge.

"Is it ruined?"

A laugh erupts from him as he swings the door open, taking out the wine.

"No, it's literally been in there for minutes. Somehow, with you, minutes can feel like hours. Time grows convoluted."

I'm not sure how to respond so I don't. My hands are covered in bits and pieces of herbs, and I rinse them before taking the glass he offers me. Then he pours the almost clear liquid halfway up two glasses.

"Let's go outside," he says.

I look back at my prepping station a little confused and he lifts his shoulders, that dimple making another appearance. "I had it all covered, just thought I'd make you work for your dinner."

I smack him in the chest, but he catches my hand and interlaces his fingers through mine. He begins pulling me gently to the patio. It's so surreal how easy and natural this feels, how right. For a moment, my mind is wandering to that place it oughtn't travel to, the one in which I share a home with Dave and we do this same thing nightly.

It's easy to envision him arriving home from work for us to cook together. Or, god forbid, if he would dare to eat something I have attempted to cook, I have that in my mind too. The cute little domesticated family.

It's pointless thinking, yet the evening is beautiful and real, and dreams—or nightmares—cannot spoil this.

Not tonight.

Not now.

Night is in full force. Out on the cliff tops, several other homes light the ledge, but below where the ocean rolls in, it's so dark that even the foam isn't visible under that cloak. There's a hint of cool air, but I have a hard time noticing it with my blood pumping at full speed.

Dave directs me to the same two-person lounger from earlier, and after I toss the apron aside, we sit in a quiet comfort while he sets a timer on his phone.

I can't help it—I analyze him as though he's a mythical creature, something so rare and fleeting. I'm worried if I blink, he'll be gone, never to be seen again.

After I take a sip of the crisp wine to wash away the lump forming in my throat again, I break myself away from those thoughts and ask over my glass, "You cook, you love your mom, you're a prodigy of a doctor, and a little okay looking. How is it remotely possible that you are single? Or is this where you confess you're married with a bunch of kids?"

"A little okay looking?" He shakes his head, adding a loud scoff. "Ouch. And here's me thinking I'm an Adonis by the way you were looking at me on the beach. And no, I'm not married and certainly have no kids, by the way."

Wiping my brow, I grin. "Well, that's a relief." He appears eager for more flattery. But it's not heading his way. "I refuse to inflate your ego any more than that."

He smiles and takes a sip of wine. "I've dated on and off over the years. Even had a couple longer relationships, but no one who's been worth taking things further."

Two words are missing from the end of that statement. I can see it in his eyes, in the way they darken in my direction, but he won't say it because I've asked him not to. "What's your definition of further?"

He sets down his glass. "Your turn. Why don't you have men at your doorstep?"

His not so-subtle deflection doesn't bother me. "Besides being a trash compactor?" I look back at the kitchen and my stomach groans. "Same as you, I guess. No one worth wanting to make it work." And I find those same two words he wouldn't say on the tip of my own tongue. *Until you.*

"How will you know when that line is crossed into wanting to make it work?"

My throat is dry again. "Besides what we agreed not to talk about tonight? I need to know."

"Huh?"

I tuck my legs under me and prop my shoulder on the incline of the lounger. "Like I should just *know.* I've yet to experience it but have heard people say when you know, you know it's right."

"Ah, I see." His eyes are up in the stars before coming

back to me. "You want that feeling everyone says they have when they fall in love."

"You don't think that happens?"

A little tic bounces between his ear and jaw, and he sets his glass down on a little wobbly table behind him. He's searching my face. It might be black outside, but I can see the glow of his blue eyes as they meet mine. "What makes you think it hasn't already happened for me?"

I'm stunned. If he were Medusa, I'd be solid rock, but he is so much better looking than a snake-headed woman, which makes me even more susceptible to his charm.

I want to launch myself on top of him, to tell him my feelings are the same. That I'm a liar and just too scared to say it out loud. But I can't.

"I have a black heart," I finally say after several beats. "Azzy and I always say that. It started as a high school emo joke, but over time, I kind of believe it." My eyes find my wine glass and I watch tiny bubbles crawl up the inside of the glass. "Especially now."

"If it makes a difference, I've seen all your scans, and I can confirm it's not black at all."

A soft laugh comes from within. "Do you know why I like heavy music like screamo and the occasional death metal?"

He shakes his head.

I tap a finger on my glass. "Wait. Why do *you* listen to it? What drew you in?"

"It pumps me up." He leans toward me and whispers not so quiet, "And it calms me down. I've never given much thought to it outside of that."

"That's where you and I differ. I feel the beats, the screams, the anguish. You can't deny these musicians are some of the most talented to walk the earth. But even more than talent if you listen to most lyrics, those artists—even in all their pain—they are all tormented by love. It's all about how deep they feel for someone." I chuckle. "Well usually, unless they're singing about anarchy or something really screwed up."

"So, your black heart is constantly seeking love even though you feel tormented and all you're wanting is for someone to make you feel the way those lyrics do? That's why you enjoy shredding your eardrums, blasting the growls and riffs?"

I frown at him. "Dr. Dave, did you just use my own words against me?" He nods. "You're right about seeking love though or maybe an affirmation. I've been on my own path to redemption with my family. Hell, with myself even. It's that pain... and love, that keep me going."

"It looks like you have a great relationship with your parents. Not sure about your sister though. That was quite the phone call."

I groan and plant my head into the cushion chair. "She's the worst but she is my sister and I still love her. I spent most of my life pushing them all away, especially her. Years ago, you would've seen a completely different relationship. I hated everything. Them, the farm, Idaho. Even myself."

"What's changed between then and now?"

"Can I say something about that medical thing we agreed to not talk about, just for a moment?"

"You made the rules."

Bobbing my head, my lips twist to the side. "This is going to sound so fucked up, so fair warning."

"Can't wait."

"But first, can you—with your big fancy degree—tell me from a medical perspective how long you think the cancer has been growing in me? A rough guesstimate will do."

He frowns and returns to his glass of wine, depositing the remaining liquid into his mouth, swallowing it with one loud gulp. "Rachel—"

"Indulge me."

Air inflates his lungs more than usual and he lets it out in a long, drawn out breath. I like the pensive look overtaking his face. He's mentally going through all his training and expertise in a split second like flipping through a textbook or a database.

"Given how much it's spread and the size, I'd say three or four years."

My voice weakens, his words confirming and finalizing a theory I had been playing around with. "Well...about three years ago, something shifted in me. It's like a light switch flicked on. Azzy went through a really bad ordeal with her own family, and I realized I needed to preserve what I had been pushing away. That's not really weird, but things clicked that shouldn't. Or should I say, things that wouldn't have clicked if something hadn't changed within me."

His head tilts. "Give me an example."

"My sister and I had had a pretty brutal falling out ages ago, but after I realized I wanted them in my life, I showed up at the farm and she hugged me and apologized." I gave him a hard look. "Chloe does not apologize. Ever. But she did."

Dave is nodding but looks a little pale. "I totally believe you and can even add to your theory."

I sit up straighter. "What do you mean?"

"Three years ago, when Kim died, I was in the ER before they kicked me out, sitting in the hallway on a gurney waiting for my expulsion. There was a scuffle with the physician on duty and interns. Some lady was going off on them for treating her friend for an overdose when really, she had epilepsy."

"Oh my god." My hand covered my mouth. "It's not possible."

"I saw you being carried out by the security guards. No, I didn't really *see* you, but sure as hell heard you." He reaches out to my hand and takes it in his. "Kragen was beside herself when it happened and it was obvious she went easy on me, recommending only a suspension for my actions because she was so consumed with *her* mistake. I remember flipping through your friend's chart while I waited, out of curiosity. You were her emergency contact, weren't you?"

I nod, quite literally on the edge of my seat.

"And you think that's something I wouldn't remember." He shakes his head, laughing. "And I didn't remember until you were in the clinic, and you said something, I can't even tell you what it was, but something clicked, and I looked at your chart and then at you and..." He whistles low. "Weird."

"See?" I say.

His finger travels down my palm. "Yes, it's all weird, but what's so fucked up about all that?"

I squeeze his hand, catching his finger in my fist. "I think the cancer has been causing my black heart to reconcile. To start feeling. It's a curse."

"Rachel, I think that sounds more like a blessing." And I'm hit by his words again, but Dave's getting up, his phone buzzing. He silences it and an awkward moment passes between us. He shows me the glowing screen. "Dinner's ready. Want to eat out here, Trout?"

I groan into the cushion. "I really hate that nickname, you know."

"I'll take that as a yes. Stay here, and I'll bring it out."

He sprints into the house leaving me with a cacophony of thoughts.

Dave's story, the lining up of our paths, has me flustered. I don't want to be pushed by fate anywhere, but it seems inevitable and the idea of dragging him into my diminishing life seems incredibly unfair and the cruelest of fates. But the idea of leaving him and whatever we have here behind in a few days makes the scar tissue in my heart rip right down the biggest of crevices, exposing fresh muscle of pain and something new. Something even more painful than anything else I've experienced: the incoming loss of new love.

Chapter Twenty-Two

DAVE'S BEEN IN THE KITCHEN FOR A WHILE NOW, AND I'm still lying out on the patio, reflecting on how I came to be here in the first place, not understanding how the threads of life have weaved such an interesting and complex pattern. A satellite catches my eye, racing across the obsidian sky. It's in these moments I wonder what's beyond that great expanse of the universe.

Spirituality is not something I've ever considered—never had to. Not sure I ever will consider it fully, but I do know that things don't *just* happen. Fate doesn't *just* intertwine. A man like Dave doesn't *just* walk into a world like mine without a reason, a purpose, a calling.

I don't accept a man of his caliber happens along my path, a man of his perfect match to my specific crazy, all because of some wonderful repeating accident. Call it faith in something bigger than myself or call it that higher power, it matters little. What does matter is that I'm feeling things that I thought wouldn't happen. Scarier still is that I want to feel them, want to be with Dave and if I weren't so goddamn selfish, I'd let him go right now, let him be free of the eventuality of our situation. Of the collective heartbreak.

But I can't bring myself to walk away from him.

I won't.

And now I have to find the strength to tell him.

He's walking across the threshold between the inside and outside of the house, carrying two plates and the bottle of wine tucked in the crook of his elbow. He hands me a plate and sets the other one on the wobbly table.

I peer past him and into the kitchen. "Where are they?" I ask.

Dave follows my gaze. "Who?"

"The actual chefs hiding in the kitchen and plating food like this?"

He grins. "I thought you weren't wanting to inflate my ego?"

"I'm not. You might be a little okay looking and a reasonably successful doctor, but there's no way you did *this*." I lift my plate toward him as if he doesn't realize how amazing his plating skills are.

"Well, you haven't tried it yet. It might change your glowing perception of me." He hands me a fork and a knife as I try to balance the plate on my lap.

"I would have thought you were the *must-eat-dinner-at-the-table* type. This seems a little primitive." I'm cutting my first bite, not even waiting for him to settle into his seat.

He's poured us more wine and hands me a refilled glass that I gladly accept and set on the floor behind me. "I would think this is elevated dining for you since you live primarily out of cardboard takeout boxes."

I stop and look over to him sitting in the lounger, positioned to cut his own first bite.

"I'll have you know that countertops are the perfect

place to sit and eat. If you're close to the sink, it's a bonus for free water refills. Saves a trip. It's all about efficiency."

"How are you even related to your parents?" He pushes a bite onto the back of his fork. "They seem so refined."

I grunt and smile, shoving too big of a bite in my mouth and sending the food to my cheek to be able to fully chew it before swallowing. Dave's eyes are wide as he sees exactly what a human trash compactor looks like in the flesh.

He's appalled and I'm trying not to laugh because the chicken will come right out my nose, and the taste is out of this world. I'm caught somewhere between choking, laughing, and in a euphoric state of foodgasm. I manage to chew the bite and get it down in four separate swallows.

"Oh my," I start to say how amazing it is, but there's a tingling on my tongue. It's not burning my entire mouth, but it's lingering, making me reach for the wine to extinguish the burn. "Holy spicy, that's delicious!"

He still hasn't taken a bite. "I think I'm in shock over what I just witnessed."

"You're impressed, aren't you? I can tell by looking at your face. You've never seen anything so perfect."

"Among other things."

He finally eats, but keeps peering over at me, as though I'm a zoo animal, but I don't care.

My plate is nearly polished by the time he's only halfway done. The last massive bite lodges in my cheek.

"That was incredible, thank you." I lick the fork tines clean and wait for him to finish.

He is better trained after he takes the last bite, putting his fork and knife side by side in the center of the plate.

Holding my hand out to him, I motion at his plate, and he hands it over which I put on top of mine, setting it near my feet.

How can I tell him how I'm feeling? How can I say what's on my mind when it's not coming together right in my mind? Letting out a huff of oxygen and not wanting to think too much about the way he's watching me internally battle, I decide I only have one option left. I have to show him instead.

There's a silence growing between us, and my time has come to act. For once in my life, it's time to stop running and face all the emotions inside head on. With every ounce of resolve I can muster, I rise from my knees and move off the lounger. Then I prop my hands on my hips.

"Will you take me to bed now?" The words come out a little too bossy with too much urgency, but the effect has landed on Dave with the force I intended. "Please."

He swallows, his whole face dropping except for his eyes, so wide he may have lost his eyebrows amidst his hairline. "I-uh," he sputters. His eyes dart away from mine toward the kitchen.

"If you say there are dishes to do, I'm going to toss these plates over the cliff."

There's no time for him to respond as I collect the plates. "I'm putting these in the sink and leaving all the rest there. I'm sure you have people for that anyway. Then I'm going into the bathroom and putting my PJs on. I plan to crawl into that massive bed, and I hope you'll be there since the upstairs is locked."

I leave him on the unlit patio, doing exactly what I say. Except, when I'm in the bathroom and digging through my suitcase that I hauled in from the bedroom, I hold up my sleep shorts and button-up shirt, the one in cutesy rainbows and hearts.

I don't feel like cutesy rainbows and hearts. Even with the severe overpacking, I didn't bring anything else.

I stay in here, staring at my exploded suitcase a little too long, trying to figure out an alternative. There's movement in the bedroom and I hear him shuffling around. He's there, waiting. I make my choice and turn off the bathroom light.

A soft glow of light pushes into the bathroom from a lamp by the bedside, and when I walk into the room, Dave's sitting on the side facing it, scrolling through his phone and oblivious to me walking toward him.

It isn't until I cross directly in front of him that he looks up, a range of expressions on his face and body screaming at me. Surprise, horror, *need.* It's all there twisting and flickering.

"Rachel." It's barely an audible squeak. "You're *naked.*" His eyes bulge while trying to keep them on my face and nowhere else. *Trying.* His knuckles have gone bone white, gripping the phone. Had he been drinking water, he would have choked to death.

I lift my arms in a shrug. "Forgot my PJs. Really sorry."

His eyes dip from my face, but it's quick and then they return and without looking away, he sets his phone on the table and wraps his fingers around the back of his neck.

"You're making this difficult."

"For you maybe. I'm quite comfortable." Only a few feet away, I take a single step toward him, and his back goes rigid, the muscles straining against his white T-shirt as he grips the mattress in a manner as if we're about to be propelled into outer space.

He adjusts again on the bed, so incredibly uncomfortable. I'm loving it, relishing the knowledge that I wield such a great power. Who knew all I had to do was take off my clothes to make Dr. Dave nervous?

He's trying to speak, his voice so low I need to take another step to hear him.

"I thought you were this innocent woman," he says.

There's slight amusement and more than a helping of bewilderment in the statement.

I bite the corner of my bottom lip then let it go. "Now's your chance to back out of my special brand of crazy."

He shakes his head at me while staying locked onto my eyes. "No chance, loser."

My face twists to the side. "Did you call me a *loser*?"

"I'm trying to match your intensity. Words are difficult at the moment. Very little is making sense."

"You're a doctor," I remind him. "You see people naked all the time."

"None of them are you." The way he says it, the way he leans the upper half of his body toward me while he's grasping the duvet, it's primal. He almost growls yet doesn't move from his seat.

"Doctor, are you nervous to be with me?" I ask and he nods twice. "You know you won't break me, right? Please treat me tonight as if I weren't sick. Isn't that what you keep talking about? Being present. Not worrying about the future?"

He's rubbing the back of his neck again, his breathing picking up. "I don't want your heart rate skyrocketing."

"My, aren't you confident?" I plant my hands on my hips and the movement draws a quick glimpse from him. He's back up at my face in a millisecond. The bed shakes in my vision as I'm laughing so much, but he's not. "Listen, if I die while you're inside me, at least I'm doing something I'm hoping I really like."

He's moved on from the back of his neck, scrubbing his face with his hands. "No pressure there," he demurs. "I can't imagine telling your dad that I killed his daughter by having sex."

"He already knows it's happening tonight. He's not dumb. Why do you think he was being so weird?"

He groans and hangs his head. "Yeah, not making me feel better about this, are you? I don't want to give your dad another reason not to like me."

"Maybe we shouldn't talk about Dad while I have no clothes on?" I take a final step to him so that our knees touch, and I study the way his hands rub along his thighs.

He watches me move closer to him. "I agree." Then his head swings to the side, as though he's afraid to really look at me.

"Good," I say, touching his chin, and he turns slowly to me. With another move, I force myself to move between his legs. He's touching a spot right above my knee, his finger moving as hesitantly as he is. "Treat me the way you would have if we'd met a year ago. Don't hold back on me. I want zero percent Dr. Trenton and one hundred percent Dave. And I want you naked too."

His Adam's apple bobs. "It's hard to argue with a beautiful woman who happens to be nude." His fingers slide up my thighs, sending a shockwave through me. They're stopping at my waist. Something shifts in his posture as if he's being pumped with energy. Like he's finally allowed to come alive.

Fingers are dancing across my waist, and I go to move into him more, but he stops me and removes his shirt. My hands can't resist, and soon, I'm pushing him backwards onto the bed, crawling to his chest, wanting to touch every inch of his skin.

As I straddle him, even through his joggers, it seems he's feeling exactly the same way as me. I rock against him once and he overtakes me with a guttural growl, shifting us, spinning me in the bed. Dave's mouth is crashing into mine until I'm underneath him and being devoured.

There's a primal hunger behind this kiss, unlike the other one. It's breath stealing and revitalizing, and I'm filling with a need to kiss him like this every day.

My heart palpitates wildly, and if Dave were actively monitoring it, he'd be stopping us because it feels as if it's going to beat right out of my chest, but this is his doing, not from disease.

It's his urgency on my lips, the hands roaming the open plains of my stomach and working upward, his touch melting into my veins, that brings me fully to life.

Dave's wrestling with his pants and then he's over me again, our frenzy waning, but he's breathing hard. So am I. The hair on his legs grazes the smoothness of mine as he leans on an elbow, forcing himself to remove his hands from me.

"Rachel, promise me you'll tell me if you get lightheaded or—"

I reach out to touch his cheek. "Stop being Dr. Dave. Just be a *little okay looking* Dave."

He leans his face into my palm and exhales. "Okay, Trout."

"You better kiss me good for that."

And he does. His upper half, all those coiled muscles, press against my side as a hand slips behind my neck, bringing me up to meet his awaiting lips. He consumes me again. Not rough, but putting a definite force behind him, a drive I attempt to match.

I arch into his chest, my breasts pressing into him as we come closer together. He balances a thigh between my legs, and it rubs against me, another shockwave igniting what already felt like an inferno. Suddenly, his hands are off and moving again, skimming down my neck, a thumb dragging behind, leaving a white-hot streak of delight in its wake. When he encircles the nearly painful tips of my nipples, my breath catches in a staccato of inhales.

It's clear he likes this noise I'm making, so he repeats it to the other side, eliciting the same reaction, his mouth moving away from mine, kissing and nipping at my jawline and then my neck and with little warning, he takes into it a teased nipple, turning my staccato into a whimper.

Is this the best feeling in the world or the most agonizing craving for more?

My hands run through his hair, gripping each time he dives in again for another taste. A hand moves south, coming to palm the apex of me as he slips a finger into the slickness of my desire for him. He groans against my chest, surprised at how much I'm wanting him, how I open my legs for him so he can nestle between them as he directs himself to me.

Stopping at my threshold, he comes back up to my face and studies me. He wants to ask about my heartrate, eyeing my neck. Worry brackets his mouth.

"Please," is all I say.

His stomach contracts over mine as a decision is made.

He dips his chin and I think he's going for my neck, but lands on my lips, parting them and diving his tongue against mine, our passion at its fullest as his weight settles over me.

In one thrust, he's inside of me and I moan into his mouth as he works his body over me. My legs are like a seat-belt, wrapping around him and locking him to me, bringing all the sensations of him inside of me closer to my surface.

He continues plunging into me until we are all skin to skin and then he pulls back out to do it all over again and I'm soaring, matching his speed and tempo, rocking my hips into him. A hand comes to my hip, pinning me to the mattress and his eyes burn into me while burying himself.

It's a warning. He's trying to stop me from overworking myself, but I can't, needing him as much as he needs me. I struggle against his hold, still able to rock enough under his hand enough that it's as though we've met a silent, delicious compromise.

I'm winding tight, feeling the tension building from within. With every stroke, my body reacts with a tighter hold and by the time I'm about ready to break free, I think I might pass out from tensing every muscle in anticipation of the incoming wave.

Dave's moving faster over me, his urgency becoming clumsy, grunting and contorting his face as he works above me, and this is what it takes for my body to hit the wall at a thousand miles per hour.

I curl up, arching into him at the same time, my body shattering into a million pieces of bright white blinding ecstasy. My hands clutch onto his back, slick with sweat as he thrusts a final haphazard time and releases into me the same way I'm releasing around him.

Our muscles are clenching and expanding, quivers and shudders rolling up my back and down again to the point where we remain connected.

He's breathing as if he ran a marathon. Me too.

He leans off my body enough to not crush me, but his face is tucked into the side of my neck, another hand trailing up my body and I spasm against the touch.

He wraps a hand around the side of my neck, checking my pulse. I want to swat him away, but also want to kiss him again. In the end, my choice is the latter.

It catches him off guard, but still he matches my kiss, his fingers in rest against my pulse and when we part, he's moved on from checking on me. A giant hand splays across my breastbone. He's staring at me with heavy lids. We aren't speaking, only breathing hard.

Then it happens. Somehow, my own hand ends up extended across his broad chest. We're both feeling the life force of the other.

Beneath my palm is everything I ever wanted, and, in this moment, it is enough.

Dave lies asleep, leaving me tangled in his arms, facing one hell of a beautiful man. His navy eyes were no match for me as he succumbed to exhaustion. We didn't even manage to turn off the lamp next to the bed, but it was good we forgot, giving me the wonderful view of him sleeping. There's such vulnerability in someone trusting another in slumber and the fact that he trusts me, that feels good. He twitches every so often and with his mouth relaxed and slightly open, looks at peace.

The lines around his eyes are softened with sleep. A piece of dark hair sweeps his brow, and I stretch my hand up, brushing the softness aside. His forehead creases a little under the intrusion.

He left the patio open, and the draft of sea air flows across us through the room, the crashing of waves muffled by the duvet covering us. I have spent years searching for this, to be tangled in bed with a man who doesn't mind being vulnerable around me.

Someone *I* don't mind being vulnerable around.

I'm trying not to think about the spots that invades my vision, about the cancer that's growing in a heart that's supposed to be so black, nothing else can survive there in its midst.

But it's impossible to ignore. And it hurts.

Not the physical pain. The pain I am going to cause this man who is sleeping so soundly. A man who a month ago, I wouldn't have believed existed. Dave bullied the cancer in my heart around and created a space for him there. I only wish he could chase it all away.

He stirs against me and given it's the middle of the night, I don't expect him to wake, but his eyes flutter open, a slit of blue peeking through. I stroke his forehead, trying not to think about anything but being in the moment with him, suspended together in time.

With strong arms, he grasps me around my middle, my naked body pressing against his. His head nuzzles my shoulder and I think he's gone back to sleep, but then find he is kissing my collar bone. Slow. One right on top of another.

"I thought you were asleep," I whisper.

He hums on my skin, the vibration drawing out an electric jolt down to my toes. I lie my head back into the pillow to give him free rein over me. No time is wasted, and for a second time, we're soon tangled in hot breath and wet kisses and traveling hands.

This time is different than the one hours ago. There's no rushing to get to the end, no whirl of hands attempting to cover every inch of skin, to explore the unknown. We're taking our time. Savoring like we're the rarest fruit we might only be able to taste once. Above all, Dave is present. He's not eyeing my neck or monitoring every moan or eye flutter I throw his way.

It might be from the sleep and his mind mostly cleared of those thoughts, but he's treating me exactly as I'm treating him, as if there is no one in the world with whom we'd rather be doing this. And there's nothing in our future that would give reason to worry.

He's ruined me. As he fills my body once again with his length, taking slow, rhythmic glides, it's obvious that I'll never crave another's touch. Time is short and if this is it, I can live with that—or die with that. I hold onto him so tight my nails might be piercing the flesh on his back.

But I need this. I need him.

We rock against each other, the building of our climax languid and in between the occasional kiss of humid breath and soft lips, he looks directly into my soul, and I his. He's watching me arch into him, my spine curving as I approach the final moments of my climb.

But he still doesn't speed up, metering us forward and as I fall over the edge, he's doing the same. We're both shaking, my mouth open against his as we tremble together.

Those strong arms pull me again to his chest and it's where I remain as sleep finds me, my vulnerabilities all in the hands of Dave.

Chapter Twenty-Three

DAVE PLANTS KISSES ON THE CORNER OF MY MOUTH AS he moves around me. I open one eye, seeing twilight bruising the sky outside the patio doors. I groan, rolling back to find the warmth of his body in the sheets, but this time, when I search for him, the bed is empty.

Sitting up, I finger comb my hair and knot it high upon my head about the time he walks back into the room with two steaming cups of coffee. He's only wearing joggers.

The view of him is magical. My toes curl involuntarily.

"Stop looking at me like that, Rachel," he tells me as he sets the mugs over by the loveseat. He grabs a blanket that rests on the seat and comes over to me. "I'd like to watch the sunrise with you, but once again you're trying to make it difficult."

"I don't know what you're talking about, Dr. Dave. You'd think someone just a little okay looking wouldn't read too much into my thoughts."

He bends down and kisses my forehead, and I don't understand why my breath catches at such a tender act and with a flick of his wrist, he's securing the blanket around me, dragging me to my feet. My eyes gaze on the blanket covering my body.

"It's for my protection," he declares as he takes my hand and deposits me on the loveseat. He opens the doors wide enough that the view is unobstructed while handing me coffee. "I can cook, but coffee is not my specialty so good luck." His mug clinks against mine.

It's decent and much better than anything I could ever hope to produce, but I pretend to gag. He's chuckling and I lean into him, curling my body on the loveseat with his legs stretching out in front of him, crossing at the ankles.

The sky's bruising purples and grays are allowing bursts of peach streaks to sneak through. We sit in the quietness, letting the rising morning do all the talking for us. When my cup is empty, he puts it to the side and pulls me to him and we stay that way the entire time the sky grows brighter.

Sun pierces our eyes and it's the only reason Dave moves, leaving me on the couch and heading back to the bathroom.

"What are these?"

When I spin around in the cushions, I catch him in the doorway, a toothbrush hanging from his mouth and my rainbow-and-heart-covered pajamas pinched between his fingers.

"A deterrent," I say, hiding my smile. "Aren't you glad I got them out of the way?"

He spins back inside the bathroom, water running a moment later. "You're incredible," he calls from the room.

"I thought I was terrifying?"

"That too." He's back in the bedroom a minute later, walking over to me. "You're a lot of things, Rachel." He takes a seat and I resume my position along his body. "Are we still not talking about that thing you don't want to talk about and the other thing *I want* to talk about? Things need to be said. What I mean is—"

"Shh." I lay a kiss on his mouth. "I know what you mean. Most of all, the things you want *me* to say."

"Yes. But I have a few of my own too. Just don't leave it to—"

"Can it wait until we get back, please?" He takes the moment of magic from me in a literal heartbeat, stealing it. It's gone now, and a wave of anxiety washes over me and I'm sure he can feel it in the way I move off and away from him. "We came here to... to get away, to enjoy."

Disappointment clouds his eyes, but I have things to say too, also needing time to gather those thoughts so they don't come out in a spew of verbal diarrhea. "You're not the only one with things to say or with needs, and I need a little more time to process."

This produces an arching brow, and he nods.

"I'll only agree if you come here and give me a reason to stay silent." A hand tugs on the blanket draped around my shoulders and it slides down my arm.

"Don't we need to start packing to go?"

He grins. "How much time does either of us *really* need?"

I move to straddle him, discarding the annoying fabric to the floor. "Doctor, I'm impressed by your stamina."

"I think I'm on the verge of collapse, but you are worth all the consequences if it means I get my hands all over you again."

Same, Dr. Dave. Same.

I LOVE DAVE'S RIDICULOUS TINY RENTAL CAR. Somehow, even with shifting gears and navigating windy streets, Dave's arm protects me, holding me safe and near him as we head back to the real world.

Driving back to Praia da Luz seems like going through a wormhole, as if we are heading to a different universe where real life awaits. Intrusive thoughts flood my brain, but I'm tired and feel hungover, though not from alcohol. From loving and missing sleep.

I don't mind being quiet and letting Dave get me back safe and sound.

Our parents are up on the café deck between the hotels when we pull into the parking lot with the sandy beach on the other side. I wave at them from the window with cheerful abandon, hoping Dad's not thinking too much into why such a big grin is plastered across my face.

Helen and Mom don't seem to mind as they smile with the brightness of the sun.

Both women are hanging over the railing, big black sunglasses on and a coffee in their hands. They might as well be twins now with their posture and the overall look of two oversized brimmed straw hats. Dad's sitting in a chair with a newspaper, but he's locked on to us, saying nothing, only assessing.

Dave's at the rear of the car, trunk open, spewing out curses under his breath. Something to do with my suitcase. I walk to the back of the car.

"Why are you yanking on the handle like that?"

It's all too clear—he's trying to dislodge it from the tiniest of trunks. Grumbling, he repositions his grip.

"What's that you're muttering over there?" I tease, cupping my ear to him.

His eyes roll at me as he tries to free the giant bulging

case. "I'm trying to figure out how the hell it even fit in here to begin with. Maybe if you didn't overpack with those extra pajamas you didn't need. I mean, hell, we only went away for a single night."

Giggles overtake me as the suitcase breaks free, coming to a loud thud on the cobbled lot. "Don't put any more scratches on that beauty!"

He grabs the smaller duffel bag and slings it over an arm and as I reach to grab mine, Dave brushes past me and swoops it into the same arm, tucking the whole damn suitcase underneath it as if the bag doesn't weigh fifty pounds.

I push playfully at his arm when the blackness comes, silently seeping in my peripherals like ink clouding water.

My eyes blink, desperately hoping this inky darkness will recede like the other times, but then the world tilts under my feet and things turn blurry in the few spots still visible. I reach out to him, grasping his forearm with a death grip. He doesn't understand at first, but then my already beat-up suitcase falls.

It hits the ground with a crash the same moment my knees buckle. I'm dropping like the bag, but Dave's faster.

He scoops me up in his arms, all out sprinting across the parking lot, yelling, "Someone grab a chair! Quick!"

As my vision is going in and out, Dave runs with me up the stairs taking two at a time, his adrenaline taking over. There's a blur of movement around me. Everything is happening so fast. Dad's rushing toward me with a chair, and someone places me into it while Mom and Helen are frozen in place. But Helen snaps out of it before Mom, reaching for a glass bottle of water and handing it off to Dave.

He gently adjusts me in the chair, taking the water from his mom, looking at it as if he's not quite sure what to do with it. He's thinking about giving it to me as silently instructed, then sets it down on the wood plank decking. We both know I'm not dehydrated.

"Give her the water," cries Mom. He does not. Because it's pointless. "She probably drank too much red wine with you. It always does that to her. You should've seen when she was sixteen and she was with her friends and got a hold of... and..."

Mom falls into silence, sensing this is not the time.

Now, it's evident this was not a mere faint.

"Leave me alone." Garbled words come as I try to whack at Dave's hands. I'm dizzy, but the blackness is receding enough to focus.

He ignores me, fingers siding under my jaw, checking my pulse. He moves onto my wrist, and I swear he might put his hand on my chest, but when I look up through the slit of my fingers resting against my face, he's exchanging a glance with Helen.

She knows.

Of course, she does. It only makes sense. He may not have even told her, but in that one sober look he gives his mother, it has to be identical to the one he had when he told her about Kim.

It's worry, helplessness, and despair all rolled into one agonizing exchange, and I'm so angry at Dave for that stupid look. Angry that he didn't warn me she would see through my omission, angry at myself for not having the courage to tell my own parents, the ones that are trying to fret over me, if only Dave would move out of their way. They do not think I need a medical professional. I need them, they're sure of it, the way parents always believe they can help their child, save their child.

Dad's look cuts right through me, and I swallow hard,

leaning back and closing my eyes. The black is almost gone when I reopen them. I'm shaky but manage to joke. "Well, that was exciting."

No one laughs, but Dad whistles through his teeth. "I thought it might be something serious for a minute there. The way your boyfriend here jumped into overdrive really made me nervous."

Dave looks up at me from his crouch and it's an unreadable expression. Maybe concern, maybe urging me to speak, maybe nothing at all.

My eyes squeeze closed again. "He's not my boyfriend, he's my doctor." The words are out before I can stop them. When I reopen them, I'm met with opposing reactions.

Dad and Mom seem utterly confused, looking from Dave to me. Helen and Dave are both frozen, but there's a cloud of disappointment trickling over Dave's features, and I even see the same expression cross Helen's.

In seven words, I've completely ruined everything in two horrible and different ways.

"Why don't we go into our room?" Helen suggests. Because she *knows.* This is a moment no parent will ever want to experience, and she knows that because the raw pain welling up behind her own eyes is all too recognizable. Nothing else could possibly look this way. "There's room and it will get us out of the sun."

"My stuff is there anyway," Dave mutters to no one in particular.

He's helping me up, securing an arm around my waist, ready to catch me if my wobbly legs go out again. I'm feeling better though, and with that comes clarity as I take notice of everyone scurrying me toward the fancy hotel with an extra star under its name.

Dad's two steps in front of us but keeps glancing over

his shoulder as though I'm going to disappear if he doesn't keep tabs. He's somehow obtained my luggage. Helen is carrying Dave's. I catch Dad's concerned stare, already able to feel the worry shared between us, but more, the pain and secrets I've suppressed for so long come seeping out of my resolve in that one look.

Dave's scrutinizing every step I take, his jaw locked tight and multiple lines of worry furrowing his brow. His and Dad's faces are similar, but Dave's is deeper because he already senses the weight of this moment. His eyes flick down to mine for the briefest of seconds.

He forces a smile.

Then, he leans into my ear. "I know you're scared. I'm not going anywhere. And I'm not just your fucking doctor." It's so quiet, but there's a potency lacing through those words.

It's not quite anger, not quite frustration, and not quite scared. It's a combination and although there's a hardness there, I sense he means every word with care.

Everyone's looking ahead toward the lobby and Dave leans to my temple and presses a kiss there. No one is the wiser and my breath catches on an emotional wave, but I shove it down.

Not yet.

There are doormen and bellhops, and I try not to but rattle out a laugh anyway. "Of course, you have doormen." Dave doesn't respond, doesn't even look at me, but gives my side a squeeze.

We're packed into the smallest of all elevators. Why is everything so tiny in Europe? Five adults in the space of a cardboard moving box makes it hard to breathe. I'm leaning into Dave, his free hand cupping my jaw, but I suspect he's attempting to check my pulse again.

The group ushers off the elevator and Helen is opening a door at the end of short hallway. I shouldn't be surprised when she swings the door wide enough for us, but the place is huge. Seems like Europe devotes its space-saving measures to only those who can't afford suites.

Dave directs me to a couch in a massive living room, doors on either side, and I suspect each leads to a private bedroom. Helen opens up the balcony to allow the breeze to sweep out the humid hotel air. After getting me settled, Dave disappears into one of the closed doors and Dad takes his place, sitting next to me on a free cushion. Mom and Helen are grabbing chairs from a table, and they create a semi-circle around me. I can't read Mom. She's somewhere between confused and maybe a little excitable, but that can't be right. She tracks Dave's movements as he walks out of the bedroom with a black nylon bag in his grip. She smiles up at him.

Of course. I groan. She thinks this is all benign and Dave is a match for me. If only it were that simple.

"Are you having the same feeling as downstairs?" Dave asks. I shake my head while he unzips the bag, kneeling near me, pulling out a stethoscope and hooking it on his neck.

It's second nature to him. He's doing what he does best, and I'm oddly turned on by how handsome he is in this screwed-up moment.

That fades when Dad pats my hand, watching Dave set aside his bag.

What is he thinking? Does he assume Dave is being a thorough love interest, or does he grasp the reality of the situation?

I'm still weak but point at Dave's neck. "You always go on vacation with your stethoscope?"

Dave's not amused with me. He's way too serious, leaning forward and pressing his fingers to my ankles. "Have they been swollen like this for a while?"

I smirk at him. "You didn't seem to notice earlier." He narrows his cobalt eyes at me and as much as I want to laugh at my joke, Dave doesn't.

"It's just dizziness," my mom is telling Helen, but Helen's eyes are wide, taking in everything. She nods to Mom, but more to appease her, not because she agrees.

Dave's lashes shoot up to mine. "How long have you been having these episodes? The blackouts and dizziness?" I'm a little intimidated.

He's all Dr. Trenton and no longer the man I'd spent the last week with.

I frown, flickering my eyes to the others in the room. "Dave..."

"Tell me right now. How many times in the past week?"

I let out a big breath. "A few times... every day."

"*Fuck*, Rachel." His eyes are boring into mine and he doesn't even care or notice that he made my mom gasp at his language. "This is really serious. Why didn't you tell me?" He comes along my side and puts the earpiece in, not even asking before he's against my heart. His eyes never leave mine, so it's not hard to see the change flash over him when he hears something he doesn't like.

His jaw clenches again, and he swallows, his head shaking from side to side.

The stethoscope moves around over my heart, Dave checking several areas. He doesn't bother to dampen his voice at all as he pulls the earpieces out of his ears and tosses the damn thing over his neck. In fact, it's louder and more authoritative than I'd like. "You need to tell them. Things have changed." When my eyes mist and I look away from him, he pulls my chin back to face him. "Now."

Dad's posture changes as he glances over to Mom.

My body begins to shake. "I want this time," I'm begging. "Just this little bit of time. That's all."

Dr. Trenton fades into the background and my Dave is back, grabbing the hand Dad isn't holding and he moves from his crouch to the seat next to me. His thumb runs across my cheekbones, and he doesn't care everyone is paying attention to us. Neither do I.

Dad's shifting, uncomfortable with everything, but Dave touching my cheek really does him in. He tries to make a lighthearted joke again.

"Thank goodness your boyfriend is a doctor. What's going on, Trout?"

Now, he's waiting too. Waiting for me to tell whatever there is to say. I clamp my eyes shut and when I open them, I shift them from viewing a man I might be in love with to the one I love with all my heart. There are a few stray tears stinging, but the storm brewing has yet to make a full appearance. "Dad, Dave *is* my doctor."

"I don't understand, sweetheart."

My mom rushes over to where we sit, squeezing in the tight couch next to Dad and almost on his lap. "Rachel, what's going on?"

I look back to Dave, as though he can help, but he seems unable to assist or maybe he's trying to let me do this on my own. Dad is holding my hand, Mom holding Dad's other hand. My vision starts to blur again, and I slam my eyes shut, falling back into the couch.

Dave's over me again. "We need to get you to a hospital," he says through the curtain of black—the pounding—the utter devastation of the moment.

"No!" I yell, my eyes clamping down even tighter.

"If you don't go, this is going to be so much worse. Please listen to me."

"I am not going to the hospital, Dave. I'm fine."

My mom's voice interjects, soft and fragile. "Why's this so serious? It seemed like a little lightheadedness. Maybe she needs some water like I said."

Her question is so innocent. "Here," she says.

"Carol," my dad says, and my mom's name sounds so foreign coming from him. So serious. "Rachel just said he's her doctor. He's a cardiologist. I think whatever is going on, it's bigger than not drinking enough water."

"Oh."

"Can someone talk some sense into her?" Dave's exasperated. He stands and I think he's pacing the room.

My dad gives it a try. "Rachel, if Dave says you should go—"

"*Dad*," I breathe out his name. I open my eyes to look straight at him. My chin quivers and it's all over. It's done. Everything is a second away from shattering.

My parents are about to be as broken as the other three of us in the room.

I'm trying to catch my breath, trying to sound normal when I speak, but it comes out with jagged raspy edges. "I met Dave a month ago as Doctor Trenton. He's a cardiologist at UCSF."

Mom's nodding as if this is all good information that they already know.

"I wasn't feeling good." I'm sputtering now. "I—they—Dave—oh god." My chest contracts against my lungs, and I swing my head back to Dave. "I can't, Dave. I *can't* do this."

I'm blubbering the words out and he jumps into the

couch, pulling me to his chest, cradling my head in his arms as I tuck my fingers around his forearms.

"You can. You must find the words. They deserve to know."

I'm shaking my head in his arms, but free myself from him, trying to recover one shred of resolve to say what needs to be said. I take the deepest breath of my life and let it out and its sharpness dries my throat. I turn to my parents as Dave takes my hand and gives it a squeeze of encouragement. "I only have five months at the most." The tears are falling, but I'm immobile. They tumble off my cheeks.

Dad gives me *that* look. The one only a dad can give. He's always stoic and carries his emotions deep within, only exposing them to my mom, to Chloe, and to me at very rare times. Like now.

It's all-knowing, pointed, and direct, but encompassing genuine concern.

It's the same look of which I've been on the receiving end countless times over the years, but this one cuts the deepest. It's the one I've been dreading to see since I first found out. Even knowing it was coming still doesn't brace me for the impact it delivers. It tears right through me because Dad doesn't have to speak to say everything that needs to be said.

But then Dad does speak. "Five months for what?" His brows are pinching together so tight his skin crinkles in all the corners and crevices that time and sun have etched into his face.

It's as if he doesn't already know the answer to his question.

He's the smartest man I know, asking the silliest question. Then he really looks at me again, that same look from when I was five and riding high on the damn horse, except he's not pulling at the ends of his hair in horror. But the fear is there in his eyes just like back then.

I see it so clear. The ability that he, as my father—my protector for all these years—can do nothing to fix this. He can't help me.

A sob rips through my center, and I think it might kill me before the cancer even has a chance. That scar tissue is ripping and shredding my heart into a maimed mess of flesh. It's the damn silly question that does me in over everything else and I can only nod a sucking inhale of a breath at Dave, squeezing his hand, begging him to help me—giving him permission to tell them everything I can't get out. I slam my eyes shut and sob as he starts to tell them.

His voice is strained, but he's trying to remain composed, trying to turn to Dr. Trenton, but it doesn't sound as effortless as before. Medical terms are jumbled between gasps and denials from both my parents. Questions are sprinkled in there too and the timbre of my dad's voice loses its steadiness into a shaking uncertainty. That causes more sobs from me, and I fall into my dad's arms while he's still trying to grasp exactly what's going on.

"We've exhausted all options. There's nothing left we can do," Dave says. It's a nail in the coffin of my story, of my life. Finality. There's no arguing, no fighting after those words are spoken and let loose in the silent room.

My mother's rapid inhales are grating against every fiber of my being, cringe-inducing and agonizing to hear. She's already started praying to her god to spare me, but even she knows that Dave wouldn't say those words unless they were true and final.

If things weren't already bad enough, the black is creeping in and even in my dad's arms, I reach out to Dave when it covers more than before. "Dave." My eyes slam shut.

I hear Helen rise, her chair falling back and there's shouting. Dave's palm is doing that not-so-doctorly thing against my chest and I'm being lifted into his arms. He's yelling at someone.

Everything—Dave, Dad, our moms, even the fancy hotel room pushes over an invisible edge into a blanket of nothingness.

Chapter Twenty-Four

THE WINDOW IS OPAQUE, AS THOUGH MILK'S BEEN spilled over top, dripping over the glass until it leaves a film behind. There's nothing beyond the window but misty tendrils of white.

Why can't I see out?

My eyes are weighted, but my heart feels heavier, as if an elephant is sitting on it. Breathing is a chore, the heaviness in my chest ridding my lungs of all the air they require but the whitewashed window draws the sliver of my one eye.

Movement occurs somewhere by my head. A chair has been tucked into the corner there and when I force an eye to open more, Dad's sitting in the chair, a newspaper wide open as he peruses the local news. I frown at the San Francisco Chronicle in bold Fog City Gothic font.

How did he get one all the way out here in Portugal? Why would he even bother?

He folds the top of the paper, and I can see from his nose up. He's watching me. Probably because I'm moaning as I try to sit up.

He's shuffling the paper aside and at my side in an instant, putting a gentle, but fatherly firm touch to my shoulder, pressing me back into the bed. His eyes have a sheen to them and the way he's eyeing me brings everything back in one snap of a split second. That look.

It's the very one I have been dreading since Dave told me about my diagnosis at the concert.

Dave.

As I try to sit up again, Dad does the same thing and when I finally settle back, he moves toward my knee and sits on the edge of the bed. He doesn't speak, but his hand rests on my foot giving it a little squeeze, and I suspect he thinks that's the only spot he can touch that won't cause any pain.

"Where..." My mouth is full of cotton, and I touch my lips as if they might have the power to bring more words forth. My hand drops to my chest, but a searing pain causes me to hiss.

"Easy there, Trout. You have a drain and stitches there." His voice has lost all the toughness of an Idaho farmer. He's a broken worried father. He's tired and helpless. Dad offers me a sip of water.

"Stitches?" I drop my chin to my chest and try to look down my nose at whatever is causing the pain, but all I see is a blanket.

"You really scared us." He's squeezing my foot again and a few minutes pass until I'm clear-headed enough to understand him. "I can't for the life of me..." His voice hitches and even through what I suspect is a cloud of anesthesia, my eyes water at the way he's cracking. "Rachel, why didn't you tell us? I understand it's scary, but we would have wanted to know from the beginning. We want to help."

A tear slips from both sides of my eyes, but I don't have the strength to wipe them. My throat is scratchy, but I have to get this out. I sip a little more out of the straw near my mouth and ready myself. "Because it changes everything, Dad. I wanted time. Good time. I've spent a lot of years being horrible. I only wanted a couple weeks of nothing but good."

Dad's brow squishes. "Rachel, you've not been horrible. You've had to figure out your own path forward. You know we've never faulted you for that. But you shouldn't have kept this a secret." He forces out a smile and then laughs softly, wiggling the bed. "But *man* we had a good trip, didn't we?"

I'm nodding, my bottom lip sticking out and I'm trying to gather courage to get everything out I want to say. "I'm sorry, Dad." Then I tell him what's been crushing me from the inside since I first found out. "I don't want to run away this time. I want to stay here. It's not fair. I want to live."

"I know you do, sweetheart." His own words are choked out and he's shaking, trying to distract me and our spiraling conversation, Dad squeezes my gray boring sock with its little non-slip stickers on the sole. He takes a deep breath and regroups. "You know that doctor loves you, right? I had my suspicions before. I knew it for a fact the second he shoved me out of the way to get you into an ambulance and to the hospital in Luz. He paid for a medevac flight for all of us home. He hasn't left the hospital at all. Not once."

"How long have I been here?"

"A week yesterday. Did you hear what I said?" He's raising a bushy brow, and I am sixteen again, asking if I took the truck without permission.

"He shoved you? I mean, he's a doctor, maybe he thought—" My eyes dart to Dad's. "Wait, did you say he's in love with me?"

"There she is. Must be all those drugs." He chuckles,

then his face is serious again. "You know his sister died of the same condition, right?"

I don't know why he's telling me this, but I nod. "You know he can't save me, Dad. No one can. Not even you." I'm choked up again, Dad's jaw working back and forth as he looks at his boots. There's probably Idaho dirt permanently embedded in those old pieces of leather. My head rolls to the side to watch him, to see his head sagging between his shoulders. My tough father, the one who could do anything in my eyes is reduced to a frail, breaking man, and all by my simple words.

All because of me.

He regains a little composure and drags a hand over his face. "You know, I'd only ever let a man take my place as your protector if he was truly worthy." He gives me a small smile. "Dave is."

There's a knock on the door and Dad rises to grab the paper and I track him to the doorway. He pats a doctor with a white coat on the arm and moves past him, leaving.

If my heart weren't so drugged, it would have fluttered at the doctor walking toward me in those damn scrubs. He's checking a few machines but keeps drifting tired eyes my way.

It's as if we're playing a game. Who will break first and speak? But I still feel like crap, so I mentally elect him to the position.

After what feels like forever, he takes a seat on the edge of the bed, closer than my dad was seated, near my hip. He studies my face as if making sure I'm actually me. As for me, I'm waiting for the sweet nothings he's going to whisper to me from that mouth I can't help but stare at.

"You're an idiot." His words make me flinch, and a puff of air comes out of him as he forces up a tight smile, but he's not amused. "You scared the living shit out of me. Did your dad tell you what we had to do?" I shake my head and he's grazing a finger on my collar bone, dipping below the blanket and pulling it back to expose blood-stained gauze, tape, and a tube going from my body to somewhere out of it. "There was a ridiculous amount of fluid in the sac around your heart. They drained it in Praia da Luz. Had we waited... had you not been near a hospital..."

He rolls back his throat and pulls back up the blanket. "You're an idiot for not telling me how you were feeling. We could have done something sooner."

"How was I supposed to know? I thought it was normal progression," my voice croaks out.

"But that's just it. You *didn't* know and you *didn't* ask. I think it's because you didn't want to know the truth because your plans would have to change. And that makes you an idiot."

"Would you stop calling me that?" I snap, and my chest sears at the pressure my voice causes on the wound. "I don't want your pity and you can't fix this. You can't fix me."

He scoffs. "Pity? Are you that dense? Do you think I'm interested in you based on what happened with Kim? Do you think that's why I am *still* here, Rachel?"

"Why *are* you here?"

"If you had let me tell you what you refused to let me say, I think you'd know by now."

Dave's rattled or unhinged, I'm not sure which, but he rubs the back of his neck then turns back to me. "I already told you that the first appointment, maybe I thought about you based on my sister's death. *Maybe.* But that went right out the damn window when I saw you at that concert. Something changed. I want to be more than your doctor.

More than a friend. I want it to be you and me until whenever the end comes. I want time with you. That's it."

I'm trying to adjust, struggling so Dave moves the head with the remote to tilt me up. "That's not *it*," I rasp out. "*It's* not that simple. I'm severely lacking in the time department."

"Stop trying to make death jokes. It's beyond self-deprecating."

"Why? I'm dying, Dave!" I'm shouting and my chest hurts so much that my hand presses above the wound. "A shitty attempt at humor is the only way I can reconcile that. Otherwise..."

"Otherwise, you'd actually have to confront what scares you most?"

"And what's that, old wise one?"

Dave hangs his head in steepled hands. "We're all dying, Rachel. You just happen to more or less know your end date—"

"Says a man who has plenty of sheets left on his calendar. I have no pages left. Nothing but skull and crossbones with a giant red circle."

"I could walk across the street right after this conversation and get hit by a car. I could die at any moment. We all could. I see it in this hospital every single day."

There's a squeezing inside of me when he talks about his own mortality and the thought of him not existing twists my insides. "But that's not what's going to happen, and you know that."

He sighs and the heaviness behind the force of air shakes the bed. Hell, it may have cleared the fog out of the entire bay beyond the window. "Why can't we take the time we know you have and make the most of it? For both of us?"

We. *Us*. He's using the words as if he wants more.

As if my disease isn't a death sentence, only a nuisance.

My lungs ache at all the energy and words coming out, and I take a minute to collect my breath. Dave's eyes are scanning the machines and I swear he wants to grab my wrist and check my pulse but doesn't move from his spot next to me.

Tears prick my eyes, the well at my lashes starting to fill and I can't look at him anymore.

"Why on earth"—I inhale a rasp of air—"would you want to put yourself through the torture of being with me?"

He gulps loud enough to draw my eyes. He's about to speak and both dread and crave what he's going to say. That scar tissue in my heart, the ashes of all my past mistakes, the cells that seem dead and lost to the depths of my life choices, regenerate with one look from Dave.

They start building a new heart around the existing, decayed one, creating a cocoon of strength. Resolve.

I'm hurting more than before, my own palm pressing harder near my center, the internal pain radiating down my arms and legs, leaving a streak of something in its wake. Something I don't want him to say because once it's out, I'm a goner but I can't stop him. A word is forming on his lips, and everything goes into slow motion. His mouth opens and he says my name like it's a deep-rooted need. A hunger and satisfaction releasing all at once.

It's the end for me.

I've given up all hope to end this and can't see anything but him. There's no certain death lurking months away. There's no calendar with no more pages.

There's Dave and there's me.

Us.

The compression on my chest releases enough to stop him, but he's already speaking.

"I'm going to tell you what you keep trying to stop me from—"

"I love you," I blurt it out, the pressure on my chest dissolving and all that's left is a stunned Dave. His mouth is hanging open and I'm crying, ugly, fat wet tears rolling down my cheeks and I might be dying here and now in this moment because the pressure returns to my chest.

I am being crushed.

It's Dave crushing me, kissing me, a hand wrapped around my neck and god—he's trying to be ginger with me, but I'm clutching at his scrubs and pulling him to my chest and he's pushing me away to preserve an inch of safety around my heart, but it's too late. It's already his.

He's the one who's fixed it on more than one occasion, the one who's built it into something new. Now, his lips are relentless, and I've officially gone backwards in the five stages of grief—smack in the middle of anger as he deepens the kiss. I'm angry our time is limited, but trying to regress even further back as I can to the beginning—into denial.

It's going to show up shortly because I want to believe—*need* to believe—that Dave and I can have something more than the next few months.

Dave stays with me the rest of the morning and as the sun burns through the fog, life outside the window finally decides to reveal itself. I'm staring out it when he conducts another check of my vitals, stepping into the doctor role so effortlessly.

He spies me watching him move over to type notes into a computer station. "What?"

"Did you tell my dad it was from us having sex?"

Dave's cheeks rise to reveal that dimple and he snorts. "No, because it wasn't from that at all."

I let out an exaggerated breath. "Whew. That would have been a real downer."

He chuckles and keeps his focus on me, waiting as I play with the tubes running up my arms. When I gaze up at him, I grin. "I'm trying to not feel guilty for wanting to rip all these things off my body and ask you to take me home."

"Now?" His brow perks up, but he shakes his head. "Not going to happen. Along with your catheter, there's also the other surgery to recover from."

"*Other* surgery?"

He pushes away from the station, the stool floating his body over to me. "I had to clear out some of the tumor from one of your arteries. We kept you under a medically induced coma so you could heal. You have to recover, and the hospital has everything we need to—"

"You *fixed* my heart?"

He's looking anywhere else but at me, swiping his palms across the fabric on his thighs. "I—uh, yes. *No*. Sort of. It's a temporary fix and doesn't change much, but it might make you more comfortable." He scratches at his scalp before running a hand through it. "And about me doing your surgery..."

"Oh no."

His mouth presses together into a tight line. "It wasn't the biggest of procedures, but it's still considered by hospital standards a major surgery. There are restrictions in place preventing doctors from treating loved ones. Technically, we—I hadn't established what our relationship was—is."

"Are you in trouble?"

He shrugs. "I don't really give a shit if I'm being honest. I'd do it a thousand times over, but I believe my days at

UCSF are numbered and my medical license might be compromised."

"Dave." I touch his hand, and he wraps mine up in his giant ones. "Why would you do that?"

"Are you kidding? There's no one else I would trust with your heart." His gaze flicks to mine and he presses a kiss to my knuckles. "No one." Someone knocks at the door, and he looks up and smiles. "I'm sorry in advance if this goes south. Please play nice."

I think he's talking about him treating me as a patient, but then she walks in.

Chloe's uber pregnant, engorged and waddling worse than the last time I saw her in the same condition. She and Dave exchange pleasantries and then he's gone, disappearing to leave me alone with my sister.

"Why are you here?" I say, the words sounding harsher than I intend.

She shuffles around the room and her head slips behind my bed before popping back over to me. "I'm trying to find the right cord to unplug from the wall." But she doesn't laugh and she's not angry. Her eyes are circled with darkness from lack of sleep and bloodshot veins scatter to her pupils. She looks absolutely miserable.

Her eyes fill with salty tears, turning into a mirror of my own.

"Why did you have to make this all about you?" she blubbers out, pointing around the room. "That's my department."

My voice is just as wet and sobby. "You seem overly emotional, even for you. Do you need some pickles and ice cream or something? I'm sure you can order some from here."

Chloe's at my side, climbing her big, bloated self into

my bed and I'm irritated. There isn't enough room, but she curls until her head is resting on my belly, the life within her resting on my thighs.

"Don't name that little shit after me," I say, running my hands through her hair.

The bed jiggles as she takes several breaths. "As if I would give you that kind of credit."

Dave finds us later, asleep and curled into each other like sisters who actually like each other. We only wake because he's redoing the checks that I thought the nurses did.

Chloe stretches as much as she can in the limited bed space. "Sorry," she says to Dave in a small voice. "I didn't mean to get in the way."

He smiles wide and says, "Not a problem, but I'm not delivering your baby if you stay too long."

We all manage a slight laugh.

Before Chloe leaves my bed, she squirms her way up to my ear and speaks way too loud for Dave not to hear. "He's wonderful. Way too good for you."

I try to smack at her, but Dave helps her climb off the bed as she tries not to tumble to the floor.

"Go back to Idaho," I say. "No one likes potatoes dressed as pregnant women."

She rolls her eyes at Dave, showing her exasperation with me. "I hate Californians," she huffs at him.

Dave is looking between us, and I think he might assume we're gearing up for a fight, but we both giggle at his face as she leaves with a promise to send in Dad and Mom.

"Has anyone called Azzy?" I ask Dave, surprised she's not glued to my side. I'm worried that she's upset at me for not telling her before I left for Portugal.

"I called her while we were in Lisbon, getting you on

the medevac flight. I'm not sure that conversation went much different than my first one with her. She makes me fear for parts of me that I find very valuable."

This produces a snort from me.

"Rachel, Azzy's been here every night with you. I even caught her sleeping in the bed with you." He raises his hands. "How do all the women in your life think it's appropriate to squeeze in that tiny bed?"

"You sound jealous, Dr. Dave."

A dimple forms under his cheek, and I like that it's making regular appearances. "No one will be sharing our bed once I break you out of here. I draw the line."

"Such a dictator. Most men would be thrilled with two —or three—women in their bed."

"Have you met Azzy? Because I did this past week and I thought you and your dad were frightening, but that woman is on a whole other level. I would never want to cross her. She went full crazy on a nurse for trying to adjust the bed setting."

"Well, she did owe me at least one crazy hospital meltdown." Dave looks confused so I shake my head. "That's why I love her. She's perfect."

"Hmm. I don't find that surprising. She'll be back tonight, I'm sure." He frowns at me. "Are you feeling okay?"

I nod. "Sore. But nothing else. Just wanting to get out of here. I really hate hospitals."

A nurse pops her head into the room.

"Dr. Trenton? Dr. Kragen and Dr. Santos are here to see you."

He lifts his chin to her in acknowledgment and turns back to me. "Judgement time."

"Kragen?"

"The very same and current Chief of General Surgery.

I'm making a habit of doing ethically questionable things in her presence. Not sure she'll be so accommodating this time around."

"Bring Azzy with you. I'm sure she'll have plenty to say."

Dave barks out a laugh and kisses me square on the mouth. "I'll be back in a few minutes."

I thought he was heading to an office but hear them talking in muffled voices outside the door. Kragen's tone rings true to the same voice from years ago and I wonder if she can appreciate this full-circle moment. I wonder, too, how tight her bun is today.

Words are flying from her mouth, and I only catch a few as she's speaking too fast for my brain to process. 'Against protocol', 'reckless', 'not your personal hospital'.

But my favorite is from Juan Santos, Dave's mentor.

"You'd do the same," and I assume he's speaking to Kragen. "Protocol was violated. Punish him if you must, but if you're going to ask the board to pull his license or threaten to take away his hospital privileges, I'd ask you to walk into that room and tell that woman that what he did was a mistake. His stupidity—"

"Thanks, bud," Dave says.

"—Is the only reason she's alive. And from my understanding, that very same woman could have had *your* privileges and license revoked years ago and she could have had a malpractice case handed to you with no problem. But she didn't."

"Sounds like you're trying to back me into a corner."

"I'm giving you facts. What about you, Dave? What do you think?"

The silence is strung out long enough that I think they've moved away from the door. Then he blows out a breath. "I don't really care, and this is taking me away from where I want to be right now. I'm taking Rachel home and you and the board can decide my fate. I have zero regrets and would do it again, so don't come at me looking for remorse or groveling because you won't find any here."

Someone exhales heavily and heels click down the hall.

Juan whistles through his teeth. "That one is coming for you. You sure you don't want to fight this?"

"Nope. I'm serious. When Rachel's ready, I'm taking her out of here and I'm going to put all my focus into that relationship. She's all that matters. To hell with everything else."

Chapter Twenty-Five

There's only one picture hung in Dave's condo, proudly displayed over the sofa. He's a man, so I didn't expect a Pottery Barn decorated space when he brought me home, but it's sparse even by man standards.

Especially with a mom like Helen.

A few touches make me believe she had a small hand in trying to make his place look like more than four pieces of mismatched furniture and stacks of haphazard textbook piles.

I study that framed art piece. It's small—too small—for the width of the wall, almost lost in the seafoam green painted walls. A black-rimmed frame, and then a single piece of paper sits between two panels of glass, the wall color acting as the mat. The waxy paper is shredded on one side, ripped from its source. The whole thing is old, aged with time and abuse, probably brittle to the touch. Where it's been folded over and over again, the color is a hint of a memory leaving only white lines of fibrous pulp.

Even smudged fingerprints reflect under the glass on the once glossy print.

Tiny vestiges, I catch myself thinking. *Imprints of another time left behind.*

The photograph on that page also causes its own mix of emotions. Lagoa, the beach where we spent one incredible day, is prominent. The cliffs are jagged, dotted with the most beautiful flowers, the waves wild and turbulent below. There's a calmer, lake-like beach on the other side of a cut-out rock, but not within the lens of the photo.

I think about Kim and of how many times she would have touched this photo to drive the point home that it was her safe space, and I find myself doing the same, but my fingerprints imprint on glass, not magazine paper. The blemished lines that lack color feel like the ones I've been protecting in my heart for years, but it's so different now.

Grabbing a blanket from the sofa, I head out onto the patio.

Ocean Beach is freezing today, and even though it's not the turquoise waters of the Atlantic, the salt spray still brings me back to our time spent there.

Azzy is watching me curl into the fluffy gray blanket and then she tucks the free end around her body and hands me a cup of steaming coffee.

We observe the fog roll in, heading to a destination somewhere within the bay, past our view.

She's been quiet ever since I left the hospital a week ago. It's not that Azzy's changed her behavior or personality to accommodate my diagnosis, it's more as if she's afraid I'm not real, a figment of her imagination. That I'm already gone.

"Where's Dave?" she asks quietly.

I'm sipping on the coffee, blowing away the steam. "Out running. I told him he can't let himself go because I might need his manly muscles and trim waist to hold onto soon when I'm only a twig." Azzy chuckles and I'm happy she gets my dark humor. "Plus, it gives him time to process me. I'm a lot, you know. A bit of a handful. Way too much for him in large doses."

She's setting down her mug, and I can see her head turn back to the waves and foam. Her brows come together the same time her mouth twists to the side. She won't look my way. "You know, just because we share half of the same black heart doesn't mean you were supposed to get the diseased half."

"Azzy," I say, unable to form another word in my mouth.

Her chin quivers. "I think I've done it to you."

"What?"

"Caused the cancer. Me. I did it."

"What are you—"

She rotates the top half of her body to face me. "I'm literally named after the Angel of Death!" she blurts out and normally, this would have been a joke between us, but her mouth is screwed up to her nose and her eyes have the all too familiar gleam of impending tears. "Maybe my parents had the foresight. I'm cursed and I somehow passed it on to you."

"You did not."

I scoot over to her, wrapping her in my arms and she tucks her face into the crease of my elbow. "This cancer is not your fault. It's not mine either. There are stacks of medical journals and textbooks in this condo that say that. I'm sure Dave can break it down for you."

Her head relaxes, cradled in my arms. She sucks in a breath. "You know what those doctors told me both times you brought me to the hospital when I was sick? They said you saved my life. But I laughed at them because you've been the one saving my life way before that. You got me out of Idaho. You stuck by my side, and you didn't have to. And now," she says, sniffling, "I can't save you and it's my fault for sharing such a fucked-up heart. For being the Angel of Death. I've doomed you."

"Azzy," I call to her, pulling her chin in my direction. "Stop that right now. You'll start to look more emo than goth if you keep crying."

She blubbers, laughing, swiping fingertips around her eyes, black streaks smearing in all directions. Her finger comes up to my own eyes and she wipes the tear-stained paint in a smear beneath them.

"There. Now we look the same." Her body returns to rest against mine and she hugs me tight. "You *are* a lot and it's why I love you."

"I love you too."

"I wish I could sew your heart the way you've always managed to piece mine back together."

"I'm a terrible seamstress," I remind her.

"That's true. And you once dated a guy named Dirk." She says the name with a sharp emphasis on the K. "Anyone who dated someone named Dir*k* can't be fully trusted. And I'm not sure I trust your judgement most of the time." She spins to face me fully. "This guy, Dave. I really like him."

I'm smiling, but there are a few stray tears left of my own. "I have something I need to tell you." I glance around the patio, pretending to be worried to say the words, biting on my nails with a dramatic flair. When I look back at her, she's not impressed so I toss up my hands. "Okay, okay. I thought you should know that I'm in love with Dave. What did you say before? Strap that ball and chain to my ankle and throw away the key because I never want another human to share that part of my heart. I want him there every day until my last breath and even then, I think there might be a place for us."

"Psh," she spits out and rolls her eyes. "Duh, Bestie. You are really easy to read. Plus, he looks at you like you're a mythical creature and he isn't quite sure whether you're real or not. I think it's mutual."

"That's pretty accurate," Dave calls out from the sliding door, startling us both. We swing our heads back to him and he's sweaty, popping out earbuds. He gives us both a confused look and points at his eye. We both laugh at the smear of makeup on our faces.

"I need to talk to you, Dave." Azzy's up in a flash, tucking the exposed end of the blanket around my feet. She's at his nose thanks to her towering platforms and honestly, he looks a little scared. "Apparently, my best friend thinks you're something special, but I need confirmation if you're truly worthy." She sticks her hand out and Dave looks from it to her to me. "Your phone, please. I need to see what you were listening to."

Azzy's about to get her mind blown and I'm here for it. Dave unlocks the phone and sets it in her hand. She's scrolling and even though her back is to me, I'm aware she's biting her cheek. She always does it when she's about to agree to something she was a little hesitant to do.

Her braids are bouncing as she nods, thrusting the phone back at him. "Fine. Your heart appears to be almost the same shade as ours. We can work on where you lack."

My hand covers the biggest grin and Dave isn't sure what to do.

"Uh, thanks?"

But then Azzy steps into Dave and wraps her arms around his sweaty body, squeezing him. His eyes are big and round, looking from the top of her head to me. He gives her back an obligatory pat as doctors do.

Azzy releases him and tries to keep her voice low, but I overhear anyway. "That's my bestie. She means everything to me so treat her well. I love her."

"So do I." But he's looking at me when he says it.

"Gotta go pick up LC from her shift," Azzy says to me over her shoulder, then turns back to Dave. "I'd like some better coffee if I'm going to be here every day. Maybe you can work on that."

"Sure, Azzy."

Chapter Twenty-Six

I HATE HOSPITALS WITH A VENGEANCE SO PURE THAT IT threw everyone for a loop when I insisted this was where I needed to be. It's the first place I found my true self, and the first place I found my love, Dave. In some weird screwed-up way, it feels like coming home.

Dave and I fought about this quite a bit, me being here. About where I would die. Such a ridiculous thing to squabble about since the end result is all the same no matter which way we go.

In the end, I won. It was the snarky comment I made about 'my death, my choice' that shut down all his arguments.

I sure as hell love Dr. Dave here. No matter how hard he tries, he can't completely dissolve his image as a health-care provider. He's not wearing the usual sky-blue scrubs and white coat that I love to tease him about. He's in jeans and a fitted black shirt and the only doctor thing about him is the stethoscope roped around the nape of his neck as though he was born to wear it.

It's as much of a part of his identity as Azzy's ring of black around her eyes.

He sits on my bed, taking my hand, but old habits die hard as his finger presses the thin skin of my wrist while he looks off somewhere in the distance. There's an expression I've not been privy to before, one that seems as if he might be having painful dark thoughts. If I were in a talkative mood, I'd probably try to make a death joke.

It's been two months since we left Portugal. The second time. And it's been nine months since I was handed my diagnosis. Guess I managed to beat those six-month odds after all. I suspect Dave's surgery is what's lengthened my timeline, adding pages to a very thin calendar.

I've spent every moment I could traveling with Dave, being around my loved ones, and living my life without worrying about the date at the end of that calendar. I got a lot out of those unexpected extra days and found my purpose—I found my love.

I'm more knowledgeable about a lot of things too. The hand that holds my wrist now has a simple platinum band around the ring finger. I have an identical one, although mine is on a chain around my neck because I've lost too much weight.

It wasn't all rainbows and sunshine these past months. I had my moments. Lots of them.

I spent one terrible afternoon out on the farm on the squeaky porch swing in my dad's arms. He comforted a grown woman who had regressed to a little girl afraid of the dark.

Some nights, I'd wake up in a panic or in a crying fit about the future and Dave would hold me until the tears stopped and I fell back asleep. There was even one night the roles were reversed and I held my husband while he fractured apart.

Everyone in my life stood by my side through it all. We laughed way too much at the most ridiculous things and teased each other relentlessly. Even Chloe and I spent an entire weekend watching rom-coms and eating terrible foods at the farm. Mom came in halfway through the marathon and sat between us and we cuddled up on her and stayed that way for hours.

Then there was Azzy. All the time we spent in San Francisco, Azzy would be present almost every day. You'd think Dave wouldn't like splitting his time with me, but they would often end up in intense conversations long after I'd had enough and succumbed to my tiredness.

Once, I found them both on the patio late at night with wine and textbooks stacked high, talking about things way beyond my level of comprehension. They weren't searching for a cure for me. None of us were that naïve, but I was sure it gave them hope to do something while I deteriorated in front of them.

Dave sighs.

It's not one of those bored sighs either. It's one that holds more weight than the room and fills the entire wing of the hospital. When he looks down to me, there's a sheen to his eyes that makes me incredibly sad and all I want to do is wrap him in my arms.

But I'm too weak to even move a pinky.

I smile anyway—try—at least. My head is a thousand pounds, and my eyes heavy under the pressure of my lashes. There's nothing steady about the beeping of the machines. And there's nothing strong about the rhythm. They're a little all over the place.

Dave reaches over me to the one machine that seems to

be slowing. The beeping silences and he sits back down. There are others in the room. Dad and Mom. Helen. Chloe and Ted. Azzy and LC. But I only see him. His thumb grazes the heel of my hand and someone else is squeezing my foot. It's my dad taking second place to Dave.

My eyes won't stay open as Dave shifts his weight on the bed.

My body dips away from his warmth only to feel the give of his lips on my forehead.

He stays pressed to me as warm tears drop from above and rain down on me. He whispers to me, and I strain to hear it through an impending cloud of haze. Their choking and hardly audible.

"I may have mended your heart temporarily, but mine will forever and always be healed by your hands, your love." He kisses my forehead once again, lips trembling. "I love you, Rachel." A palm rests on my chest, but lightly as if afraid to put the full weight of his hand on me.

There's something in the air, a familiar fragrance that I have yet to pinpoint, but it encircles Dave and me, transporting me to the flowers on the cliffside in Lagoa. And I inhale their sweet scent. It's comforting and I don't mind it taking over the astringent smell of the hospital.

I want to reach out and touch Dave's anguished face, to lay my own hand over his heart. I need to tell Dave all the things he doesn't yet know about me for there's far too much left to say.

I want to say *I love you* one more time. But all I feel is weightlessness and it's not hurting as much as it has been lately. There is nothing but warmth. I can't even begin to

Epilogue - Dave

It's been over a year now, each day rolling into the next.

And then the next.

Each one carries its own peculiar brand of pain and solace, but among the loss is extreme gratitude for having had Rachel in my life. My heart still holds onto the shock of that day as if it happened thirty seconds ago.

Some in my circle have suggested it might be time to move forward, but the truth is that no one will ever fill Rachel's shoes. A life force like hers is once in a lifetime in my eyes. It's not possible to have anything better and that's okay by me.

I've moved past the anger. Maybe I'm accepting what fate hands to me, but long gone is the day at the hospital when Randy comforted me after his first-born daughter passed minutes before. That same moment when I was a collapsed man, hanging onto barely a shred of dignity in the hallway. He nursed *me* for the bloody knuckles I smashed into the hospital wall. He held *me*, like the father I'd never had, while we both grieved. Two grown men broken by the same woman.

I didn't lose my license. Perhaps Kragen felt magnanimous and took Juan's advice, but whatever—it seemed the powers that be must have figured I'd been punished enough, having lost my wife in the long run. The board did take my hospital privileges. Their hands were tied on that. Either way it still doesn't matter. I don't treat patients anymore. Can't.

My mother worries about me. Rachel's parents too. Hell, sometimes, I even worry about myself, wondering if the pain in my own heart, the tearing and shredding of scar tissue trying to heal, is remotely close to what Rachel felt. Because if so, then it's the worst pain imaginable.

It's white-out blinding some days.

But then there are days that I see her smile in my memories. The best of those rare days is when I sit on the balcony, and the briny air sweeps into the bay. Her spirit is somewhere wrapped up in all that fog and sea spray. Then, she's here with me—that she'll always be.

Everyone's wrong, misguided about me.

All those who believe me to be a broken man and a fragment of my former self have missed the point. I am more fulfilled than anyone I know. I've had a love that was all-consuming—that *still is*, and I've known its cruel pain, but damn if it hasn't made me stronger. This is what pushes me to trudge through the murkiness in which I sometimes get stuck.

When two people you love die from the same exact cause and you think you are in a position to prevent it—and you still can't? That does something to you, fundamentally changes you.

Thank god for Juan for convincing me not to walk away from medicine completely.

But it was really Azzy who flipped me out of my

despair. She made room for me in her life and now I too share a part of Rachel's black heart. Her presence exists in the strength built between us. The amount of scar tissue Rachel left behind is immense, but it binds us as we navigate our grief together.

I may have lost my sister but gained two more with Azzy and LC. They have been my anchors in all of this, giving me purpose and a sense of direction. And fuck if we aren't the oddest family of misfits hoping to make this world a better place.

Because of Azzy's startup experience and LC's nursing expertise, we were able to combine our backgrounds and do the impossible in a wholly different way by creating our own company, Black Heart Initiative.

I dove straight into research with Azzy and together, we pour over it every day, along with my 'Pump Me Up' playlist raging in the background. In six months' time, a clinical trial will begin, one we are heading up in the hopes to join the fight and find a cure for this cancer.

I don't care if it takes the very last breath out of my lungs, I will do everything in my power to never let this disease destroy anyone else.

Of course, there are days like today where Rachel's all-consuming in my thoughts. These times don't happen as often now, but when they do, there is nothing to do other than spend hours watching the waves roll in as if she's here with me, curled up in my arms, her little hot pink painted toes peeking out from a fluffy blanket. Her hand fits in mine and the weight of her body presses into my own as she slips into sleep. I end up joining her when a flowery fragrance from the cliffs of Portugal settles over us, calming and sweet. When I wake up, the room is empty again and I'm alone and cold, the western cold front taking away all her warmth and light as if it seeks to eliminate her.

It never will.

My hand twists the ring on my finger mindlessly. It's become such a habit that at some point, the metal is going to wear down to only dust. I put my hand to my chest to feel that I am still alive but break into a thousand pieces when my fingers graze her ring that hangs around my neck.

But I move forward regardless. She's still with me and always will be.

Despite Rachel's assertion that there would never be a happy ever after for us, that's simply a bold-faced lie. Our love—even with as short as she got to experience it—was something that could only be written in the stars. Rachel sure as hell got her happy ever after, I made sure of that.

Luckily for me, not all that happiness and love died with her that terrible day. I'm miserable right now, that much is true, but I'm also incredibly grateful to know what love—true love—feels like. I'm so happy I experienced its limitless highs and the devastating lows. That will be something I will never regret or take for granted.

Rachel died.

Simple as that.

But I don't worry, because like she always told me—a black heart can never truly die.

Acknowledgments

Black Heart(s) is one of those projects that sits a little nearer to my heart than most. Inspired by a bout of sadness, I turned to my playlist. Fate landed on a couple of emo songs that had sat firmly in my past for way too long. I ended up pouring that gloomy energy from those love songs into this book.

Although I instructed them repeatedly to never to read my work, I doubt my parents will listen. Thank you both, I think? My parents have always been my rock, supporting me through every obstacle in my life, each providing me with a strong landing pad, whether I thought I needed it or not. This story, although wildly different from my own, attempts to showcase the unique understanding between a father and daughter. It doesn't begin to do my own father justice, but there are pieces of him sprinkled within these pages.

California, Idaho, and Portugal are meaningful places where a lot of personal growth for myself occurred. It felt only natural to use them. There are people in each place that have inspired me. None more than Nicole – you know you're a big reason I still have a black heart. Once inseparable, we're now rooted in adult lives and don't talk as much, but one fact remains: you'll always be my emo-listening, black-heart matching, college BFF that introduced me to 'real' coffee, wine, and a plethora of VHS tapes. You're not Azzy at all, but maybe in another life, I could see you painting on black lipstick and covered in tattoos as we make our way to every concert we could afford.

I must thank HEA Author Services – Jessica, Emily, and Kimberly – for their attention to detail, ability to deliver ahead of schedule, and for keeping me in line with my writing. I've learned so much from you three. You've kept the integrity of my work while giving gentle guidance. It's exactly what I needed!

To all my beta readers, especially Raquel and Claire – As far as readers you were quite literally the first line of defense and every word of feedback given meant so much.

Jules – your cover art is exactly what I envisioned. The fact that I can give you a short description and you transform it into this? Just amazing!

To all those bands that got me through all those times in my life that I needed something to make me feel... The Used, Breaking Benjamin, My Chemical Romance, A Day to Remember, Mayday Parade, Beartooth... the list goes on and on. As does the love I have for your lyrics. *cries in sad mascara tears*

Finally, to all the readers that have or will read this – thank you. Every time you pick up a novel, you're supporting an author that has spent countless hours trying to make a perfect world for you to escape for a short time. Hopefully, I achieved this.

-Calli

About the Author

Calliope Daniels is a proud veteran, emo nerd, world traveler, and occasional baker. Lately, she's been spending her evening and weekends writing in the rainforest of southeast Alaska. When she's not working or writing, her time is spent on hikes, drinking lattes, and eating any and every pastry within sight.

Read on for an excerpt from Calliope's debut novel, Dare Me to Love

Chapter One

"*Opa* to my best bitches!"

"*Opa*!" I chime in, raising my drink.

I've never been into calling my girls bitches, but it's April's newest term of endearment so Karissa and I go with it, clinking our Champagne flutes together and giggling at the full week of freedom in front of us.

I needed this. I needed them.

Things have been imploding in my life for a while. A silent and destructive depression has poisoned me. The fear and dread that I'd end up like my mother twisted every thought I made to the point of inaction. That, coupled with losing my job *and* my husband acting more like a roommate than my lover is exactly the reason I agreed to this trip to Greece. Time away could only help me push through everything and develop a plan to get my marriage and life back on track.

What better way than with the biggest support system a girl could have?

For the past decade, Karissa, April, and I have traveled for a girl's-only vacation at least once a year, but after spending the last year and a half in my head and canceling two trips in a row, it was time to do something other than feel sorry for myself.

If I'm being honest, after figuring out that getting away might help not only my mood but give me much needed time away to sort my marriage out, none of this took much convincing.

A week spent on the island of Crete with my two best friends sounded like the perfect solution. Having an escape from the reality was enough to click the 'Book It Now' button on my flight.

Sipping casually, the bubbles tingle on my tongue as the other two women down half their glasses in one gulp. We met up two hours ago in Athens, then boarded a small regional plane. Although the last twenty-four hours were filled with long layovers and connecting flights, this seems all worth it. Even the horrendous line at passport control in Athens, and the lack of Ubers at the small airport in the coastal town of Chania, can't take away the sigh of relief we all released the moment we arrived at the resort.

Travel weary and giddy to be together, my girls and I recline against luxurious, fluffed cushions. Perched high above rocky, jagged cliffs, a clear glass railing gives us a view of the turquoise waters of the Mediterranean. April's flowery pink dress skims the marble patio as she stretches long bronze legs toward Karissa who's found the world's largest brimmed straw hat, obscuring her face from the nose up.

Karissa leans toward me, shoulder-length auburn hair brushing my upper arm as she downs the remainder of her Champagne. I tuck the side of her hat between us so it stops smacking me in the face and pull her into a hug.

"This is already amazing. Thank you guys for

suggesting we come." I exhale slowly, looking to April. "How did you ever find this place?"

April sets her flute on the low glass table and flashes a brilliant smile. Out of the three of us, she is by far the most glamorous. Some would say she's perfectly sculpted by the Greek gods themselves. Others would argue that's the plastic surgery and fillers, but the woman is beautiful regardless. As a plastic surgeon's wife, she has anything and everything her heart desires. Money? That's a yes. Free Botox? No question. Paying for this resort in Europe for her two besties? Didn't even blink twice.

April waves a hand at me, her sparkler of a wedding ring glittering in the sunlight, "Josh, the anesthesiologist from the practice, came here with his wife last year and told Braxton about it. When he came home and started talking about how we should go I told him I'd prefer to see the island with you two instead."

Karissa chuckles into her glass and then drains the remaining liquid. "I'm sure that went over well. If I know Braxton, he probably thinks you're running off to find another husband and is worried sick. There's pacing involved, I'm sure."

Karissa is April's polar opposite. Tomboy at heart, the fact that she's currently wearing an off-the-shoulder black and white maxi dress, delicate strappy sandals, and that ridiculous hat is blowing my mind. To get her out of what April calls her lumberjill outfit of flannel, jeans, and hiking boots must have taken quite a bit of convincing. Even her hair is out of its usual ponytail and down in a wavy style. My guess would be that April made it a requirement for Karissa to not bring any of her own clothes and instead wear ours.

"Believe me, I left Braxton with no doubt about how I feel about him." April's eyebrows dance up and down as she snatches her drink and flicks the rim of her glass several times with her tongue.

"Gross, that's my brother. And why am I required to wear dresses this whole time?"

There it is.

Karissa lasted a whole two hours in a dress and she's already whining.

April scans her sister-in-law, taking in the whole look before issuing an approving nod. "You look amazing, Risa. You'd think you would be thanking me for loaning you a designer dress."

With a graceful and experienced raise of her hand, a waiter is summoned. Within a minute he deposits another round of drinks in front of us without a word spoken.

"Anyway," April continues while sipping on a new glass. "We should make this trip interesting. Who knows when we will get to do it again?"

Both Karissa and I let out identical groans.

"Sure, we'll get right on that," I say dripping with sarcasm. "The last time you wanted to make a trip interesting we were in Thailand and ended up in one of those little tuktuk car things and you"—I tip my glass to Karissa and nudge her shoulder—"were experiencing the lovely and infamous Double Dragon while we tried to navigate back to our hotel because April insisted you try some roadside grilled meat that was undercooked."

"Both ends for thirty-six hours." Karissa sighs, dreamily gazing off into the glittering sea as if she were reliving a cherished memory. "I had to buy monster-sized pads to line my underwear to make the flight home without worrying about a terrible blowout. If it wasn't for Ana, being my backup pads holder, we might never have made it home with most of our dignity intact." She sips with a smack of her lips. "You can't buy memories like that from a tour company."

"That wasn't my fault." Both Karissa and I swing our heads over to April and she throws up her palm in defense. "Okay, it might have been my fault, but this time will be different. I need a spark of something fun. Maybe we can skinny dip or—"

"No," we say in unison.

"It was one time." April pushes her sunglasses up her petite nose and shakes her head. "You'd think you both would let that one slide."

"Maybe," I start, "if we had known that we were skinny dipping in someone's private pool—"

"With a security system," Karissa adds.

"And armed guards."

April scoffs into the Aegean breeze. "Bruno was a gentleman when he handcuffed my naked ass."

"His name was Officer Jimmy Bennett, not Bruno. Do you know how I remember that?" I don't wait for her to respond. "Because he was at my arraignment and told the judge that we should be given community service teaching children about water safety."

Karissa laughs and bumps my arm. "I mean, not all was lost on that one. I learned how to properly don a lifejacket and you learned that you can hold your breath for more than thirty seconds."

April mutters into her glass. "You'd think you two would be grateful for all the memories. A girl only wants to make life interesting for her best friends."

"Forgive me if your 'adventures' have turned into disasters." I use air quotes near her nose.

April sinks into her chair and sets her now empty second glass down. "This is going to be such a lame vacation. What are we supposed to do? Sit around the pool and beach while sipping drinks and doing nothing?"

"Yes," Karissa huffs out. "Why do we have to do something crazy?"

April pops back up, a delighted spark flashing across her face. Karissa sees it too and we both cringe at whatever outlandish idea is about to come out. We love our friend and even though we give her a hard time, we truly have had some great adventures due to her scheming. And now it seems we are on the brink of another one and like always, we'll end up going along with it like all the times before.

"What if we do something lower key?" She studies us, gauging if we're going to bite. When neither of us respond, she pouts. "Hear me out, okay? We're all married and live these boring lives of—"

"Says you," Karissa interjects. "I'm quite happy in my career and marriage."

"I didn't say you weren't. I'm saying that maybe we break out of the mundane routine and—"

"We're literally in Greece," I point out.

"Yeah," Karissa agrees. "How is this not breaking out of our routine?"

"Would you let me finish?" April is exasperated and both Karissa and I chuckle as the woman braces her forearms on her knees and steeples her fingers. She leans in with a sinister glint in her eye. "Truth or Dare."

"I am *not* playing that with you." Karissa crosses her arms and sneers. "There's no way in hell. You'd have me doing something so crazy it will make international news and Paul will get a call from the Embassy that I'm in a Grecian prison and have a prison wife. I might wear a lot of flannel and drive a Subaru, but I'm not ready for a prison wife. No way."

"You could pick Truth," she counters.

"Sorry April," I jump in. "I'm on Karissa's side on this one. It shouldn't even be called Truth or Dare. It's always just Dare and we escalate way too quickly. It ends up being a death-match between all of us and someone always ends up being burned."

April bites at the corner of her lip as she inspects her perfect French-tipped nails. "One round and I'll concede after that. We'll spend the rest of the week poolside without a single complaint out of me."

Karissa flicks her gaze over to me and shrugs. I'm not convinced. "One round of what? A dare per person?"

April nods. "You can even start, Ana." She extends her praying hands in my direction. "I need an adventure, even a small one. Give me this before I go back to L.A."

"And when does this start? Now?"

Her smile reaches up to her crow's-feet-free eyes because she knows she's won. April launches her body off the chair into a victory dance complete with high stepping and fists punching the air. "Yes! Today only." She composes herself on a half-breath, dragging a chair closer to us. It scrapes along the marble tiles ominously.

Reaching for my untouched drink on the table, and she downs it before I can rip the glass out of her hands. "I'm ready! Give me my dare." She rubs her palms together and lights up like a kid at Christmas. A psychotic kid.

"Careful, Ana," Karissa chuckles. "She's got that crazed twinkle in her eye."

I stand up and smooth out my dress. "Give me a minute to look around and see if I can come up with something worthy of your neediness."

April claps her hands together and steals my seat so she's next to Karissa. "Take your time. Make it a good one, I need memories to get me through the next year."

www.ingramcontent.com/pod-product-compliance
Lightning Source LLC
LaVergne TN
LVHW100518110826
845146LV00002B/692

9798892830720